THE CITY
ALWAYS WINS

THE CITY ALWAYS WINS

OMAR ROBERT HAMILTON

MCD 〰 FARRAR, STRAUS AND GIROUX NEW YORK

MCD

Farrar, Straus and Giroux

18 West 18th Street, New York 10011

Printed in the United States of America

First edition, 2017

Library of Congress Cataloging-in-Publication Data
Names: Hamilton, Omar Robert, 1984– author.
Title: The city always wins : a novel / Omar Robert Hamilton.
Description: New York : MCD / Farrar, Straus and Giroux, 2017.
Identifiers: LCCN 2016059405 | ISBN 9780374123970 (hardback) |
    ISBN 9780374716332 (ebook)
Subjects: LCSH: Dissenters—Egypt—Cairo—Fiction. | Protest
    movements—Egypt—Cairo—Fiction. | Egypt—History—Protests,
    2011– —Fiction. | Egypt—Politics and government—1981– —Fiction. |
    Maydān al-Taḥrīr (Cairo, Egypt)—Fiction. | Cairo (Egypt)—Fiction. |
    Political fiction. | BISAC: FICTION / Literary. | FICTION /
    Historical. | GSAFD: Historical fiction.
Classification: LCC PR9375.9.H36 C58 2017 | DDC 823/.92—dc23
LC record available at https://lccn.loc.gov/2016059405

Designed by Abby Kagan

Our books may be purchased in bulk for promotional, educational, or business
use. Please contact your local bookseller or the Macmillan Corporate and
Premium Sales Department at 1-800-221-7945, extension 5442, or
by e-mail at MacmillanSpecialMarkets@macmillan.com.

www.fsgbooks.com
www.twitter.com/fsgbooks • www.facebook.com/fsgbooks

1   3   5   7   9   10   8   6   4   2

For Alaa

This would have been a better book
if I'd been able to talk to you

PART 1

TOMORROW

Never underestimate the wisdom of the
naive . . . #Jan25 long live the revolution.
@Alaa
8:17 PM–28 Jan 2011

1

October 9, 2011

She stopped counting the dead an hour ago. These corridors are so compressed with bodies and rage and grief that something, surely, is going to explode. Everywhere are the cries of a new loss, a shouted question, a panicked face, a weeping phone call. *They are dead, they are dead, they are all dead.* The hospital's morgue is full. It was not built for this. There are twelve people locked in this infirmary with her. Eleven are dead. She can hear their parents through the thick metal door. *We must bury them now! Tonight!* Eleven inside, at least four still coming, ten in another room, who knows how many more still to come, how many still running from the army? *The coroner is coming. Just another hour. Please wait.* Eleven here and a woman sitting on the floor, clutching a man's limp fingers to her breast; her face runs with tears. His eyes are closed—her husband, her brother, her beloved—his clothes are ripped and bloodied from the serrated metal of the tank treads. His chest is covered with the embroidered face of Jesus. Eleven in here, in this room getting hotter with every minute, and how many more are coming? How long will the killing go on? How long will we be locked in this room whose air is thicker than any air ever breathed before, whose every atom is death? Blocks of ice are melting between the bodies of the fallen, vapors whispering off the flesh of the silenced. She breathes deeply. This room. This tiny room where every breath breathes in the dead. We will carry you forward. We will carry you in us. Breathe in. *Nafas.* Breathe in. *Nafas.* These molecules of scent rising from your bodies, your final offering to the upper world. I will breathe you in. I will carry you in me.

"We must bury them now." A man's voice. Mariam can hear shreds of the shouted argument slipping through the door. "Justice is for the next life. Leave justice to the Lord. We must bury them now."

Breathe in. Smell the fruit, sweat, dust of your brothers, sweet like blood, heavy with the coming rot. Soon the sun will come. Breathe in. We are together now. We will make them pay.

"But"—a younger voice, polite, frustrated—"if we have no autopsies, no proof, the army will deny everything." Mariam recognizes the voice as Alaa's, the first person she saw in the hospital, the curls of his hair framing his face as she had seen it on television. "We need the autopsies for justice."

Breathe in. Be strong. We will get justice. Be strong, be strong for this woman whose name you don't yet know, for her tears, for her beloved. Ask her her name, if she needs anything. She needs her husband to wake up. Leave her alone. Ice. We need more ice. Who knows how long we will have to keep the bodies from their burial. Breathe in. Breathe in the heavy air curling in your lungs, settling in their passageways, coating them forever with this night. These bodies will become what the mind cannot forget.

"What right do you have to say the word *justice*? What justice? What justice? There can never be justice, don't talk to me of justice, don't insult me with words. My son is dead. My son is dead inside and we talk of justice? What justice for the poor? For the weak? For the Copts? There *can never be* justice. What justice? How will you get justice? The priest says we must bury them now, now before the dawn. Forget about justice. Forget about autopsies. We must bury our children."

"Please. Let's be calm." Another voice, a woman's, low, with great authority: "My brother's inside next to your son, sir. These are their friends. They trusted them. They made the revolution together. We should listen to them."

"And we see now what your revolution brings us."

The march was to Maspero. To the state television and radio building. The army opened fire. No hesitation. They crushed people under their tanks. How many dead are there in rooms throughout this hospital? How long until they come for us here? Outside the gates a crowd waits nervously. Will the army come to seize the bodies filled with military steel and dispose of the evidence? Mariam ran from the bullets and hid in a building and carried a young man's bleeding body into the back of a car and pressed on his wound with her shirt and told him it would be okay and brought him here, to the Coptic Hospital, and then a doctor took him and left her dazed in the fluorescent corridor.

"Mariam," a voice said. A doctor. A friend of her mother's. "Are you okay? Yes? Come with me. The morgue is full. We're using a ward. I need someone in there. To keep people out. Can I ask you for that?"

They paused before the infirmary. There would be no stepping back through this door. There would be no unseeing. She turned the handle.

The woman with her beloved's hand to her chest has not moved. Mariam pulls her phone out of her pocket. Flat. Where is Khalil now? She left him. They carried the injured man together, put him in the car. Go, Khalil said. There's no room. I'll find you later. She turned back and saw him, his white

T-shirt brown with drying blood, heading back into the field hospital. Where is he now? Is he outside somewhere, among the families of the dead? Go find a charger, some water. Go get this woman some water. Ask her if she needs anything. No, no one can give her what she needs.

Outside, the woman's low voice, again, its authority heavy with belonging and loss and patience, is slowly turning the families. *Yes. Yes. We must fight. We will have justice.* Grief by grief the voices join together into a shield of shared purpose. There will be no swift burial of bodies and truths. There will be autopsies. There will be evidence. There will be justice.

Mariam steps out into the corridor. The world is calmer now. The sun is rising. She looks for Alaa but can't see him. The floors are lined with people sitting against the two walls, waiting, still, for the coroner or the attack or whatever's coming next. She walks down the center of the corridor, looking for water. The air is thinner, she feels it moving against her cheeks, her lungs reach for it greedily but she tries to keep her breaths shallow. Out of respect.

In the hospital courtyard a young woman wearing a black hoodie sits with an open plastic bag full of water bottles.

"Could I get one?" Mariam asks.

"Yes, of course," she says, handing her one.

Mariam sits down on a low, dusty wall. An older woman wrapped in black sits in stillness. "You're good kids," she says in an almost silence, almost to herself. "My son . . . maybe you know my son? His name is Ayman. He's . . ."

Mariam waits, doesn't say anything.

He is inside. She knows. Ayman is inside, under the ice. Again and again they've come for us. Once a month, every month with clubs and masks and guns and boots and bullets, again and again and again and for what? Mariam moves closer to the woman, gently placing her hand on her shoulder as new tears swell. "My son . . . he . . . he said he came alive in Tahrir."

2

The elevator up to the office is a thrilling ride: the halting climb up to the tenth floor a repeated act of faith in a higher power. But the risk is worth it for the classical expanse of wooden floors and high ceilings and the late afternoon light streaming in from the balcony that looks out over the lower buildings of Downtown and onto the Nile and there, in the center of the landscape, the ever-smoldering ruins of Mubarak's National Democratic Party headquarters, the sun setting perfectly behind the charred concrete skeleton. Khalil loves that building, loves that it stands there every day as a testament to all that's possible and all that's impermanent to the tens of thousands of people who drive past it every day. A symbol in cinders of our victory, our antimonument to the future. A giant billboard stands tall amid the scorched ruins. Untouched by the flames, its meaningless electioneering slogan become flesh: *For your children's future.* What poetry the city gives us. All around from this balcony Cairo sings out its history to

9

him. The once-modern internationalism of the Nile Hilton, its wide and welcoming facade overlooking the shuttered gardens and their mysterious excavations; the muscular terra-cotta of the Egyptian Museum still standing firm despite the years of horror inside it, from the shadowy corruption and shameless thievery to the whippings and beatings dealt out by the occupying army. And then to the east and the buildings surging inland, their modernist balconies and flat rooftops pushing toward the chorus of Talaat Harb Square and, his favorite, the great sloped mansard roof, the dramatic gradient of its gray tiling more appropriate for the rains of Köln than Cairo's heat, but beautiful here in this city of infinite interminglings and unending metaphor. Cairo is jazz: all contrapuntal influences jostling for attention, occasionally brilliant solos standing high above the steady rhythm of the street. Forget New York, the whole history of the world can be seen from here, flows past us *here*, in the Nile streaming from its genesis north and out into the waters of empires and all the brutalities and beauties they bring, emerging riotous and discordant and defiant into something new and undefinable and uncontrollable. These streets laid out to echo the order and ratio and martial management of the modern city now molded by the tireless rhythms of salesmen and hawkers and car horns and gas peddlers all out in ownership of their city, mixing pasts with their present, birthing a new now of south and north, young and old, country and city all combining and coming out loud and brash and with a beauty incomprehensible. Yes, Cairo is jazz. Not lounge jazz, not the commodified lobby jazz that works to blanch history, but the heat of New Orleans and gristle of Chicago: the jazz that is beauty in the destruction of the past, the jazz of an unknown future, the jazz that promises freedom from the bad old times.

Yes, Khalil thinks, this will do. All the work they've been

doing from cafés and their homes and in Rosa's apartment can now coalesce here. Chaos: their magazine, website, podcast—this will be its new home. He turns and steps in from the balcony to see Rania kicking up bits of splintered floorboard, her short frame dressed in black, her hair cut to a stylish buzz on the sides, a spider tattoo illuminating her left shoulder.

"What are we doing here?" Rania's saying, her voice always louder than all others. "The cobwebs are older than the building! This floor is all ripped up. Did you go in the kitchen? It looks like a murder scene."

"Come on, Rania," Khalil says. "The ceilings are high, the elevator works, and the doorman's so old he doesn't care anymore. It's perfect."

"Did you see the bathroom?" she says. "It looks haunted. I'm all for industrial chic or whatever but this place is going to collapse on top of us. We don't have time for this. I don't know how to fix up *apartments*. I can barely work the *kettle*. I turn it on and sometimes it just sits there staring at me. We're in the middle of a media war. We need to keep working."

"But look at the balcony," Khalil replies. "Clean it up and the whole world'll be hanging out here."

"You don't want the whole world."

"We want enough of it."

"Well you'd better get ready to fight the rats because that's *their* balcony. Do you know what happens when you get a rat into a corner? Have you ever got a rat into a corner?"

Hafez is watching the exchange silently, leaning against the doorframe of the balcony, taking in the new view. As always, he is smartly dressed, his hair cut close, glasses fashionably thick-rimmed, a paperback squeezed into the outside pocket of a light jacket: Herodotus, Joyce, Gramsci, no big deal. Two years into a PhD in London, he's clearly fashioning himself in the Said model of the academic sophisticate.

"Shall we go finish this argument at the Greek Club? There's a party tonight and I need to get warmed up."

"Fine," Rania says. "But just tell me how you think we're going to pay for such a big space?"

"We can crowdfund," Khalil says. "And then room rentals, a café. Rosa did the numbers."

Rosa is holding her phone's flashlight under the kitchen sink, the shaft of light shining unbroken through a gaping hole in the ceramic. "It looks like someone's been disposing of evidence in here."

"Great," Rania says. "Very comforting."

"Don't worry," Rosa says. "There's plenty of money out there. We'll work it out as we go."

"And if the numbers don't add up," Khalil says, "we'll get some Swedish aid money or something."

"Didn't we say no funding!?" Rania's voice rises, filling the enormous room. "My God, I take my eye off you for one second! *Swedish aid money*, he says! *Swedish!* First you make us take an apartment we can't afford that's ruled by an army of rats and has no plumbing! Then, once we've signed the contract and have bills coming out of our asses, you'll come sliding up to us with ambassador Bjorn or cultural attaché Helmut and a couple of application forms. You know what happens when you start taking funding?"

"Relax, I was joking."

"So . . . ," Hafez says. "Greek Club?"

"I have to work," Khalil says.

"On what?"

"Maspero."

"Shit. Can't you finish it tomorrow?"

"It should have been finished days ago."

"You want to come with me out of Cairo tomorrow?"

"Where?"

"I got a tip. The army is loaning out conscripts to work some businessman's farm. Will try and go get some photos. Conscripts, man. It's damn slavery."

"Sure. If I finish the edit."

"Do it in the morning. We'll do the party tonight, work yourself up a nice creative hangover and I'll pick you up midday. Easy."

"All right, Hafez."

"All right yourself. You're making me feel bad."

Rania turns to survey the room again, flicks open the rusted circuit-breaker panel and two small spiders scurry out. "Well, there you go. I rest my case."

3

A whole universe can hinge on a glance, a cigarette, a joke.

He heard her voice first. "We're not going anywhere," she shouted.

"You've made your point." The officer's voice was loud, firm. "You've made your point and that's enough. Now, please . . . ," he said, and gestured to the streets leading back into Downtown. He wore sunglasses, of course, even though it was the dead of night. Fifteen commandos in balaclavas formed a semicircle behind him. But Mariam was unafraid: "We're not going anywhere until the revolution's demands are met!"

The officer's jaw clenched against the insubordination: "What," he said coldly, his look fixed on Mariam, "will make you go home?"

She didn't miss a beat: "The arrest of Ahmed Shafiq and all his ministers. That would be a start."

A commando flexed his shoulders, cricked his colossal neck. Someone else always runs first. If a herd of buffalo stands together, the herd is impenetrable. But the wolves skirt the edges.

The crackle of tasers snapped through the air. The crowd split. The wolves gave chase.

The long yellow streetlights shaking in the running of the open street, the shouts of the scattering crowd, the men with guns and sticks: all were as nothing next to her hand rising and falling in a running fist next to him, and all he can see is the coming decision.

Whole futures are born in the touch of a hand. Whole worlds that could have been are destroyed.

And now she's here, living with him, in bed next to him, reading the news on her phone.

"You want breakfast?" he says.

"Sure."

"Want to learn to fry an egg?"

"Not today," she says.

"Surely everyone has to learn to cook one thing?"

"I can cook." She puts her phone down.

"What can you cook?"

"Toast."

"Toast is not cooking."

"It gets hot."

"Hot's not enough."

"Heat changes it. So that's cooking. And anyway, I can fry an egg."

"We'll make pasta one night."

"I hate pasta."

"You hate pasta?"

"You can't tell if you're buying from the army's factories."

Her phone buzzes and she picks it up again:

Rania: six active strikes right now. We should do a special strike edition next.

"Rania's talking about doing a strike episode."

"I thought we needed to get out of Cairo? Do the Liberation of Suez piece?"

"I know. But we could do that anytime. The strikes are now."

"Sure. I'm going to get us breakfast." He gets up, pulls his trousers on.

As he rides the elevator he thinks again of that moment, her hand, the two of them running, how they ducked into the dark doorway of a building hanging heavy with foliage. Khalil nodded at the ancient doorman. She kept her hand in his as they made their way up through the spiraling shadows of the staircase, a single shaft of yellow light cutting in through the dusty windows.

He stopped, turned back to her. "Your name is Mariam, right?"

Her hand slipped quickly out of his: "How'd you know that?"

"I was camped near you in the square," he said. "Was just . . . I must have heard someone say it."

They sat on the balcony, watching the soldiers slowly wandering back from their chase toward Tahrir. "The assholes," Mariam said, and flicked her cigarette off the edge of the balcony.

Then she turned to him: "So what do you do?"

"I worked as a fixer—," he said.

"And then?"

"Then the revolution happened."

"Right."

"Now I'm going to build a radio station."

"Really?" she said, interested. "And how do you do that?"

Once they started talking they didn't stop. When the soldiers had all gone, she said she needed to find her friend but she stopped at the door. "So," she said, "how come we never met in Tahrir?"

"Because my friends are useless."

"You could have said hello."

"You react kindly to men hitting on you at political protests?" he said, smiling, and she laughed.

4

October 27, 2011

An island of white floats illuminated on a distant billboard and with an effort she can make out the words: "WE MUST EDUCATE OUR CHILDREN TO BECOME LIKE YOUNG EGYPTIAN PEOPLE" —BARACK OBAMA. There's a little rush of pride; she swallows it. An involuntary reaction. Fuck Obama. And fuck Mobinil more. She turns inside. She has phone calls to make. There aren't enough hours. Lists. Her pockets are always hiding little lists on scraps of paper, her jeans are stained with the ink of a thousand cheap pens. There aren't enough hours. If she lets herself think about it too much, about the lifetime of work lining up before her, the unending city of sores and scars and needs that will never be sated, all that is to be fought for and all that needs to be won, if she lets the thoughts take over, the blood comes rushing to her brain. She should have been a doctor, there's no questioning the value of a doctor, how can both parents be a doctor and their daughter not? Her blood-flushed brain is dizzy for a moment and she holds on to the railing and looks down from the horizon at the ground to see a line of ants adventuring across the dusty tiles, their lives' work laid out before them in the carrying of a leaf; hundreds of dutiful workers labor on repeat until the end, unquestioning of themselves, working only for the greater good. A lifetime of lists and websites and sleepless nights can never do the good a doctor does in a day. But what could she have done? Leave her mother to go study in Minya? Leave the clinic? Or go begging to her father and watch the happy relief on his face as he bought her a place in a private university? There was no other way. She's an organizer, an engine, break it down and take it on. The time is now. You're lucky. You were born for this. She can feel the papers in her pocket, takes a glowing strength from the lists, the active strikes, the calls to make, the coming protests, the events to push, the grand projects and passing thoughts, the people to remember and books to read and skills to learn and ideas for actions. She looks up at the city again. You are not alone. Tahrir is everywhere, the bonds forged, the lessons learned an unstoppable floodplain of possibility.

Her phone buzzes—

Brilliant new episode from @ChaosCairo. Essential listening for the week.

Evidence compiled by @ChaosCairo on Maspero killings should be used at the International Court of Justice.

Since the phone is in her hand she flicks open Twitter without thinking—

Today at 11am. First meeting to discuss plans to establish a public broadcast service.

Click. The phone locks. A twitch reflex. She's not ready for news of another martyr. She needs to prepare herself.

Website and podcast up and running already, a print monthly in the works. Every week Mariam produces the show, Rania does the interviews, Khalil records and cuts, and Rosa writes the continuity and spits her soulful *Señorita Love Daddy* intro: "Hello, dearly liberated from the streets of our revolution, today we've got news from the front lines, tunes from the underground, and every political beat you need to get through your week." The Maspero edition has been downloaded seventy thousand times—has played on nearly every independent Egyptian television channel—the analysis of the military's bullets has been picked up by a dozen foreign papers, a thousand new followers flock to the Chaos Twitter feed every day.

But what if people don't take to the streets again? It's been nine months now since Mubarak was forced from power and the army took over, but the sit-ins and small battles of the summer have left everyone exhausted. There is an anger, of that there is no doubt. But if Maspero is not the spark, then what? How many do they have to kill? When will the unconquerable numbers return to the street?

No. The revolution is unstoppable. Chaos will carry news, and tactics and triumphs from Bahrain, Libya, Yemen, Syria, Palestine. Start with the Arab Spring countries, then open to the whole Arab world, then: who knows? They can't keep up with us, an army of Samsungs, Twitters, HTCs, emails, Facebook events, private groups, iPhones, phone calls, text messages all adjusting one another's movements millions of times each second. An army of infinite mobility—impossible to outmaneuver. All they know to do is pull the plug, cut the line. And the world saw what happened when they tried that. They have no moves left. We have an irreversible tactical advantage. Divide and rule is no more for we can no longer be divided. How can they control us when, at last, we can all see one another, talk to one another, plan together? First in Arabic and then the rest of the world in English. Empire sows the seeds of its own defeat.

They pulled the plug and we fought them, we burned their police stations to the ground, we drove them out of our cities. Let them come again. They are the ones afraid of us now.

5

November 16, 2011

"Look at this," Khalil says, turning to the French documentary crew. "I love this neighborhood. They get fuck-all from the state and look. Streets are clean, walls are all painted, plants everywhere, everyone's safe."

The roads are so long, so straight, so narrow that you can't see to the end of them. Redbrick mountains lean in on the shaded street below, barely wide enough to fit one car. A tuk-tuk ambles past them. Khalil makes eye contact with an old man sitting outside his shop who gestures at two empty chairs in welcome; Khalil places his hand on his chest in thanks and carries on.

Cairo: the future city, the new metropole of plants cascading from solar-paneled roofs to tree-lined avenues with whitewashed facades and careful restorations and integrated innovations all singing together in a chorus of new and old. Civil initiatives will soon find easy housing in the abandoned architectural prizes of

Downtown, the river will be flooded with public transportation, the shaded spaces underneath the bridges and flyovers will flower into common land connected by tramways to dignified schools and clean hospitals and eclectic bookshops and public parks humming with music in the evenings. The revolution has begun and the people, every day, are supplanting the regime with their energy and initiative in this cement supercolony that for decades of state failure has held itself together with a collective supraintelligence keeping it from collapse. Something here, in Cairo's combination of permanence and piety and proximity, binds people together. There is a value to society here, he thinks, a neighborliness on a massive scale.

"The streets don't look so clean to me," the crew's director mutters, pushing his sunglasses up over his white hair and casting a suspicious look around him.

Khalil turns from him. It's just a job, he tells himself. You're a fixer. You don't need to be friends with them. Every day new journalists, filmmakers, and artists arrive. There's no easier money to be made right now than fixing. Two jobs a month covers half the rent on the Chaos office. He keeps pace ahead of them.

When the graffiti grows dense he knows they are close.

THE REVOLUTION CONTINUES

DOWN WITH MILITARY RULE

THE MARTYR BASSEM GOUDA, HERO OF MAADI

They climb the narrow stairwell. He can hear a television murmuring through the floor from above. He climbs the stairs to the home of the martyr quietly, respectfully. The television grows louder:

23

Yes, Alaa is strong in his resolve. He absolutely refuses to answer any questions in front of a military judge . . .

At the top the door is open, a single pair of shoes sits outside. Khalil takes his off and signals the crew to do the same. He knocks on the door, but there is no answer. The lights are off but the television is on.

He is a civilian and so he must be tried as a civilian. Thousands of Egyptian civilians have already been tried in military courts—and his arrest has brought attention to that fact.

Through the narrow corridor he looks into the first room. Abu Bassem is sitting in front of the television, a phone in his hand and two more on the small table in front of him.

"Abu Bassem?" Khalil says. He doesn't know his real name, he is simply known as Abu Bassem, Bassem's father.

"Ah, yes." Abu Bassem gestures for them to come inside. "Come in. One moment. Come in. I'm just doing a tweet for people to watch this show."

Abu Bassem's concentration is split between his phone and the television, so they each take a seat in the cramped room and watch quietly. He is thin but firm, his grief is all in his shoulders.

Above Abu Bassem, in the center of the small room, hangs a vinyl poster. BASSEM GOUDA: MARTYR OF THE REVOLUTION. The young martyr's eyes stare straight through the camera, the patron saint of his own home.

Alaa knows that the whole world is watching and that the country is behind him and that is giving him strength right now.

Before long the director is making noises of displeasure, checking his watch. But Abu Bassem's attention is fixed on the television. The whole country is talking about Alaa, his stand against the army, his imprisonment, the countdown to the birth of his first son. Abu Bassem doesn't say a word until the interview with Manal, his wife, is over.

"I'm sorry about that. Some tea? A Pepsi?"

"Thank you, we're fine," Khalil says. "As I said on the phone, these men are from French television. They want to hear about your son. And, if it's all right, I'd also like to record for an internet broadcast."

"Of course." Abu Bassem sits gracefully in the seat under his son's poster.

Behind them the cameraman sets up.

"So . . . how do we begin?"

"Obviously we just want to hear about his son," the director declares, in English, to the room at large.

"We think it's important," Khalil says, positioning his body between Abu Bassem and the director, "to hear about your son first, about his life."

"My son was a great boy. A great boy. Always a help. He always helped me. Always smiling. Whatever we asked him for he would do it. He couldn't wait to be grown-up."

Abu Bassem's dignity is somehow unbearable. He doesn't cry or curse or swear vendetta. But he is not defeated. Khalil feels somehow animal in contrast to the older man, his stillness, that he must be enraged for him, that he must do the crying, the stumbling.

"My son wanted to be a musician. On the computer. He and his friends made several songs."

"What's he saying?" the director whispers in his ear.

"He's talking about his son," Khalil replies.

"Tell him we need to hear about his killing."

"Relax," Khalil says, but Abu Bassem has stopped talking. "Sorry, sir"—Khalil concentrates on him—"please carry on."

"My son went down against Mubarak for all of our rights. He went down on the twenty-fifth even, not just the twenty-eighth like the rest of the Brotherhood. He didn't want to raise his kids with just the same chances he had."

Khalil looks up at Bassem's poster, at the eyes staring out into the world. He wonders if he saw him. January twenty-eighth. The day we beat the police. Qasr al-Nil Bridge. Maybe they stood next to each other in the crowd. There was a young man. The first life Khalil saw slip away that day. An inch to the left, a gust of wind, a glance at a watch—the unknowable differences between life and death.

"What's he saying?" the director whispers.

"I'll tell you later," Khalil says. "So you said Bassem wasn't Brotherhood. Are his friends?"

"No, not his friends. But both I and his uncle are."

"I see."

"I'd hoped he would join when he was a little older. Maybe for these elections. But he was his own person. Did you hear his music? I didn't understand it but his friends . . . We could go down to the cyber maybe?"

"You want to go down to his son's cybercafe?" Khalil asks the director.

"No. We need to hurry up."

Khalil feels suddenly, burningly foreign with this crew behind him, a tour operator cashing in on other people's misery, a cheap Virgil to guide foreigners through the city's labyrinth of martyrdom.

"I'm sorry, sir," he says to Abu Bassem in Arabic. "They've had a long day. But I'd like to go with you."

"What did you say to him?" the director says, aggressive now. Khalil feels the blood rising to the back of his head.

"I said I'd like to go to the cyber."

"I told you we don't have time."

"No, *you* don't have time."

"Well, our insurance won't cover us being here so late."

"Here?"

"Yes, here in a neighborhood like this."

"Then you should leave," Khalil says.

He turns away from the director and back to Abu Bassem. He understands enough French to catch some insults before the camera clicks off its tripod.

"I'm sorry about them," Khalil says. "They got a phone call. There's some news they have to cover urgently. Shall we go?"

Abu Bassem stands up to shake their hands and show them out as they bluster through the door. Khalil feels his heart slowing down, feels slowly clean again. No more fixing work. For the first time in a hundred years we don't need to sell our stories to France or England or America. We'll win or lose it all here.

"But you're not in a hurry?" Abu Bassem says.

"If you're not, I'm not."

Abu Bassem puts his arm in Khalil's and they make their way slowly out of the apartment, down the stairwell and through the long passages of memories.

"We fought the morning of the twenty-eighth. I was having some difficulties. But he was never rude or disrespectful. He knew how to handle people. He was good with people. I snapped at him. Said something cruel. On the day he died. I think about it every day. All we want is for him to be recognized as a martyr. We'll have justice when this street is named after him."

ABU BASSEM

He zips his coat up to the collar. He ties a scarf around his neck and quietly opens the front door, makes his way down the dark stairwell's concrete steps and past the graffiti that punctuates his world with a sorrowing pride. He walks through the narrow streets, holding close to the sides to avoid the winter puddles that will rot in the craterous center until the sun comes out again, walking the same route he walks every day now. He knows, he knows, he knows he should do it less. That he needs to get his life back. That he needs to love and protect the ones he still has. But not yet. Soon, but not yet. We will have our street named after you. He turns left. The naked bulb hangs over the doorway. He steps inside and sits down at the third booth in, the deepest one, the most private. He nods at the young boy sitting at a cracked old laptop—who bows his head respectfully. He puts his hand on the mouse and starts moving through the learned motions. Click two times on the orange-and-blue circle, move the arrow up to the white space at the top, click again and type: يو تيوب. Two words he learned months ago and never questioned their meaning. When the screen changes, press on the first of the large English words: YouTube. Next he takes the folded paper from his wallet and types out the English characters one by one: *kiko mahragan*. And then Bassem appears, his face furrowed into a serious expression, his cap turned slightly to the side, his right hand pointing toward the camera, his left holding a microphone, the young man, the musician, his son. The picture doesn't move, will not move, it sits in front of him and from behind it comes the music, Bassem's young voice manipulated by a machine almost beyond recognition, but there, and all the same feelings come rushing back again as his chest cracks with sorrow and pride and anger.

6

In the video the boy is not moving. His blood has turned black on the pavement. Nobody knows what to do. Nobody knew his name.

Khalil hits pause, holding the moment, the intimacy of his sound studio with its low roll of acoustic cotton hanging down from the ceiling, the wide wooden desk with two microphones, Mariam's VISIT PALESTINE poster above it. He takes a breath before placing the headphones over his ears. The conductor before his orchestra. A moment, and he will begin flicking through the sound files one by one; scanning for highlights and grabbing them with loose, brutish cuts to drop them into his five categories: *essential, secondary, ambient, cutaway, effect.* Five colors for five pillars with which to build the week's aural architecture. Five colors with which to make the listener see Abu Bassem's pain, to join his vigil. He presses play on the video once more. We know his name now. We know his name is Bassem.

He feels the weight of the older man's hand on his arm and an old music stirs in his heart:

I've been in
the storm
so lo-ong

The record player in the linoleum corner. The LPs long off-limits. The old man sitting alone in his labyrinth. A silent bullet, a cracked skull, a phone call from the morgue.

Khalil's father went to study in America and never came home. He was supposed to be a violinist, his parents sending him to Juilliard to concentrate on his career, to get away from the fundamental unpredictability of life in Nablus. Life settled down. Certainties were erected. Nidal became Ned.

They never talked about it. Palestine. Home. They never talked in a real way about anything. Only music. Music and its shared contemplation. Music could explain more for Nidal than words ever could.

Khalil sees the cyber, the lone light in a dark alleyway, feels how carefully Abu Bassem treads, feels his arm and wonders if, for even a moment, he can fill in for his son. Bassem watches over us all. The martyr is a witness who speaks of the injustice he sees. He stands before the violence and falls before it. Rachel Corrie before her minotaur.

"And now people ask us why we keep protesting. People who are happy and eating and getting married and acting like people didn't die for them or that people are out protesting and being beaten for them. I say one thing to those people: Don't ask us *why*. My son died for them and now I'll die for them and everyone in Tahrir will die for them—so don't say it's time for calm, don't say we shouldn't protest, don't tell us to stay home, don't ask us *why*. Who are we dying for? For ourselves? Here we were alive and happy and everything. We're dying to stop the killing and the corruption. We're dying for respect. We're dying for bread, freedom, and social justice. And we're dying for you. Just don't ask us why. Please. You can stay home. Tomorrow they'll do to you what they've done to us. And more. Because enough people let them. Stay home, eat, relax, have a nice life, and see what happens to you tomorrow."

The martyr dies for his testimony and you, Abu Bassem, you are the shahed of your son the shaheed, the martyr's witness, the one who will not be silenced, the one who sees and speaks the truth.

A simple church organ pulling together a few unexceptional notes to gather the people's attention. And then the voice rises—

> *I've been in*
> *the storm*
> *so lo-ong*

Khalil hears the music in his head, replays the day he tried to ask his father. Palestine. What's it like? It was a simple question, though they both knew the real one: Why is it not home? And the answer, the look, the deep pull on the cigarette, the pause. His father stood up from his armchair, buttoned his shabby waistcoat, smoothed it down, and went over to the record player. There's not one answer, he'd said. Khalil could see the LP cover, a black-and-white-photograph: the Reverend Franklin. They listened to it in silence, the Reverend's voice rising into his chorus and holding that deep note of long woe before crashing down in lamentations to the Lord. The voice, heavy as a mountain, filled the room with the loss of generations.

> *I've been in*
> *the storm*
> *so lo-ong*

Khalil's fingers hover over his keyboard, waiting for his music. He will watch the video again. A gust of wind, a turn of the head, blood black on the asphalt, the cold of the morgue. Today I am a brutalist and will build in logical, unquestionable blocks: news, interview, music, finish. Today I am a modernist and will slice between segments to reveal hidden truths through catalytic combinations. Today I am Gothic and the spectacle of music will tower over the logic of the interview and empiricism of news. Today I will find your music.

> *I've been in*
> *the storm*
> *so lo-ong*
> *children*

The fluorescent emptiness of a dead son's bedroom.

His father, the snowy solitude and silent cell. Absence, an empty fluorescence.

> *I've been in*
> *the storm*
> *so lo-ong*
> *Oo-o-o-oh*
> *Lord, give me little time*
> *to pray*

7

"You've got to help. Mariam, you've got to. He was painting the walls of Umm Ayman's house and they took him and we don't know where and his phone is off you've got to help they took him last night and we didn't even realize until this morning and we don't know where he is you've got to help, Mariam, I don't know what to do."

"It's okay, Tante, take a breath," Mariam says. "It'll be okay. Just tell me everything you know and we'll find him. Where exactly was he arrested?"

Within the hour Mariam is marching up to the steps to Qasr al-Nil police station, Rania and Malik, a lawyer, keeping close behind her. She doesn't break stride as she steps up to a young officer sitting at the splintered desk in the entrance hall.

"You're holding someone illegally."

"What? Who are you?"

"This man here is a lawyer with the Egyptian Initiative for Personal Rights." She gestures at Malik but doesn't give his

34

name. "We're looking for a young man by the name of Abdul-rahman Ahmed. He was arrested illegally last night for decorating someone's house."

"Decorating?"

"Yes, decorating. We know that you have him and we demand that he be released immediately."

"*Demand?*"

"Yes, demand. In ten minutes the media will be alerted that a young student who was kindly helping the mother of a martyr decorate her house is being illegally detained. In an hour a crowd of five hundred people will be on the street. If he's not released by tomorrow morning five families of the martyrs will have a press conference—"

"Okay, okay. Hang on."

The officer is stunned. He gets up and slips into the dark corridor behind him.

Mariam thinks of Umm Ayman's house, of the walls now illuminated with her son's face, his name. Every week Mariam sits with the families of the martyred in Umm Ayman's apartment, drinks tea with them, discusses their plans and their dreams for their fallen children's memories. New networks of trust and consolation and revolution have formed. Statements from the martyrs' families carry a political weight heavier than any other.

"Please." The young officer is back. "Please take a seat."

Malik paces before them, Rania composes tweets and emails and saves them in drafts, waiting for the signal to go public, Mariam calls Abu Bassem and asks him to prepare the families to make an appearance in the morning. The cells are underground, under her feet. She listens for noises, vibrations, covert communications. But the walls are thick. Ninety-nine police stations burned to the ground but Qasr al-Nil still stands.

Her phone buzzes—

Umm Ayman: Please update with news about Abdu. Shall we call the press conference now?

Umm Ayman has grown so strong. My son, she says, my son died for this revolution and I will now give my last drop of blood for it.

"Shall we call the press conference?"

"Give them an hour," Rania says.

"Okay. Well, talk loudly on the phone as if you've got Yosri Fouda on the line."

Rania puts her phone on silent and joins Malik in his pacing. "Yosri?" She booms down the line, "Yosri, can you hear me? Yeah, we're still at the station. They're holding him. No, I don't know if he's tortured. People are asking? Say we don't know. Yeah, Qasr al-Nil station. Decorating, that's right."

Mariam has to step outside to keep herself from laughing. She lights a cigarette and in its first breath remembers anew that her old life has been entirely washed away. School friends, old colleagues, young dreams, ex-boyfriends—all have vanished from existence.

"Yeah, all right, Yosri, you'll tell everyone then? Yep. Great. Okay, see you in a bit."

It's not long before a door swings open from the dark of the corridor and a young boy appears, grinning like he just scored a goal.

UMM AYMAN

She thinks, every morning, of the way he would prepare the cheese for breakfast. Ayman, her boy, her Ayman, and his moment of pride and presentation to the family every day. The soft whiteness scooped out of the packet and spread with a swirl in the shallow bowl, the herbs—zaatar usually, mint sometimes—then an almost flamboyant drop of olive oil and the look of quiet satisfaction creeping into the corners of his mouth as he whisked the bottle away. His contribution. The thing he could give to us each morning. She makes it his way, the herbs, the swirl, and places it down in front of what remains of her family. Gathered, now, every morning, in mourning and absence. She is thankful. She will be watchful. And when breakfast is over there is always a little left. She makes sure of it. She places it in the fridge. She does not think in reasons. It should just be there. Heba, her youngest, always watching, takes it out first thing in the morning and washes it before her mother wakes up. And the day begins again. The relics of the dead. The cloth of the saints. The guidance of the stars. Do they hear you? Do you hear me? Again and again and forever. The rhythms and rituals that keep us alive, keep us strong in our faith and our work through this cruelty. She knows it's pointless. That it's ridiculous, even, to think about it, but she cannot shake the thought. That he was hungry. Why did we not eat together? Were we all so consumed with the news? Her boy died hungry. He went out like a man to stand up for his people and his church and his family and he marched, and marched hungry. Don't worry. She can hear his voice perfectly. I'll eat, I promise. Don't worry, Mama. My boy. My darling boy. Would you have been able to run that inch faster? Stand that second longer? Breathe even one breath more?

8

November 19, 2011
6:09 p.m.

Mariam opens her backpack and quickly moves through the apartment: phone charger, water, two packs of cigarettes, two lighters, small notepad, antiseptic spray, pen, painkillers, toothbrush, spare underwear, socks, T-shirt, ID. Money, phone, keys in pockets.

She pulls out her phone and writes a tweet:

Everybody: go to Tahrir now. Tell everyone. The police attacked the "injured of the revolution" protest. Huge numbers are out.

"Ready?" Khalil asks.

"Yes," she replies. "Let's go."

In four seconds she can pull the kufiyyeh up around her face, tie it around the back of her head, can become a boy. She practices once, in the bedroom mirror. He watches her hands, so deft in the knot.

He pulls her close to him and they stop for a moment before stepping out into it. It's finally happening again. The streets are full. She kisses him, moves herself against him; the clamor of the riot rises up from the streets below.

"Don't do anything stupid," she says. "Or brave."

"It's not me I'm worried about."

She pushes against him for a last moment and he is in their first night together and the echo of bullets ricocheting through the air and the blood rushing as his hands pulled her body against him—but the front door's open, it's time to go.

There are no cars on the street. The elegant boulevards of Downtown are all but deserted. What few people there are hurry toward Tahrir. In the square a police truck is on fire. Khalil and Mariam hurry through the crowd, toward the reverb of shotguns down Mohamed Mahmoud Street. Throughout the square the same words ring out, again and again:

Down, down with military rule!

Mariam cannot help but smile to herself.

Down, down with military rule!

It's finally happening again.

Burning tires light the long and narrow dark of Mohamed Mahmoud Street. Silhouettes slip between the flames. The police form a dark line of men ahead. At the front, the conscripts. Behind them the officers wait darkly, their trucks and shotguns ready. Behind them both lies the Ministry of the Interior, still standing despite all those who gave their lives in January trying to take it. Motorcycle ambulances race the injured away from the front line. She squeezes Khalil's hand and is gone. He pulls his phone out and sets it to record through the binaural microphones in his headphones. He stands to one side for a moment, watching the shape and rhythm of the battle.

A hundred people make up the front line at any one time, informal ranks of stone throwers and shit talkers hurling everything they have at the cops. Behind them a middle section stretches down the street, the immediate backup, people taking a break from the rocks or gearing up the nerve for those final few steps into the firing line, people pushing up for a better view, the fire starters and gas catchers hurling the smoking canisters back where they came from. Behind them, where Mohamed Mahmoud Street flows out into Tahrir, are the spectators, the chanters, the drummers, doctors, quarriers, and hawkers.

A rock crashes into the tree above Khalil and cracks into his head, another grazes his shoulder and another bounces off the tarmac onto his shins, and he picks one up and hurls it back at the police. He can't see where it lands. He pulls his hood up and slips into the crowd, into a unitary anonymity, and with each rock he slings out into the no-man's-land he feels a growing potency as more and more bodies press up to the front. Each shot rings like a ripple through the crowd, each person who falls hurried quickly away to the doctors, each rock in the air an invisible fate, an invigorating fatalism.

A siren sounds and a panic of blue light flashes through the darkness. A shotgun sounds. Two APCs charge forward, showering buckshot, and a gas canister lands at his feet and the poison takes hold in seconds and cramps at his stomach and burns his eyes and he runs in the stampede back to Tahrir, holding his breath until he's doubled over, dry-retching, waiting for his stomach to unclench itself. Through the salty mucus filling his eyes he sees a boy in a hood, feels him rubbing his back, and it's only when the breaths come again that he sees it's Mariam.

41

"You okay?" she says.

"I'm good."

She takes her bag off her back and pulls out half an onion, holds it under his nose.

"Does that work?" he asks.

"Try it."

He breathes it in.

"Isn't this an old Palestinian trick?" she asks.

"Is it?"

In the crowd behind her at least three people are splashing Pepsi into their eyes, desperate to soothe the burning.

"I was doing the Pepsi thing before," Khalil says. "This is better."

A man with a large cardboard box on his head weaves through the crowd: "Gas masks! Ten pounds! Get your gas masks!"

"You're good?" she says.

"Yes."

"I've got to find my mother," Mariam says, then squeezes his hand and is gone.

Khalil lights a cigarette. The gas has cleared and the crowd is flowing back down Mohamed Mahmoud Street for another round. His chest swells with a warrior pride.

Down, down with military rule!

A woman with a bottle of Pepsi held high looks for patients.

Khalil takes his phone out of his pocket, checks on the recording.

"Beautiful sight, no?" comes a voice from behind him. He turns to see Hafez. Even in the middle of a riot, Hafez is well dressed, a casual but decent jacket over a rugged dark shirt. He stands with an old Hasselblad camera slung over one shoulder and a standard digital around his neck.

"It's good."

"Only took the army nine months."

The flames from the police truck lick high up into the air.

"You been here long?" Hafez asks.

"Couple hours."

Hafez is watching the crowd pulse back and forth, studying its movements, alert, always, for the image.

A man's body is carried among eight people. *Field hospital*, they shout. *Where's the field hospital?* and two boys start running with them.

"You see how it started?" Khalil asks.

"I heard they came and the filth beat up the injured-of-the-revolution's protest camp."

"That's a dumb move."

"Or a provocation."

Every time he looks at Hafez he remembers January 28. Thrown together and inseparable since then. The day of days. The day we won. The day the police fled. The crucible in which new bonds, a new chemistry, was catalyzed. Khalil sees it still, always, a frozen moment in the sun, the sky a brilliant blue, the glinting metal falling like a mechanical animal homing in on them, the crowd parting and running and covering their eyes as it comes for them until from out of the sea of hesitation steps Hafez and it's trapped under his foot, the hissing gas canister pouring its malice out into the world and then it's up and in the air again and the crowd is back all around him and roaring in defiance as the last of the poison trails down toward its grave in the Nile and there's Hafez with a wild pride in his eyes and a red welt of seared flesh across his hand and the crowd surging back toward the bridge.

"They're hot!" he said in surprise, almost laughing, shaking his burned hand against the wind. We didn't even know they were hot. January 28. Just a bunch of kids out on the street.

A man breaks out of the crowd. He has three tear gas canisters in his hand. "Photograph these!" he shouts at Hafez. "Photograph these, sir! It says *Made in America*, right? Nothing's changed! Photograph these! Fuck Tantawi and fuck the army!"

Hafez takes a shot, says thank you, and the man moves on.

A doctor in a white coat is picking her way through the crowd, a black gas mask raised over her face. An old man sits on the ground with his head in his hands. "Are you okay, sir?" she asks. He nods, puts his hand up to her, and she helps him stand and steady himself and head back to the battle.

"Fucking Tantawi," Hafez says, shaking his head. "What do they think they're doing?"

"They don't know what they're doing."

"No? They come beat up a bunch of invalids live on TV by accident?"

"That was the cops."

"You think the police do anything without an okay from the top?" Hafez says

"Police and the army aren't necessarily friends."

"Right now, they're friends," Hafez says.

"They were humiliated," Khalil says. "Maybe they want revenge and Tantawi can't control them."

"There's an election in five days," Hafez says. The police truck blazes in front of them. Three news cameras record the hungry flames. "It's no accident. They left that behind for us to burn."

"But the army *wants* the elections," Khalil says. "They don't want this."

"Nor do the Brotherhood," Hafez says. "That's why they're not out here."

44

A roar of triumph echoes out from the front line. Hundreds of people are streaming into the street and Khalil follows, excited about getting back into the fight, about getting home and listening to his new recordings, about stripping the gas-sodden clothes off and falling, alive, into bed with Mariam, about posting the next podcast to Facebook and watching the downloads spike, about the stories they'll tell for years to come.

November 19, 2011
8:47 p.m.

"What'd you need?" Mariam asks as she slips under the rope separating the field hospital from the street. She'd spotted her mother from afar, her gray hair tied back tight, the headlamp, the rapid movements.

"Betadine, cotton wool, gauze," her mother says without looking up from her patient's buckshot back.

Mariam knows her way around the supplies and quickly places each item carefully next to her mother.

"Dress it?" Mariam says.

"Yes."

They work quickly together. Mariam loves watching her mother work. When she was young Mariam had a vision of herself as an emergency room doctor, quick and clear in command, calm under pressure, compassionate with her patients, an example to her colleagues and immaculate in scrubs.

"You okay?" her mother asks.

"Fine."

"And Khalil?"

"Everyone's fine."

"Good . . . You'll be all right, son," Nadia says to the teenage boy, gritting his teeth against the hot metal in his body. "There's nothing serious, thank God. We'll clean you up and you'll be just fine."

"Thank you," the boy mutters through clenched teeth.

Mariam's phone buzzes:

Have the supplies, where should we meet?

Ten minutes later she meets the old friend of her parents by the Borsa. He smiles as he sees her, opens the trunk of his car.

"Pretty much everything on the list," he says.

"Great," she says, counting the boxes quickly. "Thanks."

"I'll be back with more tomorrow. Be careful."

They can't get the car to the field clinic but she can't carry all the boxes alone. Four teenage boys sit smoking in a street café. "Hey," Mariam says. The boys look up at her. "Yeah, you guys," she says. "Come help me carry this stuff to the revolution."

They jump to attention, grab two boxes each, and follow behind her, through the crowd to the field hospital.

Her phone vibrates—

Rosa: Any injured take them to Qasr al-Aini Hospital and call me. Some doctors there we can trust.

Every thirty seconds a new motorcycle ambulance arrives carrying another young body riddled with bleeding buck-shot.

"Excuse me, miss," a deep, formal voice says from above her.

"Yes," Mariam says, without looking up.

"Would you please wear this?"

She snaps her eyes up. Wear this? What the fuck does this asshole have the nerve to try? *Wear* this? If there's a fucking cap or headscarf in his hand, I'm going to—

He's holding out a white helmet.

"Please," he says. "We bought helmets for the doctors. You have to stay safe. We need you."

November 20, 2011
2:19 a.m.

Rania commands the room, her hands full of papers and phones; she shouts out instructions over the television blaring in the corner: "Gas masks! Tell them to buy gas masks and food. Bananas, biscuits, cheese sandwiches. Nothing greasy. And gas masks! Everything goes to Omar Makram Mosque—that's the distribution point now. And juice! Juice in small cartons. Got it? Keep people's blood sugar up. How many cameras do we have down there? We need to be putting videos out already! We need a list of people with cameras, editors. We need videos out tonight!" She is the center of a web of information relaying out and across Downtown.

The dining table at the center of the Chaos office is crowded with laptops busy with news, videos, photographs, tweets, and press alerts. Mariam's friend Ashraf the Enormous is rigging up cable extensions while Hafez threads USB wires from a massive hard drive up to the waiting computers above. Rosa is fixing a bulletin board to the wall for new information: *camera-people, editors, medical runs, food buying, food distribution, media contacts.* The Chaos office has become a cerebral cortex at the center of the information war.

In the corner the television has state TV on loop.

We can assure our fellow citizens that tear gas would only ever be used in circumstances of national security.

"Have we sent out the shotgun video to the press list yet!?"
"Make sure it goes to domestic *and* foreign."
"How many languages can we get it into?"

And there is not an atom of truth to the malicious rumors of live ammunition.

"Did Nancy ever buy that night-vision camera?"
"Who's putting together the list of hospitals we trust?"
"Where are those instructions about how to make a catapult?"

Do not believe unverified rumors. Do not rely on foreign-owned media for your information.

"Will someone turn that shit off!" Hafez shouts from underneath the dining table. "Hey, Khalil! I have a great interview for you." Hafez has his two cameras out on the table. "I talked to a doctor about the effects of the tear gas. Here." He hands Khalil an SD card.

Beware of troublemakers. Beware of infiltrators. Beware of those who would bring Egypt to her knees.

November 20, 2011
7:45 a.m.

Khalil quickly cuts the gas testimony with street battle sounds
and interviews—

> *In all my years as an emergency physician I have never seen*
> *reactions like this. The government is using an experimental*
> *new gas. Possibly a nerve gas. People are dying of*
> *asphyxiation.*

Next is news in brief about the protests to come and the
supplies needed for Tahrir. He finishes quickly, exports, and sets
it to upload.

Within minutes the hashtag #egywarcrimes is born; by
midnight half the nonstate TV show hosts in the country are
talking about it and grilling the military spokesmen; by morning a dozen foreign news websites are quoting the doctor; by
the next evening emails have arrived from NGOs and activist
organizations and academics asking if samples of the new gas
can be smuggled out for testing, and by the day after a U.S.
State Department spokesman denies any security assistance
funds to the Egyptian government were ever used for the pur-
chase of tear gas.

November 21, 2011
2:36 a.m.

Her hands are cut from the rocks. The sky is filled with jagged
fists of paving stone crashing around their heads. When the
rock hits her she thinks that she's been slapped and spins toward

the men, but when the pain focuses on her cheekbone she understands and stumbles to the side of the road behind a tree. A burning tire illuminates enormous words flickering on the wall behind her: WE'LL GET THEM JUSTICE, OR WE'LL DIE LIKE THEM.

Her phone buzzes:

Mama: It's time for you to call your father

She has a flash of anger. This is not a time for phone calls. She is angry but she is cold and she wants to stay here near the danger. She wants to stay on the front line. It can't just be poor boys who keep dying.

She collects herself. People are depending on you. The field hospitals need supplies. The hospitals need medicine. Time to call your father.

She drops the rock in her hand, walks away from the front line, the headlights of the motorcycle ambulances carving a path through the forest of human silhouettes, racing new injuries to the field hospitals.

She turns into the McDonald's alleyway and dials her father. They used to work together, her parents. Used to do real work, used to hold a whole hospital together between them. The best public cancer unit in Egypt, they said. He was, maybe still is, the best administrator in the country. But it went to his head—as it always does—and he left it, left them, for the blue glass and creamy marble of a private hospital out in the desert.

"Hi," she says. "It's Mariam."

"I know my own daughter's number," her father says.

"We need help. With supplies."

"For this chaos you're causing?"

"*Us* causing! Do you see guns in *our* hands?"

"You're being manipulated by the Brotherhood. They want

to disgrace the army. You're disgracing all of Egypt in front of the world!"

"The Brotherhood has nothing to do with this. They're with the army now."

"Doesn't mean they're not playing you. They're using you to force the elections before anyone else is ready."

"Please. We can talk about this another time."

"Listen to me, Mariam. This is what they do. They always sell you out in the end. Ask your mother."

So where are *you*, Father? With your years of experience. Why are you not out here helping us outplay them?

"If you were here you'd see there's no way anyone's controlling what's going on out here. We're winning. We just need supplies."

He's silent for a long time.

She lights a cigarette.

"The usual stuff?" he says. "Same as in the Eighteen Days?"

"Yes. But we need things for the gas." She pulls a list from her pocket. "Naphcon, Prisoline, Prefrin, Ventolin inhalers, masks. And the Eighteen Days stuff, too. You have that list still?"

"It won't be hard to find. I hardly have any messages from my daughter."

She doesn't say anything. This isn't the time for family drama.

November 21, 2011
1:12 p.m.

Khalil and Hafez stand a few streets over from the battle, a quick break for a coffee and a cigarette. Umm Ayman is on the television in the corner, she is speaking in the camera. The qahwa falls silent as her words fill the alleyway:

51

Record the blood of the martyr. They shot him with bullets and ran him over. Go, Tantawi, and see. See. He says they're not shooting anyone. Go. See. See what is being done to the young of Egypt. What's being done to the youth. Those thrown in garbage piles. Our youth were shot and thrown in the garbage. But every one of them in Tahrir there is Ayman. Every one of them in Tahrir is Ayman. And Ayman's blood will not be lost as long as they are in Tahrir. As long as they hold their ground. I will say Ayman's blood is lost when they leave. If they kneel before them and leave, then my son Ayman's blood is gone. As long as they remain firm, my son is alive. My son's blood will not go willingly. Every one of them is Ayman. Each and every one of them is Ayman. Every girl among them is Ayman. Every boy is Ayman. They've all become Ayman. All those in Tahrir are now Ayman. And they will avenge his death. They'll not leave until the whole state is torn down and built back up again. They'll not leave until every policeman and soldier who fired on their own people are tried and jailed. I swear they will get him justice. And God will not let this pass.

November 21, 2011
7:49 p.m.

A young man lies semiconscious on the ground, leg elevated, trousers sodden with blood. Mariam's mother is before him, tying the wound tight.

"Femoral artery," Nadia says as Mariam kneels next to her.

"I can take it," Mariam says.

"It's okay."

"Mama—you have a lot of patients. I've got this."

Nadia pauses, and Mariam takes over the tourniquet. Femoral means he's lost a lot of blood.

"Just try and be calm," Nadia says softly to the boy. "You're brave, son. You're really brave. This is one of my best nurses." She strokes his forehead and turns quietly to the next case. Mariam pulls the improvised lever out of the bandage, ties it. The tourniquet can stop the bleeding but without an ambulance he'll lose the leg.

The boy looks up at Mariam as she finishes the knot. "You'll be fine," Mariam says. "The ambulance is coming."

"Where will it take me?" he says.

"To the hospital."

"But the hospitals are Mubarak's."

"Not all of them."

A motorcycle's tires screech to a halt. *Hey!* someone shouts. *We need help here!* Two doctors carry in a new casualty, wheels burn, the bike speeds back to the front.

"Come with me to the hospital," the boy says.

"I can't."

"It's a good hospital? It's with the revolution?"

"Yes. We need to stop the bleeding. They have better equipment."

"You'll visit me? To check they've done it right?"

She looks at his face for the first time and is struck by how pretty he is, his high cheekbones and delicate nose.

"I'll try and find you in the morning."

"Thank you."

"It's a fucking generational war." Malik shouts over the echoing reverb of shotguns and the clattering rain of a thousand rocks. "It's all-out fucking *war* and if we don't *do* something we're gonna be down on our fucking knees until we're fucking dead! 'Cos they're not gonna let go of shit until they're all dead! Here! Have some fucking elections, you wankers. There you go. Shut up now, aye? We've got no choice but to rip it from them, the *old*. It's not about right or left anymore— they're all the same. It's about young versus old. They'd send us all off to war to die if they could, the bastards. Everyone under forty, off you go. Take your debt and your stupid student loans and your useless fucking university degrees and fuck off! It's a *war*, man. Young against old. Whole fucking world over."

Malik: another diaspora returnee. Back from Glasgow to build the new country. A lawyer, working on a police reform initiative. In a less intelligent person Malik's voice and volume would be intensely annoying. Khalil keeps his eye on the mouth of Mohamed Mahmoud Street, for sirens, panic, for Mariam's kufiyyeh.

His phone beeps with a Facebook message—

I've been following your posts. Am so impressed with the bravery and courage you're all showing. Promise me you'll stay safe.
Diane x

Khalil feels his back straighten with a virile pride; the whole world is watching. All your ex-girlfriends are watching.

Essential listening from @ChaosCairo. Huge pressure mounting on Egyptian Army and now toxic gas.

"You know what it's like?" Malik is as unrelenting as the battle behind him. "The world they've so carefully fucking constructed? It's like one of those *humane* fucking mousetraps. Here: have a little glimpse of some fucking cheddar in there and you'll walk yourself right in because (a) why *wouldn't* you? (b) you're *hungry*, and (c) you're a *fucking mouse* and then schloop, oh sorry, oh excuse me, the door seems to have closed behind you and now here you are humanely fucking fucked and left to enjoy the little crumb of cheddar they bought you with for the rest of your useless life."

Hafez watches the crowd. Khalil flicks through his phone.

Incredible mismanagement from EgyArmy. Demand they cede power to civilian rule now!

The One silently listens to Malik's rant. The One is an old-school European immigrant-drifter, has lived in the same Downtown apartment for decades, was married briefly to an Egyptian woman; a traveler from the times when you went somewhere and didn't turn around and leave on the next budget flight out. Khalil can never remember if he's Bulgarian or Hungarian and he can't ask him again. No one even remembers why he's called the One anymore.

Khalil sees Mariam walking over to them, pulling the kufiyyeh off from around her neck. She looks exhausted but invigorated.

"You okay?" Khalil asks.

"Yes," Mariam says. "Hungry."

"What's happening with the new council?" Hafez asks.

"What council?" Malik butts in.

"A revolutionary council," Mariam says.

"For the army to cede transitional power to," Hafez takes over.

"Who's in it?" Malik says.

"Martyrs' family members. Lawyers. Religious figures. Academics. Legal experts. It's not a bad list," Hafez says.

"You think the army might go for it?"

"If they see this shit's not going to end without a major concession, then maybe. Every minute of this makes them look weaker."

Khalil's phone vibrates—

Strength and solidarity from Athens to my Chaos Comrades! You are an inspiration to the world!

Malik leans forward. "They say they have planes ready at the airport for SCAF to escape."

"Shut up."

"Yep."

"Well, what are we doing here then? We need to get back in there."

November 22, 2011
3:34 a.m.

Khalil stands back from the front line. His shoulder aches from days of throwing rocks, but he is wide awake.

Hello mate. Jim from Huffpost. Thnx for interview tonight. Wondering if you know anyone in the Brotherhood I could talk to?

Under the yellow streetlights he sees Ashraf, Mariam's friend from childhood who laughs loud enough to silence a room and has hands big enough to crush your skull and whose footsteps make glasses of water tremble and who is not, Mariam insists, a rival or a threat or interested or an ex or anything—but he has become her personal bodyguard.

"Khalil," Ashraf says with a smile and an open paw.

"Hi," Khalil says, and grips Ashraf's hand with a manly but uncompetitive firmness. He's not worried about Ashraf. He's glad, in fact, that he watches out for Mariam.

"I'll see you at home," Mariam says. "We have to go to the morgue."

November 22, 2011
4:28 a.m.

He's there, as Mariam knew he would be. The color drained from his body, the tourniquet soaked in dry, blackened blood. And there's the phone number, written in careful marker up his left forearm.

"Hello," a harried voice answers. A baby is crying in the background.

"Hello, miss," Mariam says, unsure how to carry on. "My name is Mariam."

The boy doesn't move and she doesn't know his name. The boy doesn't move. Of course he doesn't move. He's never going to move again. Did you tie the tourniquet tight enough? Should you have left your mother to her work? Did you cost him a crucial second? Did you take the reins before you were ready? His hand doesn't move. His hand will never move again. Could one second, one breath more blood have made the difference?

"Yes?"

"This is your phone number?" Mariam stalls.

His body lies cold before her under the glare of the fluorescent light. His shirt is ripped, his slenderness exposed to the

57

cold, to the aluminum fridges, the metal of the coroner's table.

"What do you mean, is this is my phone number? You just called me, didn't you?"

"You're right. I did."

There is no sheet to cover him with. There is nothing but dampness and mold and stained steel. The clerk does not enter. Nobody would have called the number.

"I'm calling you from the city morgue."

"Oh God. What's happened to him? Oh, God have mercy. What did they do to him?"

"Your son was brave."

Nobody would have called her. He would have been buried in the desert with all the other nobodies. How many other mothers are out looking for their children still?

"Your son was brave. He's a martyr now."

November 22, 2011
4:59 a.m.

His hand lies cold on the chromium table. Mariam wants to reach out and hold it. She still doesn't know his name. His hand is still, will be still forever. If I held it, nothing would happen. If I held it, maybe he wouldn't be so alone. If I held it the coroner would walk in and there would be a scandal.

She keeps her hands by her side, waiting for the boy's mother to arrive.

How many have we lost now? What does this do to us? How many times did we warn people? You could have done more. There is always something. Nothing is fixed. Nothing until death. We could have stopped this. We could have fought back harder, earlier. What if we hadn't left the square the day

Mubarak stepped down? If five minutes had been different. If one word had been spoken different. We should have been different—because you only know one way. You with your trucks of malnourished men plucked from the countryside to throw rocks at their own people in strange cities and stand as cannon fodder for the officers and their shotguns and their body armor. This is what you have? This is the miserable power you want to cling to? Your slave army to work your factories and fields on conscription, your pasta production and air-conditioning units and men's clubs and salmon-pink walls? This is what you'll go to war against your own people for?

She picks up the boy's cold hand and holds it gently in hers, she hears the rain of bullets and the echo of death and remembers Khalil, that first night, hiding off Tahrir as the army's metal ricocheted across Downtown. Months ago now. April eighth. They ran and hid and stopped in the dark of the stairwell and she pulled at his shirt and ran her hands over his body. "Are you shot?" she kept saying. "Are you shot? Are you shot?" As she checked his trousers for the wet warmth of blood: "Are you shot? Are you shot?" And then his hands were on her and he wasn't shot and his hands were in her hair and on her back and neither of them were bleeding and neither of them were dead.

November 22, 2011
5:21 a.m.

The mother will need help. And how many more mothers, too? How many bodies are waiting inside the aluminum fridges for their uncles to wash them? She wants to open a door but she's afraid. What if each fridge has five bodies stuffed inside it? What if they are rotting unrefrigerated? She does not move from next to the boy, his body turning yellow under the cold strip light. She strokes the top of his hand and sees now Verena clasping her husband's hand to her chest in the morgue after Maspero, tastes the last breaths of the dead coating her throat, lying deep in her lungs. The end comes so quickly.

We could have done more. We could always have done more. We should have made people listen sooner. We were too slow and now they've made their deal with the Brotherhood and all we have is rocks. The Brotherhood keeps the peace and the army keeps their bank accounts. The elections are upon us, the trap is set. They think elections can end the revolution? They think that's all it takes. Khalil is thinking about voting. How can he even think about it? What is he thinking? What are we supposed to do—pack up in the morgue and quietly file into the polling station? That's what this is for? That's what this death is for? To be forgotten with a ballot?

November 22, 2011
5:44 a.m.

Once, deep inside the fluorescence of a government building—it must have been the Mogamma3—standing in the eternal queue, she broke down in tears. Mariam remembers it perfectly. The cruelty of it. The bureaucratic disdain for our precious breaths vanishing into our eternal, untouchable wake; seconds gifted to us by millions of unrepeatable accidents and divine chemical coincidences burning up before her eyes, evaporating off her body, out of all their souls into the earthly certainty of state bureaucracy. She clutched at her chest and ran out into the waiting winter. How short life is. Life is to be lived and death is to be feared and hated and remembered and resisted every day. There is only now, there is not even tomorrow. A life that others will talk about when it leaves us. That's the goal. A life that conquers death with memory. She does not know the boy's name.

Her phone vibrates:

Hello. My son is missing. I was given your number. I think the army has him. I was told you can help.

She pulls a pen and battered notepad out of her back pocket and adds the new phone number to her list for the morning.

UMM X

She saw the pen in his hands, saw the numbers climbing up his arm, her numbers. She hadn't seen a pen in his hand since he stopped school. A part of her was proud. Then she understood better. Then she should have locked him in the house. She should have taken his phone, called her brother, and barricaded the door. She should have called her brother and sent him out of the city to the village. She should have taken his shoes and cut them up. She should have locked the door and melted the key. She knew, she knew he was watching that video on his own in his room. What kind of mother lets her son do that? How could you hear it, the pleading in the dead of night, and not take it from him? *Please, basha, please, no more. Please, please, no more.* How many times did he watch the video, the grainy image, his father's humiliation, the policeman's stick, the bloody ropes. *Please, basha, please please I beg you.* Words that have haunted us all for years, words I hear in the glint of every knife, in the shine of this metal table. How can you hear your son listening to that filth and not take it away from him? Were you afraid of him, a little? Did you know that he wouldn't give it to you? That he would have to have his revenge? You couldn't have taken it from him. You knew from the first time you saw him, sitting in the corner, the phone in his hand, his father's voice pleading from the past, the police whip cracking through the night. You knew, you knew. And now they've taken your boy too.

November 22, 2011
6:47 a.m.

Mariam emerges into the daylight and doesn't understand when she sees Khalil sitting on the low wall outside the morgue. Someone else is dead, she thinks.

"What are you doing here?" she says.

He stands up. "I thought you'd need a ride home."

"Thank you." She puts her arm around his shoulders and when she sees the car her body wakes to its tiredness and her legs tremble a little. She sits and melts into the deep seat, her bones, skin, hair all heavy with relief on sitting down. She puts her hand on his knee.

"You want to go home?" she asks.

"Why? You want to go to the front?"

"Let's just take a look," she says.

November 22, 2011
7:39 a.m.

In the dawn there is a waiting. A comedown. The dark possibility of the night is over and the real world has survived it and is growing in strength all around her as shops open and the first buses roar past, and soon all that'll be left is the need for a shower to wash off the night's chemical accelerants. The rising sun seeps a dull gray into the streets, slowly lighting the long and ruined road between the few remaining revolutionists and the police. Khalil and Mariam sit side by side on a car parked in Bab al-Louq, smoking and watching, legs touching. A gas canister chokes out its last few breaths. The police, in full body armor, stand at one end of the street, all Wild Bunch shotguns resting on their hips. The revolutionists, cigarettes hanging out of their mouths, wait with rocks in their hands, the stretch of road between them too long to make the throw.

November 24, 2011
6:47 a.m.

They come at dawn with a crane and trucks. The army soldiers push the crowd down Mohamed Mahmoud Street, away from the Ministry of the Interior. The crane drops concrete blocks on the asphalt. Block by block a wall is built. Doctors from the Muslim Brotherhood, dressed in their white coats, their beards cut close, climb onto the wall . One stands hand in hand with a general and shouts out to the crowd over a megaphone:

"Go back to the square. The revolution is in the square! The army has put this wall up for your own safety! Go, you can safely protest in Tahrir! Go back to the square. The revolution is in the square! The revolution is in the square!"

Some people shuffle back toward Tahrir.

A voice shouts out: "What do you mean, in the square? What the fuck kind of revolution happens in a square, you assholes!?"

"Get out of our way, you traitors!" another man shouts. "This is between us and the police!"

"The revolution is in the square! Protest safely and democratically in the square!"

A line of Brotherhood men stand in front of the new wall. They carry long steel poles between them and together start pushing the crowd away, away from the wall, back to the square. It's been coming. Since Mubarak's fall the Brotherhood has been courting the army. Everyone's been courting the army, but the Brotherhood must have given them the best offer. The army returns to backstage with all its privileges while the

Brotherhood wins the elections. Easy. The two don't need to be in opposition. The army should not be seen to be ruling. Each can look after the other.

"Get off me, you sons of bitches! You fucking collaborators! We were winning! They were running! Traitors! You're traitors! You've sold us out to the army! You've sold us out, you fucking traitors!"

But the Brotherhood line is strong and the crowd is pushed back meter by meter to Tahrir.

9

November 26, 2011

The elevator door opens and a small middle-aged man enters, nods his head good morning. After a moment he takes off his gold-rimmed glasses and looks at Khalil with a disarming earnestness.

"What's happened with your friend?" he asks.

"Excuse me?"

"Your friend in jail. With the long hair. The sticker on your door."

"You mean Alaa?"

"Yes."

"He's still in jail."

"I'm sorry to hear that."

Khalil leans heavily on the elevator wall. The gas does strange things to people. People are sick, vomiting. He couldn't get out of bed. He lay down and woke up sweating, confused, the world dark again. The older man waits in silence for him to say something.

"But there's a lot of pressure now. They've been forced to move his case to a civilian court."

"Good. Good." He turns away with a sharp little movement to face the door again, then twitches back toward Khalil, in the mood for more conversation. "Your accent—you were not born here?"

"No. In America."

"Well, welcome home. It's disgraceful what they're doing to him, you know? The army thinks they can just frame him like that. Everyone knows what happened at Maspero."

"They're denying it."

"But that's impossible now. You kids and that Facebook of yours—impossible."

The elevator arrives at the ground floor and they walk together to the street.

"It was nice talking to you," the neighbor says. "And, I wonder, if you happen to have any *more* of those stickers?"

"I'll get you one."

"Yes, thank you," the neighbor says. "I would be so grateful."

Khalil nods goodbye, crosses the wide street and cuts sharply into an alleyway. Downtown is all about the shortcuts, the hidden footpaths slipping through clusters of buildings, the quick duck to the right and away from the crowd to the stilled fountain in front of Grillon, the swinging doors into Estoril, the qahwa chairs that line the narrowness up to Umm Dahab's street kitchen, the quick dash behind Townhouse up to Odeon for a last drink before calling it a night. Cairo's alleyways, for a moment, become complicit in your roguishness.

From a taxi's sound system comes the thump of electro-shaabi music: the new flex from the ghetto. What would my father think of this new music, of its rebellious genesis in the street and the young and the disenfranchised and the newly empowered? The hip-hop of our time, coming live from the ghettos on USB sticks. Would he feel the connection between there and here, see the line binding Run-D.M.C. to Oka & Ortega? Or would he turn it off and tune it out and keep it locked in whatever strongbox he has reserved for this side of the world, keep himself listening to the A-side of his history?

It was music that brought Khalil to Egypt. He would learn the qanun, would navigate the worlds of meaning bound tight in its seventy-two strings and speak in subtleties beyond language through its quarter tones. The qanun. The Law. Whole universes of potential wait tight and tense in its hollow. The qanun would be his home. He would be the one to reclaim that most majestic of sounds from the Orientalists, he would carve out a place for it in the future, in the modern, bring it bright and new into the digital world.

Who would have guessed, just a few months ago, that we would be here? How far away now, those long weekends in Kofi's garage drinking PBRs and scratching away at songs; Friday afternoons dragging on in the library waiting for the clock to hit six and apologizing to the homeless men returned out into the cold; sleepless nights in Diane's bedroom with its black curtains and Hopper posters and small green chair piled high with clothes and her unrelentingly innocent desperation to understand. Do they have internet in Palestine? Yes, Diane, they have internet in Palestine. But doesn't the wall save lives? No, Diane, the wall is an apartheid landgrab. Couldn't they just go to Jordan? Who, Diane? The . . . Palestinians? No, Diane, that would be ethnic cleansing, let's not talk any more about it. Oh, but I want to *understand*.

He turns into an unmarked door and heads up the granite staircase to the Greek Club. You don't need to call anyone, just walk in and there'll be tables of revolutionists, men and women thrown together in Tahrir Square and working now to push the revolution on into the future. Activists and filmmakers and journalists and psychotherapists and urbanists and historians and lawyers and more arriving every day: diaspora Egyptians returning to help build the new country; international activists looking for a way to unlock the new world; artists and academics intrigued by the great surprise sprung that is changing everything.

Khalil pushes open the high wooden door, greets the manager, and catches a glimpse of himself as he walks past the mirror, his black hair growing untidy, and even from here he can see the first grays emerging at his temples. He walks through the bar, past tables of familiar faces talking unfamiliar ideas: the dissidents of the early blogosphere discussing how to crowdsource a new constitution; the cineastes of Adly Street drafting a manifesto for a new union of regional artists; the journalists raising funds to establish a publicly owned television station; the media activists hatching plans for a global archive of political film; the experimental coalition of actors and therapists building a public art space for at-risk children; and at the back of the room a man is tinkering out a Lionel Richie song on the grand piano.

Khalil stops for a moment to listen. Then hears Rania.

"Arash!" Rania shouts. "Come in. Meet everyone." Arash, tall, smartly dressed, bookish, signals hello to the group. "Arash here has made the most brilliant film. Did you see it, Khalil? It's about the Iranian revolution and he's organizing a string of screenings across Egypt."

Khalil pulls up a chair at the long, crowded table, orders a drink; Lionel's silken notes work their way between the words. There is an idea Khalil has of the world, a balance he thought he could express in music where he failed with language. *Music*, his father liked to say, *is the only way to understand the world*. And it was music that first brought him here. It is music, he told himself, that can express the inexpressible. There are answers in melodies and social values in harmony. Music can unlock the future and through music he tried to build his connection to the country, the land, its history.

"Layla!" Rania shouts. "Come sit down! Meet everyone." Layla, all blazing smiles and quick, compact movements, pulls up a chair. "Layla's written a brilliant book about Denshawai and Egyptian resistance and she's giving a talk—when is it, Monday?"

"Hanan!" Rania shouts. "Come talk to us, you genius! Hanan's working on Mubarak's toxic loans and getting our—what did you call it?—'odious debt' wiped out by those bastards at the IMF."

But Khalil's fingers were not equal to the demands of his ears. After two years of ever slower progress he quit. He spent time studying the law, working as a news fixer and a translator, began drawing a graphic novel, taught English and worked with refugees to help get them documentation, worked on water sanitation with an NGO and solar energy with another, learned some French and played chess every Tuesday, volunteered to play football and run drama workshops with street kids. He worked as a copy editor and a journalist on an English-language paper and earned flutters of cash translating written words into English and spoken ones into Arabic. He bought an old camera and learned to develop film, rolled his own cigarettes, and made friends and lost them again—all, he sees now, in search of an idea, a way to be in the world.

"Lizzie!" Rania shouts. "How are we with the diplomatic pouch? We need to get those tear-gas canisters to the lab in Brighton quickly."

10

"Palestine," his father said, long ago, and Khalil had looked up from his computer to see him standing in the doorway, the faint orange light of the hallway barely silhouetting him. "What's wrong with Palestine?" There was no masking the hurt in his voice as he strained to understand how his son could be choosing Egypt, choosing *any* country, over his own. Nidal had only been to Egypt a single time, before Khalil was even born. Ugly, offensive, arrogant, he said. Sold us out, he said. What was that look on his face now? Was there disgust mixed in with that jealousy? Disappointment? As if the old man had ever shown half a moment's commitment to Palestine or done any-thing about it or even spoken as a Palestinian. *Ned.* As if he hadn't spent his life hiding from Palestine out in the fucking snows. As if he'd sat and read bedtime stories from the home-land and cooked chicken infused with zaatar and quoted Mahmoud Darwish, as if he'd built our Palestinian refuge in the diaspora and I was tearing it down. What *is* wrong with Palestine, Ned? At least my mother tried to make me watch the old Egyptian films, took me to the beach those summers to meet my cousins. At least she was still Egyptian. I'm dying for you to tell me what's wrong with Palestine. Tell me why we only went once, and that was for your mother's funeral. Tell me what Palestine did for you to abandon her in the framed map at the end of the hallway? Tell me what's wrong with a schoolboy trying to talk to his father about this thing they call our Catastrophe and being quietly handed a book of Handala cartoons with a look of, almost, pleading for silent understanding, for us not to have to do this with each other. Tell me, tell me about my name. Tell me why you put this all on me. Turned away from me until there's no wall left to turn to. Let's not do this. Let's not do this. So who was I supposed to do it with? Tell me what you found out there in the cold you can never call home. Tell me, when did you decide you had to choose between the two? What sewed up the Arabic in your tongue? Did you wake up one day knowing you would never speak it again? Did you forget it at the bowling alley? Tell me. Tell me what's wrong with Palestine. I'm dying to know.

11

December 7, 2011

Mariam keeps her headphones in when she walks, keeps her pace brisk and her expression set to *fuck off* as she navigates the street's assault course of words and sounds and unwanted invitations. The small can of pepper spray smuggled by a traveling friend lives on her key ring, waits tight in her hand as she picks her way through the little swarms of men; grinning, whistling men, men in packs along the narrow sidewalks, men who spit and men who stare, men who make sure they're in your way, men who follow you through the dark streets, men who like to scare you for their miserable midnight erections jerked off in dark bathrooms. From the street to the top it's all the same, same animal urges, same violence of hands, same paunching weight, same father's flesh, same buffalo words, same brute language. Virginity tests. The army doctors' vaginal violations they call virginity tests. The police's hosepipes forced into the anuses of young prisoners. The grabbing hands of kids on the street ripping at clothes, grabbing for flesh. The same siege, everywhere.

Cap D'or and its miserable barmen. A man mouths something at her but she can't hear him, doesn't look twice at him. Above her the Kodak building folds in and closes itself over the alleyway below. She climbs the narrow stairwell that bends up around the iron gridwork of the elevator shaft and pulls out the headphones.

A meeting table runs through the center of the room with, she quickly counts, sixteen people around it. Familiar faces: lawyers, journalists, filmmakers. She's late.

Or, more accurately, the meeting began on time. She mouths an apology and stands with her back to the wall by the door.

"—and even if we will never have the exact number, what we have are hundreds of names of people martyred for the revolution. We need to know their stories. They are central to our narrative, they're the reason the revolution must be kept alive."

Leading the meeting is Ashira; her voice is strong and firm and considered, her seriousness embodied by her straight jet-black hair, her face imbued with a sharp and somber authority by her cheekbones. Her daughter, Horreya, is asleep in her baby throne.

"We've got to take all the different lists of the dead and the missing, combine them and see where the gaps are. We think that at least a thousand were killed. But there's no accurate number for January twenty-eighth. And we don't know how many are still missing. How many in jail. So first we have to make a master list."

Mariam sees a familiar grouping of four women she met doing square security through the long weeks of the July sit-in. Dalia works in a small factory and as long as she has a job her family won't force her to marry; Rasha is a student in the faculty of arts, is drawing a comic in her notebook, and has badges of the martyrs pinned to her backpack; Fatma's son was killed in a motorway crash so she says she's here in his place; Lina is a doctor but gets claustrophobic whenever she tries to help in the field hospitals.

At the back of the room is Verena, her dark hair falling down over her black clothes.

Mariam's phone vibrates in her pocket—

Announcing free weekly clinic in Tahrir. Every Friday from now on. 10am–3pm. Please forward this message.

"Then," Ashira continues, "we have to map the master list. How many contacts do we have? We need to find a route to every single family of every single martyr. We need to visit them. We need to know their stories. Where they were born, what their job was, why they joined the revolution. What did they hope for Egypt, what did they wish their life would be? We need to sit with each family and listen until we have a story for each of the thousand people we've lost."

So many dead. So many still missing. Mariam glances at Verena and feels the thick air of the Coptic Hospital coiling again in her lungs and her throat.

"Finally," Ashira continues, her voice pitched with total control, "there will come the question of what more can we do for people. Are we going to talk to them about reparations? About their demands as martyrs' families? Or are we an archival project? We have to decide this today, because when we talk to the families we have to be very clear about what we can and cannot do. Did I miss anything? No? Then I hand over to my colleagues to talk about the methodology."

We all take strength from one another, yes, but how many

harvest theirs from Ashira? Ashira was four months pregnant when her husband was killed. January 28. "He went out that day," she said once, "for all three of us." Who could possibly show weakness or doubt in the face of her conviction? Mariam feels again the rising heat of the long nights with the dead and the cold of the chromium table and the sodden darkness of the city morgue and the hard skin of Umm Ayman's hand in her own. Toussi, Ayman, Amirah, Khaled, Hadeer, Bassem, Mina. Streets of our cities will be renamed in your honor. Glory to the martyrs. Your names will be taught in history books. You have given what we have not yet been asked for.

ASHIRA

Ashira waits. She is always waiting. She can't stop herself waiting, can't switch it off, that part of her that's always listening for the quiet click of metal, the vibration of a phone, a tread that pauses outside the door, the dream that doesn't end on waking.

She calls his phone sometimes. She holds her breath through the long seconds of silence, then collapses in exhausted tears at the voice of the machine.

She goes to the morgue every Wednesday.

He went out on January 28 for all three of us. He went out on January 28 for all three of us. She woke with a start. He was gone. No, he was in the shower. He came out, a towel around his waist, his body, his warmth filling their tony bedroom. She was so pregnant.

"Is your phone working yet?" he asked. It wasn't. Nobody's was. Then he was on top of her, shaking his wet hair onto her and they were laughing and his hand was on her stomach and then his ear as he listened to the baby. "Baby?" he said. "Baby, can you hear me?"

"We can't keep calling it Baby, you know?"

"I know."

"So let's give her a name."

"Tomorrow. We'll spend the morning in bed together and not get out until we have a name."

When he got up to get dressed a chill came over her.

"I'm coming with you," she said.

"No," he said, not smiling. "It's not safe."

"That's why I'm coming."

"No. I'm going for all three of us."

She checks the hospitals still. The police stations. They are all liars. They are all Mubarak loyalists. Maybe he's alive. Alive and chained to a hospital bed or locked in a desert prison or alone in a coma.

She doesn't find him. She comes home.

What does a year do to a body?

He died gloriously. Sacrifices have to be made. Prices have to be paid.

12

Stella is Khalil's favorite Downtown joint. Wooden furniture decades old, ancient yellow and blue tablecloths, air ever thick with smoke. Saad has his seat by the door and Saad keeps the count; Saad likes the regulars who don't cause trouble and shakes your hand and learns your name if you tip a bit and signals to Marwan, wire thin with slicked-back hair and eternal patience, who picks up a new table and carries it above his head and for all of six footsteps you're in *Goodfellas*.

"I got another busload of Italians today," Hafez says.

"What now?"

"Fixing job. Cyberactivism and the revolution or something."

"A film?"

"TV."

"Paid?"

"Nope. They offered the spirit of camaraderie. Or was it comradeship?"

"Hard currency."

"We'll be parachute journalists one day," Hafez says. "We'll show up in Rome and demand free labor to tell the Roman side of the story!"

Marwan places two beers on the table.

"To bloody battles and bruised arms," Hafez says. They clink bottles.

Hafez's head drops and he starts scribbling in his notebook. Khalil lights a cigarette and checks Twitter:

@jona9898: What's become of the army's investigation into the "virginity tests" of female protesters. It's been 8 months now.

@Nadiaidan: Eleven months of SCAF rule now and still police are unreformed and unjailed. What is going on???

Hafez is scribbling away in his notebook while Khalil smokes in silence. Marwan reaches up to switch on the radio and Umm Kulthum drifts into the room. Khalil listens while Hafez writes, the Lady's voice filling him with a subtle excitement for the future, his next project: as soon as he has five minutes he'll go through the albums one by one, a new way into the language, he'll learn the songs, he'll study the lyrics, he'll teach himself to feel them.

After a few minutes Hafez looks up, an epiphanic grin on his face as he polishes his glasses:

"I got it!" he says. "It's a *movie*! The twenty-eighth is a movie! It's the only way to do it. You can't write a thesis about it or poem or a song or a book. It's too big. It's too cinematic. January twenty-eighth: it's gotta be a movie. The whole country pours out, takes the streets, beats the pigs, burns down their police stations. It's not about one hero, it's not about feelings or interiority, it's just too big. Nothing can do the twenty-eighth justice other than cinema."

"So you're saying you want to set up a shoot featuring thousands of people waging a street war in five cities? You'd better call your old man."

Hafez prickles a little. His grandfather was a film director back when Egyptian films were legit, but Hafez's father produces today's schlock and his son holds him responsible for the whole industry's downfall.

"Oh, shut up. With a good script we'll raise the money in no time. Just think about it. Cairo, Alexandria, Fayoum, Suez. Think of all the stories. The guys running into the burning party headquarters looking for evidence of disappeared family members, people breaking out of prison, the Brotherhood *leaders* escaping, the guys in Luxor who held a troop of cops under siege for days, burning down Sayyeda Zeinab police station, the police running out into the night in their underwear, SCAF's meetings and plans, Gamal Mubarak freaking out as he's watching TV. Shit, there's just so many scenes!"

"Sure. But how do you hold it together without a hero?"

"Time. Or some theme ties each scene together. And in the end you have forty, fifty scenes that—taken all together—give you the picture."

Hafez orders another round and scribbles a little more in his book until Nancy walks in and takes the seat next to him. Nancy and Hafez are a nascent revolution couple. They met in the dark romance of Tahrir, smoking and watching the battle down Mohamed Mahmoud Street. Marwan comes over and asks if she wants a beer.

"Yes. Thank you," she says. Then, with a flourish of volume, adds, "We'd better all drink up while we still can, eh? You've seen what they're doing, of course? You saw that video on Facebook we all saw? Buying votes! They're out there buying votes! Brotherhood buses handing out bags of food. It's disgusting! They should be disqualified!"

Hafez, pen still in hand, looks up from his notes. "It's not totally clean but anyone can take a bit of initiative and go hand out food."

"Yes, but *we're* not!"

"And that's the Brotherhood's fault?"

"They're the ones pushing this criminal timetable through. They've had decades to prepare. Who can compete with that?"

"Who do you mean by *we*?"

"You know very well, Hafez, who I mean by *we*. Liberals, secularists, whatever—whoever's not going to segregate the beaches and pour all the alcohol out into the Nile."

"But it's not the Brotherhood setting the timetable," Khalil says. "It's the army." He points at the newspaper headline on the table.

SCAF SPOKESMAN CONFIRMS TIMELINE
FOR TRANSITION OF POWER

By June 30 we will have an elected president and the army will have only one role to perform, which is to protect the country. The Supreme Council of the Armed Forces does not seek continued authority, and we will not interfere in political life.

"The army is stuck," Nancy says. "They made a promise to the nation and they have to stick to it."

Mariam walks in, and Khalil can feel every man in the bar watching as she kisses him on the cheek, as her hand finds his knee for a moment.

At the table in the far corner Khalil can hear Malik talking at top volume. "We *are* crisis! We *thrive* on crisis! Our fucking job is to *create* crisis! Without the *crisis* there's only the fucking *regime* or the *system* or whatever *the fuck* you wanna call it. Without the crisis everything just stays the fucking *same*!"

The One is sitting opposite him, a minefield of empty green

bottles and overflowing ashtrays and cigarette packs and cell phones and plates of cheese and tomatoes and chickpeas between them.

"And what," Hafez calls out across the bar, "what if what's coming next is worse? You can't have crisis forever. People are getting tired of this."

"People can't expect a revolution to be tidily wrapped up in ten months. These things take years."

"Well, then people have to be convinced that it's worth years. They have to make that choice. We have to show that there's a plan. They need concrete ideas."

"And what exactly, dear Hafez, is a *concrete idea*? You can't *design* an anarchist utopia, that's the whole point. You can only have principles. It's all about *principles*. They're all out there banging on about democracy but you and I can agree that it's not democracy that they're talking about. Elections are a billion-dollar distraction. Actual democracy is everyone having an equal *stake*. So we can only get to the principles—and then you build from there."

"This is all well and good," Hafez says. "But you've still got to give people something to hold on to. Why's revolution better than not-revolution? If you can't answer that in a sentence, you're losing people every day."

"Everything's encapsulated in one chant: bread, freedom, social justice."

"People don't want to hear a poem. They want a plan."

"Do they? Or do they just want to be told that everything's going to be all right? The fact is, it's a fight among five percent of the population because there's only five percent willing to actually *fight*. Everyone else'll just fall in behind the winner."

"You've just summed up everything that the revolution *isn't*," Hafez says.

"The revolution is a story told to get people on your side. But in the end, most people stay home."

"And what"—everyone turns their heads; the One rarely speaks—"what if one side is paid and the other side not? Or when your half of the five percent gets bored and wants to stop playing revolution and get on with their lives? Or when your half splits?"

No one leaps to respond. Hafez lights his cigarette. Malik is too polite to say it, but Khalil knows what he's thinking, he feels it, too: our days of listening to drunk old Europeans lecture us about democracy are over.

"So who are you voting for?" the One continues.

"I'm voting for Hamdeen," Nancy says, and Khalil can feel Mariam's eyes rolling next to him.

"Everyone else is boycotting," Mariam says.

The One nods sagely.

"I'm undecided," Khalil says.

"You're not serious?" Mariam says.

He's been thinking about it constantly. The Brotherhood wants elections. The army wants elections. America wants elections. So surely we *shouldn't*? Elections are the death of politics. The ballot box exists to quell the revolution. Democracy is always for sale to the highest bidder. We want another way, a way as yet unknown. Khalil can hear the words, can see the argument. The young do all the dying and the old go to the polls to vote for other old fucks to tell the young what to do. It's clear. Just say *no*. But he can't stop thinking, what comes after saying no?

"How else do you take power?" he says.

"But it's a *sham*. How can we vote when the army controls the voting districts *and* the polling stations, when the Brotherhood is handing out free food across the country? It's all theater and voting legitimizes it."

"It's already legitimate," Khalil says. "People want it, and the boycott won't stop it happening."

"But it's all *theater*!" Mariam repeats. "It's already decided what's going to happen. The army and the Brotherhood have *agreed*. So having a high turnout only helps them."

"But if you don't ever engage in elections, how do you come to power?"

"I don't *want* to come to power! Do you? Do you want to be a politician? We're the opposition, we're the disruption, we're what's going to keep power in line."

"We're *crisis*!" Malik shouts.

Mariam nods approvingly. "I don't want power. I want to trust the street. Something new is coming that we can't see yet. And we have to keep the crisis alive long enough for it to happen."

"Whatever's coming ncxt," Khalil says, "I think you still have to try and take power."

A silence falls between them.

After a moment, Hafez steps into the breach: "I've been reading a book about the independence movements in Africa, decolonization. And in pretty much every single case it goes the same way: The revolution arrives, it seems glorious and popular and invincible, something goes a little off course so the army stages a coup, people are massacred and jailed, then another general overturns the last one with promises of democracy and so on. And on and on it goes. Every single time."

"Won't happen here," Malik says, with instant confidence. "It's different now. Mobile phones and the internet, mate. You need more than just an army to control people. The whole world's fucked off and everyone's *talking* about it. The *idea* is too strong. And you can't kill everyone."

13

The bats went home. Alone in the dark of the studio, he often thinks of that night, its infinite silence, the bats looping through the dark air above the river, the tank sitting in stillness in a pool of yellow light, the wide, empty street, the night's hunters gliding silently between the great riverbank trees, ecstatic in this, the first silence in generations. How did they know to go back there? Had they been waiting, watching, hoping we would finally extinguish ourselves and our incessant noise?

Above the desk is Mariam's poster. VISIT PALESTINE. Her first addition to the apartment those months ago. The dark tree framing the promised land in the art deco distance, the Dome of the Rock triumphant at the heart of the eternal city. It used to be easy. A train from Cairo to Jerusalem. One land, one people from Casablanca to Baghdad. No, not one people. One language. What better basis for cooperation can there be? The United States of Arabia. Is that what we want? Nothing short of that would be strong enough to change the world order. And then what? Then we have borders keeping out everyone else? No. The United States of Arabia will not be enough.

He clicks back to the recording of the bats, to the simplest, most glorious nights. The city waiting silently, the people united, the crumbling dictatorship, the bats set free. He can hear the trees hanging heavy over the Nile. No one else is there. Just Khalil and the bats. We could all breathe again. He reached his hand out over the railing, strained out over the black river. Look at the new world, the unthinkable happening around us. This is your doing, Bouazizi. There is no one else. Did you doubt yourself, for a moment? Were you scared when you lit the match? This is all for you. Everything, now, is for you.

14

A stone river of blood drags through the asphalt of Tahrir. On its banks the mourners. The stain of a life slipping away. He walks silently along it. The square is empty now, dark and cold. This new battle has been long. Khalil follows the bloodline, follows the careful stones lining this new holiness. This must be where the bleeding began, the dark heat in the center of the square. They attacked in the afternoon, bullets racing ahead of men in body armor. This must be where he fell. He sees the men heaving a young body between them, sees clothes heavy with blood, the police giving chase. The death leads north. The square is silent now. They will attack again soon.

Khalil sits down carefully on the ground next to a woman in a doctor's coat. All along the bloodline are men, women, young boys sitting cross-legged on the banks with heads in hands and tears in eyes.

"Who was this?" he asks quietly, without looking at her.

"I don't know," she says.

"Did he survive?" Khalil asks.

"I don't know."

How many people are carrying him? Does he know what's happening? All we know is he's bleeding fast. That blood dries thick. They know about blood work. The bloodline stretches on. It takes so much to keep us alive.

The report of a shotgun echoes through the square.

They are coming.

Hundreds of police are sprinting across the square. Everyone is running. He is slow to react, he is somehow the last, and when he does the attack truck is already upon him, its headlights blinding down on him, and he hears a shotgun and he's running and he stumbles as an arc of light cuts across him and a siren screams and white light floods through his body as a lashing of fire cuts across his back and he stumbles and falls and in a moment is everything, is a dozen final conversations in a heartbeat, is all the things he should have done differently as he aches for his mother, watching him die, a death in the family, a crowbar and a laughter, a wheelchair and ramps and a new life on wheels and weak arms now alone in a dark apartment without Mariam, alone in a sea of a thousand mourning posters, the breath in her chest as she allows herself to cry, as she feels the break inside her. Will you remember me? Will my name take its place among our fallen constellations? Do I take comfort from it, do I relax now, let go? I have stood and I have fallen. You would be proud of me. You'll all be proud of me. Mother. The night is so long. Unmoving forever next to each other in the dark. Have you been here long, Mom? You saw me, we could have been together, let me show you around, but stick together—it's better to be in pairs. You know that. I'll show you around just stay with me and we can talk and you can tell me some things. I was too young, you know I was too young to know about burials. We would have been together. We should have brought you here. We would lie together, all together still bodies wrapped in linen and laid out in the darkness for an untouching eternity, you and your boy. But what if forever is spent in desperate loneliness, lying together in the family tomb, next to each other but untouching, a shadow of yearning through the dark unmovable night of nights? What if every second of every minute of every night of our eternity of death I want nothing more than for you to reach over and touch my arm? You have to tell me and tell me now because my father will be getting on a plane soon and he doesn't even have Mariam's phone number so who's going to meet him, how will he find his way to the morgue?

15

The light in the apartment is off. When Mariam comes into the bedroom he doesn't move. Khalil is lying on his side. Dark bloodstains rorschach across his bandaged back. She walks around the bed. He is awake, his eyes are bloodshot. So are everyone's. The gas makes you sick. She kisses him gently on the lips.

"How you doing, darling?"

He gives half a nod through the opioid fog.

"We should change your bandages."

"They're okay," he says. "Tomorrow."

She sits on the bed next to him and gently strokes his hair. He can feel her phone vibrating. She ignores it.

"I called your father," she says.

He tries to answer but he needs to sleep. Is he coming? Am I going home? Home? *Home?*

Her phone vibrates again and he feels her move and then she's leaning over him and kissing him on the cheek.

"I have to go," she says. "I won't be long. Sheikh Emad's widow is giving a statement about his autopsy. She's going to say it was an army bullet that killed him."

"Okay," Khalil mutters.

"I won't be long."

"It's okay."

She kneels down next to him, kisses him again. "I won't be long."

"Mariam," he says, and she pauses at the door. He tries to tell her to take a microphone, tries to tell her to record something but he can't remember what he was trying to say and his arm is so heavy hanging pointlessly in the air so he puts it down slowly again and just lifts a finger to say goodbye before closing his eyes again and he can hear her phone ringing outside and maybe it's my father calling her, maybe they talk all the time, yes, she says, your son is in a military prison, yes I understand, she says, what does she understand, it's so hot in here under this sheet, so hot in my home, new home, cold home, home, home please stand for our brave servicemen and -women, and stand, maybe you'll never stand again maybe their steel will dig into you and gnaw away your spinal cord and you'll never be able to enlist, because you *would* enlist, wouldn't you, Kaleel? if your country called on you you're a good kid Kal I know you, I know your father, if your country called you'd answer, right? Right? Turn left to exit, press escape to escape, press now, press on, pray tell did you read that Nick Kristof book it was a present from a colleague's daughter I told you all about her I'm dying for you to meet her and dialogue because you moderate Muslims are the ones who should be speaking out don't you think don't you think about pork, *there's no escape*, because let's face facts the Buddhists aren't out blowing themselves up so come meet her, she's good people, her parents are part of the peace movement in Tel Aviv but oh, my, gosh, *you'll never be free*, look at that beard, Kaleel, you're not going fundy on us are you darling because I know we can agree that we've just got to get Bin Laden and the very strangest thing is, every Muslim I've ever met loves pork and I summered in Israel once and it just has to start with dialogue but it was a beautiful country so funny all your virgins in suicide paradise but you wouldn't want your sister wearing a veil praying five times a day and not even having a sip of water through all that month of Ramadan checking Facebook, is it all about Facebook, do the Arabs want freedom because they saw that we have it on Facebook?

16

December 24, 2011

He hadn't spoken to his father for weeks, months maybe, but he's called every day since Mariam told him.

"Will you be careful now?"

"Yes. Don't worry about me."

"You were shot. I have to worry."

"I'll be careful."

"And Mariam?"

"Mariam, too."

"What are you doing, Khalil? You're going to get yourself killed. What can you possibly do in the face of this?"

"You've been asking that since day one," Khalil says, impatient.

"Look around you. You've no guns, no bombs. Be realistic."

"Let's not say those words on the phone."

"This is a new game now, son."

"And you know all about the game, right?"

"You think it's only you who knows anything?" He's silent

95

for a moment. "You think that you and your friends are the only ones to have stood up? There have been hundreds of generations."

"I didn't mean . . . ," Khalil says. "I'm sorry."

Khalil's father waits in the silence of the wounded, then says: "There's a reason you were born in America, you know."

17

January 2, 2012

He uses Hafez's grandfather's cane on their walks. Every day Hafez rings his doorbell at eleven. At first Khalil's legs would shake and the pain would overcome him. But now, with the cane in his right hand and his left in Hafez's arm, he manages. The anniversary of the revolution is upon them. By January 25 he must be able to march. By January 25 he must be able to run.

"Come on, Rambo," Hafez says, as they tread carefully along the unpredictable sidewalk toward Mohamed Mahmoud Street. Cairo is alive, as always, with its sounds immeasurable. The coded language of car horns communicating endlessly in animal impulses of greeting and warning; the chorus of birds that fills the dusk air in Zamalek with chatterings before sleep; the echoing of the pleasure boats under the Abd al-Moneim Riad overpass; conversations private and public all shouted for the world to hear; the polyphony of grizzled adhans puncturing the predawn silence, announcing it is finally and unquestioningly time to leave the twenty-four-hour bar at the Odeon Hotel and go home to bed. And then the army's wall, and silence as it severs Mohamed Mahmoud Street, the graffiti covering its cement blocks a chorus of demands. WANTED, it threatens in a frontier font—

LIEUTENANT MAHMOUD SOBHI EL-SHENAWY, A CENTRAL
SECURITY FORCES OFFICER ACCUSED OF SHOOTING DOZENS
OF FREE REVOLUTIONISTS' EYES OUT.

On other blocks are freehand scrawls desecrating the military and exalting the martyrs and stencils of a blue bra:

NO TO STRIPPING OF PEOPLE.
NO TO VIRGINITY TESTS.

"I quit," Hafez says.

"Quit what?"

"The PhD. I can't go back to London now. Not with all this."

"Good."

"There's no point. The images are all here." Hafez half gestures out to the desolate, divided street. "You just need to be in the right place at the right time."

Khalil's mind flicks to the famous video of Toussi; the young body, broken by the police, is dragged into the garbage piled up on the corner of Tahrir Square. His name, we know now, is Toussi. Toussi. So alone in his last moment that pulled so many out to the streets for his vengeance.

"Remind me your title?" Khalil says.

"Don't bully me."

"Come on."

"The Politics of Tracking Shots in American and Cuban

Cinematic Political Self-Representation of the Nineteen Sixties and Seventies."

The laughter hurts Khalil's back.

The wind blows a newspaper up against the wall. Again and again the paper rises and slaps itself against the cement blocks and falls again.

HAMAS INFILTRATORS UNCOVERED WITH CACHE OF WEAPONS AT CABINET CLASHES.

"Hey girl, nice hair!" someone behind them shouts, and they turn to see Mariam walking toward them, a teenage boy cycling quickly away with a glance over his shoulder. She doesn't look at him. She comes and stands next to them. She is looking at the stencil of the blue bra, seeing the jackboot smashing down on the young woman's chest.

If you look at the picture you'll see it's not actually a boot. He's wearing running shoes. Which is proof that these men were infiltrators. Sent to discredit the army.

He has to get back to work. It's been two weeks since the last podcast. He must start collecting material. The radio commentariat sicken him. The Facebook warriors. The sycophants working through the night to poison people's minds.

Why was she wearing this sultry blue bra? Where did she think she was? And she's clearly not wearing anything else under there, so what's really going on here?

"Oh, fucking hell," Hafez says, his phone in his hand. "Guys, you're not going to be happy about this."

"What is it?" Mariam says.

"The people, apparently, have spoken."

Hafez's face freezes in seriousness.

"Well, come on then," Mariam says.

"Honestly, you're not going to be happy," Hafez says.

"Seriously, what is it?"

"*People* magazine named Bradley Cooper the sexiest man alive."

"Oh Christ, Hafez, you had me fucking nervous."

At the end of the street a small crowd is gathering. A young man on a ladder is painting the final touches on a mural. In the crowd, Abu Bassem is watching the colors climbing together to draw his son's face, the black contours of his eyes bold and forward-looking. They embrace in silence and wait for the artist to finish. All around Bassem's portrait are sketches of pharaonic figures stretched to modern brushstrokes imparting timeless lessons for good governance. This, he thinks, is Egypt. The new, here, does not destroy the old but carries it with it, builds on it, talks to it. The connections, the foundations, are stronger. It's what you do with the old—that is what's new. We are New York in the twenties, the music and the modern driving forward together, forging the future with brass and steel but keeping our histories alive with us, keeping our fallen living among us. The mural complete, Abu Bassem steps carefully forward. He runs his finger over the careful black outline, alone, for a moment, with his son.

ABU BASSEM

He's walked through it a dozen times. The clap, the crack, the fall, the blood. The last breath. The phone call. The word was Bassem but the voice wasn't. Too late to the hospital. Bassem's friends in the gray corridor, faces dark and downturned. There was no doctor. He just picked up his son and walked.

At least he had his body. At least he could say goodbye. At least we'll lie together through the next darkness.

He had the body—and now he has a name. Captain Mokhtar Ibrahim, Imbaba police station. He finds himself pacing the long sidewalk opposite the station, running his hand through the sharp brush shading the houseboats beneath, the relentless traffic a hot barrier between him and the squat concrete across the freeway. They are afraid. They do not come out alone. They wear their weapons heavy. He watches every move, counts the breaths filling Mokhtar's fat paunch, runs the words he'll speak through the bars of the courtroom cell as his son's killer is dragged away to justice. In darker, weaker moments he sees other things, a sweating brow under a single lamp, an open hand landing on a terrified face, a knife forged for small cuts. But he shakes them from his mind. That is not the justice Bassem died for, that is not the new world he went looking for on the twenty-eighth. We must be patient. The orders are for patience.

"We will avenge your son" is the message. "But we must play the game, we must take power, we must create a smooth and orderly path to the elections and we must win those elections. If a police station were to burn to the ground tonight, could there possibly be elections tomorrow? Of course not. So we must be patient, trust our leaders, they will lead us all to justice."

He hears the words, he hears their logic, but they do nothing to unclench the fist in his pocket.

18

January 14, 2012

A fragile shaft of light shines. A widening cone of shifting colors caught between two perfect lines beaming out from the projector cradled in Hafez's arms to the cotton screen hanging at the base of the metal monument to Talaat Harb, the curling smoke of dozens of cigarettes rising from the crowd between them, catching the image's chromatic shifts racing to the screen, the eyes, the brains of the audience: the shifting consciousness of the future.

Mariam and Khalil stand toward the back of the crowd, her hand subtly in his down by their sides. Every night street screenings are happening, young men and women across the country, gathering equipment, rallying their friends, and taking over the squares and alleyways of their cities to illuminate the old walls with the new truth: The army lies, the state media is its mouthpiece, everything you are being told is untrue.

Toussi dies a thousand times a day, his young body raked

across the screen. The chaos of Maspero, the suffocations of Mohamed Mahmoud, the rain of bullets on April 8, the battle for Qasr al-Nil Bridge on January 28 plays out again and again. Images and dates and names of the dead are our history, eternal rebellion our future.

When Mariam hears Umm Ayman's voice she feels the ice vapors of the morgue curling in her lungs. "My son." The image cuts from mother to son. "My son was martyred in Maspero." An army APC crashes through a crowd of protesters. "The Egyptian Army killed him. I have no doubts about that." Soldiers open fire on the fleeing crowd. "But my son died for a reason. All our children died for a *reason*. They died for this revolution. They died for this country to be a a place *you all* can have children in." The image cuts to a marching crowd. "We will see our children's killers in jail. We will see the Supreme Council of the Armed Forces and the police in jail. Go to Tahrir! Hold your square! As long as each of you are in Tahrir my son is alive! As long as each one of you are in Tahrir all our martyrs are alive! Don't give them an inch! We will see all the killers in jail. The revolution *continues*!"

The crowd erupts.

> *The people! Demand!*
> *The field marshal's head!*
> *The people! Demand!*
> *The field marshal's head!*

Khalil leans lighter on the cane now. Mariam presses her body close to his other side. She removed the final bandages this morning, carefully peeling the gauze off the sealed skin of his back. The doctor said the body will slowly push the pellets out of itself. One by one. The doctor said it can take months.

No one can question your commitment now or snip about the passport in your pocket or ask when you're going to leave. You're a real Egyptian now.

"Not long now," she says. The anniversary of the revolution is coming up fast and everyone expects big numbers to turn out. "We have to take the TV building. The numbers will be big, we need to use them."

"The army will be heavy round it," Khalil says.

"So we have to overwhelm them. More people than they can shoot."

"You don't want the Ministry of the Interior?"

"Of course I want the Ministry of the Interior, but we can actually *take* Maspero. If fifty thousand people march at it and calmly dismantle the barbed wire, the army won't shoot. They won't be able to. We overwhelm them and march in. So we have to make the marches go to Maspero and not Tahrir. Once everyone's in Tahrir you can't move them again."

The credits roll on a video and a group of Ultras fire up a familiar chant:

> *We haven't forgotten Tahrir*
> *You sons of bitches.*
>
> *We gave you a beating*
> *Like you hadn't had for years.*

Khalil feels the metal quivering in his body, alive with audiographic excitement as he takes in the street sounds, the ambient bustle farther down the avenue, the distant dark spots waiting to be filled by a siren pulling around a corner and charging into the bullring.

How long will they let us stand here insulting them? Let

them come. No one will run. *Raise your head high, you're Egyptian.* You're a real Egyptian now, real as the steel under your skin.

A face he knows but whose name he can't remember is smiling at him. "Hey, man! How you doing? How's the back?"

"Fine. Better."

"That's great, brother. That's great. You need anything?"

"I'm good."

He feels Mariam press closer against him. He's never been more attractive than in these days of heroic recuperation.

"The projector's holding up well," Mariam says.

"It's been through a lot with these screenings," Khalil says. "I got it last year. I took this terrible job. A Canadian crew on a TV spot about temples and ley lines and shit."

"Like in Dan Brown," Mariam says.

"The very same. I spent days with this idiot director trawling around the pyramids looking for an 'indigenous wisdom keeper' and scanning the ground for—what did he call it?— 'conductivity discontinuities.' It was awful."

"What was his name?"

"The director? I don't remember. Jim something."

"No—Tom Hanks's character."

"Dr. Robert Langdon."

"Wow. No hesitation."

Then the words, stark and clear, appear on the screen: February 2, 2011, and Khalil feels the crowd hush in anticipation. The camera moves through Tahrir, toward the museum, up into the Camel Battle and the Molotov cocktails raining down from ornate rooftops onto the revolutionists below. Cairo is a new map of memories. He can't walk through Tahrir without thinking of that night, without a heartbeat of pride at the victory over Mubarak's final assault, the parting gift of the ultimate Orientalist: to attack a political protest with a camel.

The wretched bastard. The wind ripples through the screen. A Molotov falls through the image but the revolutionists are unrelenting. The crowd holds its breath. They will hold the square. They will fight off Mubarak's militias. The revolution will prevail. *This*—he smiles to himself—this is cinema. He has no time for the regular movies' expensive ticket, sniffling audience, and formulaic stories, can't bear the inconstancy of popcorn and the heartbreak of the stale batch. Add to that Cairo's triple alliance of terrible sound, soft focus, and the impeccably timed interval and a lousy experience is guaranteed—and often garnished with an audience engaged in insistent conversation: with each other, with their glowing smartphones, with Mr. Cruise himself. When invited out he cites with dullard regularity the time he was told the impermeably dark projection of *Harry Potter* was "meant to be like that" or the projectionist on *Shutter Island* who insisted the out-of-focus picture was uncorrectable or the night he had to actually go into the projection booth during *Step Up 3D* (don't ask) to get the corrupted file playing from the right point again.

The crowd breaks into applause as the credits roll. The revolutionists won. Here we are. The revolution continues. Forget cinema. *This* is cinema.

"Show me your list again," he says.

She pulls out a series of folded papers from her back pocket, checks one, another, and hands him the third.

SCREENINGS TO PUSH ONLINE
Ain Shams Uni (every day, midday)
Helwan (Sat, 6 pm)
Luxor (Sat, 7 pm)
Mansoura (Mon, 3 pm; Wed, 3 pm)
Matareyya (Mon, 6 pm)
Sohag (Mon, 6 pm; Tues, 6 pm; Thurs, 6 pm)

Agouza (Mon, 7 pm)
Mahalla (Mon, 7 pm)
T5 (Tue, 6 pm, Swedish mosque)
Rod al-Farag (Tue, 6 pm)
Helio (Wed, 6:30 pm)
10 Ramadan (Thurs, 5 pm)
Qalyubia (Thurs, 6 pm)
Maadi (Thurs, 6 pm)
Fayoum (Thurs, 6:30 pm)
Zaytoun (Thurs, 7 pm+march)
Zamalek (Thurs, 7 pm)
Warraq (Thurs, 7 pm)
Sadat City (Thurs, 7 pm)
Haram (Thurs, 7 pm)
Cairo Uni, Faculty of Arts (Mon, 10:30 pm)

This is cinema. These people, the revolutionists, these images moving elegantly across this screen, this street in the winter wind. The screen cuts to an image of Alaa, his newborn son in his arms as he strides triumphantly out of prison. He stops for a camera:

> *We all know who killed the martyrs at Maspero. There won't be justice until General Hamdy Badeen is picking his nose in a courtoom cell.*

The crowd cheers. The revolution continues. This is finally it. This is art that can truly change the world.

19

We lack a killer edge. Of course we do. Our weapon is mass. The revolution's anniversary passed. January 25 is gone for another year and Maspero remains under military control. The streets were filled with people, twelve marches all zoning in on Tahrir, bodies all pulling one another toward the center, a mass building up its own gravity. There were more people on the street today than ever before, millions, but only a few hundred were pulled toward Maspero. Can the crowd be made to think tactically? Can there be tactics when there is no leader? It's been a year now of asking the same question and we are no closer to an answer. We have to take Maspero. Two hours, one year ago. That's all we had. Two hours between the police retreating and the army deploying, two hours to take the right buildings.

A few hundred stood outside Maspero. An unmarked microbus circled through the back streets, picking off lone stragglers. The happy crowd cheered in Tahrir. The police wait with their fingers on the trigger.

20

February 1, 2012

Someone has died at the Masry–Ahly FC match
5:43 PM–1 Feb 2012

Confirmed one Ahly supporter has died in the dressing room
5:53 PM–1 Feb 2012

News coming in of three people dead at Ahly match in Port Said.
Tens wounded.
6:07 PM–1 Feb 2012

3 are dead in the players' changing room. At least 15 bodies in
the hospital now.
6:35 PM–1 Feb 2012

What the hell is going on in Port Said?
6:42 PM–1 Feb 2012

Got a phone call from Port Said. My cousin says dozens of Ultras are dead in the stadium!!! It's a massacre!
6:49 PM–1 Feb 2012

35 people now confirmed dead in Port Said.
6:51 PM–1 Feb 2012

35 confirmed dead?!? What the fuck is happening in that stadium?
6:52 PM–1 Feb 2012

35 dead in Port Said. The police are taking their revenge on the Ultras. What are we going to do?
6:55 PM–1 Feb 2012

And now Cairo Stadium is on fire. What is happening?
6:57 PM–1 Feb 2012

They welded the stadium gates shut. The Ultras are trapped inside. They're massacring them!
7:27 PM–1 Feb 2012

At least 50 people now confirmed dead in Port Said massacre.
7:34 PM–1 Feb 2012

It's on the TV. Security forces stand by while Masry fans attack the Ultras.
7:37 PM–1 Feb 2012

Why were the Port Said governor and the Head of Security not at this match? They always attend. This is a setup!
7:41 PM–1 Feb 2012

They turned off the stadium lights as the attack began. This is all planned.
7:55 PM–1 Feb 2012

Health Ministry confirms at least 73 killed.
8:25 PM–1 Feb 2012

When the Ultras bring their friends' bodies home they count seventy-four dead.

Mohamed Mahmoud Street is flooded within hours, the army's wall is ripped down, and the crowd advances on the Ministry of Interior. Khalid moves through the sounds, the invisible world of the battle, the rain of stones, the hiss of a fire extinguisher, the echoing crack of a shotgun, the insults volleyed at the cowards in armored uniforms. He checks the mics in his headphones. A doctor's coat flits between the bodies moving in battle through the street, catching Khalil's eye with its movements. He stands to the side and watches her move confidently through the crowd, the flashes of her white coat a private Morse code between them, unrecordable to his microphone.

A shop is on fire. Voices bark in different directions. *Sand, bring sand! Step back! Clear a path!* A supply line of boys rush sand to men at the front to be hurled onto the flames. The crowd shouts at the neighbors above to evacuate, to hurl water, to attach a hose. Another civilian response to the emergencies unleashed by the state. A huge round of applause breaks out as an elderly woman is carried out of her building in her armchair. She looks as if she's not been outside for a long time.

Mariam slips her arm subtly into his: "Have you seen my mother?"

"She's in the hospital behind Hardee's."

"Okay, thanks. See you later." She squeezes his arm and is gone.

He moves closer to the front line. A group of teenagers hurry past with a plastic crate full of rocks. Another has three Molotovs in his arms. How much longer can we keep fighting with rocks and fireworks? How long until we see the first gun on our side? Something is going to snap. With each report of a shotgun the metal pellets in his back vibrate. We are one, still. Your steel lives on in me, poisoning me, seeping chemicals into my bloodstream. His muscles twitch in readiness with the sirens of the attack truck but he doesn't move, determined to suppress the Pavlovian reaction.

The doctor in the white coat stands still in the middle of the crowd, watching the police lines ahead through her industrial gas mask.

He can see the flashing blue of the attack truck's beacon in the distance. They are coming. He doesn't run. The truck charges and unleashes a volley of heavy buckshot and the crowd splits—but the doctor is still. He watches her, unmoving as the crowd parts and pushes, as gas canisters land around them, and as the truck pulls closer an armored policeman appears out of a roof hatch with a spark of light. Her white coat crumples to the ground. The truck pulls closer but she doesn't move as the police leans over the edge and unloads another round into her. A gas canister lands by her feet, pouring a white cloud into the air around her but she doesn't move and Khalil is running toward her into the cloud and the tears are streaming and burning little salt runs of acid down his cheeks his eyes are raw and sealing shut and his chest is heaving when he kneels down before her and pulls her up into his arms as another canister lands behind them and he turns to run but his eyes won't open and his chest is closing and with every breath he's gasping for air while his lungs try to vomit themselves out of his body and he's running half-blind and arms full into the tear-burned world and you'll be okay you're gonna be okay and every muscle is working to keep him moving and his chest closes while he trips blind through the debris and a wrong breath and you're finished so run but don't fall, run fast but don't breathe run *faster* but don't breathe and don't fall just run and run faster without breathing and without seeing, keep running until through the stinging crack of an eye he sees a faint shimmering of a line, a shape as the world begins to define itself again and he can see now two doctors and with his last strength drops to his knees before them as she spills from his arms.

He gasps for new breath as the medics remove her mask and quickly unbutton her coat, its white fabric mapped with an oozing constellation of bloody points.

The doctor's hand reaches up, grasps for something, grips his. Her breaths are short, shallow; her eyes are open and she is looking up at the world; she knows where she is, what's happening: and she's afraid.

She breathes short—shallow—breaths.

A crowd is gathering around them. "Get back!" a medic shouts. "Give us space to work!"

She is trying to say something but the breaths are pulling in so fast she can't form a word. She grips his hand tighter.

"No!" someone shouts. "No! What are you doing!" A medic is cutting away her shirt, revealing her skin and the little red ruptures across her chest. "What are you doing? You can't disrespect her like that!"

"We need plastic wrap!" a medic shouts out to the crowd. "Plastic wrap! Her lungs are being crushed! If you don't all start helping, this woman's going to die!" The crowd erupts into activity and young men set off running and others reach for their phones. "Now—help! Turn around! Link arms! Make us some space and give the doctor her privacy." As soon as people are given a clear instruction they snap to it.

She is looking at Khalil. Each little breath collapses her rib cage tighter onto her lungs. Short. Sharp. Breaths. The plastic wrap will plug the holes. Her hand is holding on tight to his, but she is looking past him. Short. Sharp. Breaths. Each breath snatched for life brings her closer to death.

She grips his hand firmer.

"I'm here," he says. "I'm here with you."

Each breath comes shallower than the last. The doctors work quickly but the wounds are too many. Her skin trembles. Her grip loosens. Her eyes scan the dark sky for a comfort that will not come.

21

There's that tree, on the corner of the square, in front of Safir, that blooms blood-red flowers early every year. The people waiting for the bus on the street corner crush its soft body bleeding underfoot. The red cotton tree. It prepares us for the coming heat.

PART 2
TODAY

With a constitutional assembly on the brink of collapse and protesters battling the police in the streets over the slow pace of change, President Mohamed Morsi issued a decree on Thursday granting himself broad powers above any court as the guardian of Egypt's revolution.

The unexpected breadth of the powers he seized raised immediate fears that he might become a new strongman. Seldom in history has a postrevolutionary leader amassed so much personal power only to relinquish it swiftly.
—*The New York Times*, November 22, 2012

She hurls another rock. Throws it so hard that her shoulder might rip out of its socket, and before she can see where it's landed she's stooping to pick up another.

"You bastards! You stupid sheep bastards!" Mariam's never been so angry. "You stupid sons of bitches! Think what you're doing! *Think!*"

They came in the morning to attack. Since the new president's constitutional amendments there have been protests every day around the presidential palace. So they came in the morning to remove them.

"You fucking thug sons of bitches." She hurls another rock. "Your pimp of a president is fucking elected! *Elected!*"

The Brotherhood has made its move. With a parliamentary majority they played their hand to force through the country's new constitution in betrayal of all their revolutionary promises and alliances. The new constitution that will shape the country's future and define its laws and seek to forge its postrevolutionary identity. The new constitution that doesn't protect any minorities, that subjugates women, that allows for torture, that invites privatization and protects the army.

"You think that's it!?" Mariam hurls another rock into the no-man's-land of debris between them. "You think it's that fucking *easy?*"

Ranked against them, their backs to the presidential palace,

121

are men, hundreds of men. Men with long beards and heavy jackets booming instruction, men with lighter beards and the anger of an impotent youth, men following orders, men with nowhere else to turn, men lost in their blueprint for divine salvation and those burning with the need to cleanse the land.

Then gunfire and the crowd flinches. She can't see the gun. People are running and Ashraf's hand is on her shoulder. We need to go. Something hits her on the back of the head but she doesn't fall. Ashraf is running, they're both running. They don't know which streets are safe. "Flatten your hair down," she tells Ashraf as she tries to slow her breathing. "Try and push it to the side or something. Look less revolutionist." She takes off her kufiyyeh and feels it is heavy with blood.

"Which way's the
palace?"
                    "I'm sure it's this way."
"Which way did we
come? I don't
recognize this street."
                    "When we chased
                    those boys did we
                    turn right or left?"
From the shadows Mariam can see eight men, wooden sticks, two kitchen knives.
"You guys know this
is a Christian
neighborhood."
                                        "The sons of dogs
                                        clearly have money."
"Of course. They have
everything."

          "A curse on Sawiris and
          Hamdeen and
          El-Baradei the traitors."
      "And on the Pope,
      the son of a dog."
She puts her hand on Ashraf's shoulder. Hold still. Keep
quiet. There are too many of them.
      "And *you*. What are we
      going to do with you?
      Who paid you? *Huh?*
      Who paid you?"
The slap of a hand on flesh. She strains to see through the
ironwork of the door.
          "Who paid you?
          Was it El-Baradei?
          Just tell us. We
          already know so
          just tell us."
A man, shirtless, bleeding. His ripped shirt is tied around
his neck like a leash. His eyes have bruised shut. They came in
the morning. They came on hired buses to drive away the protesters camped outside their new president's palace.
          "You're Christian,
          right? So who
          paid you? El-Baradei
          or the Pope?
          Who paid you?"
      "Boy, I'll cut your
      lips off if you don't
      start using them!"
      "Who paid you?
      Look, you're on

camera. How much
did he give you?"
"We'll cut your
throat, boy! How
much did El-Baradei
give you!?"

Another slap lands hard on the back of his head. She feels Ashraf flinch next to her. Blood drips from the prisoner's lips as he moves his head in dazed confusion. All he can say is "no, no, no."

"We know you have
money. We saw what
you all had in your tents
this morning. Cheese!
Three kinds of cheese!
Nesto cheese, you
perverts!"

"A plague on your houses."

"The filthy sons of shoes,
so much food, all living
like kings on their
American dollars."

"May they ask forgiveness."

"All paid for by the Americans."

"And the Israelis."

"If they have the Americans
we have the Quran."

"Thank the Lord."

"Thank the Lord."

"We have the Quran and we have the president."

"Thank the Lord."

"We should to get back
to the palace."

"Let's take this filth to the palace."

"Are there a lot?"

"Of what?"

"Of prisoners?"

"We'll find out."

"Sheikh Yassin said check their hands. If they're dirty, cut them off because they've been throwing rocks and you can be sure they're traitors and cut off their hand!"

"Come on. I'm sure it's this way."

"I don't recognize this street."

"It's this way."

"Come on, dog."

Another hard slap lands across the man's face.

"WE'RE WITH YOU, MORSI!! ANYONE WHO INSULTS YOU GOES HOME IN A BODY BAG!!"

"MOR-SEEEEE! MOR-SEE!"

"God's the greatest!!"

DECEMBER 5: SIX REPORTED DEAD IN PRESIDENTIAL PALACE CLASHES

Khalil is leaning over the balcony, trying to make out the street fighting ahead, the sound of the occasional bullet drifting toward him. This is the nightmare scenario. He's been thinking it all day and with each rock thrown at the Brotherhood militia the feeling grew in his stomach. This is it. This is our *Africa, darling, terrible mess, isn't it?* moment. This is a shit show and this is an excuse for the army to roll back in, to take the reins again. And what comes next will make Iraq look like a playground. Because if this plays out with Morsi overthrown, then Egypt has no shortage of veteran jihadists and fiery ideologues and lifetime fighters who are all going to go home, tool up, and come out guns blazing. And then we'll be sorry. Then there'll be no one who can do anything except the army and the fucking police. The country will be begging them to take the streets again.

"They're holding people in the fucking palace!"

He turns to see Mariam and Ashraf walking into Nancy's apartment.

"Yes, we know," Hafez replies, turning his computer around to show Mariam a video, "they're boasting about it."

A dining table full of laptops runs through the center of Nancy's parents' dining room. Hafez, Rania, and Rosa all uploading, editing, and writing. There are several other faces he doesn't recognize.

He steps inside to see Mariam and sees blood smeared across her forehead.

"What happened? You okay?"

"I'm fine. Just a rock."

"Did you black out?"

"No."

"You're sure?"

"I'm sure."

"Good. Sit down."

He gets water and a towel and antiseptic spray and sets to work cleaning the wound.

"The Brotherhood are torturing people in the palace," she says.

"I know."

"What are we going to do?"

"What do you mean?"

"We have to get them out."

"We can't storm the palace. They're too many."

"We can get numbers. If we have ten thousand people outside the gates, they'll have to let their prisoners go. Where the fuck *is* everyone?"

"Let's just fix your head first."

Once the wound is clean he sits down next to her.

"This is bad," he says.

"We'll get the numbers out tomorrow," she says.

"This is giving the army what they want."

"What do you mean?"

"There's people calling for them to intervene."

"There are always people calling for the army to intervene," she says.

"And what if they do? If they try and get rid of him . . ."

"They're not going to. They're working together. This is just a test. This is the Brotherhood showing they can control the street. The army couldn't be happier right now. This shitty constitution gave them everything they want."

"But maybe we should be doing something different."

"Like what?"

"I don't know."

"You want another election, do you? Now that we've seen how well your last one went."

"Right. It was *my* election."

"You voted, didn't you?"

"Whatever."

DECEMBER 6: MORSI: "FIFTH COLUMN AND MUBARAK LOYALISTS WORKING TO DESTABILIZE EGYPT"

In the nights he sees her: her chest rising and falling, faster, shorter, rising, falling, feels the doctor's hand gripping his tighter, squeezing his chest closed. He is straining for breath, he is lying on the ground and the world above him is spinning but she's there, her hands on his chest, she is above him: an eternal darkness inside the gas mask. Her hands are on his chest. His father stands above them. Pump, he says. Pump. He flicks a ruler into the air, the conductor keeping time. One, two, three: pump. Her hands are on his chest. One, two, three: pump. She's leaning now, down and into him, and he's kissing the mask, kissing the glass darkness and his chest loosens into a breath and into a sudden waking sweat.

He goes into the bathroom and pulls off his T-shirt, then turns, strains to see over his shoulder, to see his back in the mirror. The wounds have long healed, leaving scratching scars across his skin. How close were we to the same death? The file waits for him on his computer: Doctor_02022012.mp4. He does not open it.

DECEMBER 9: MORSI'S CHIEF OF STAFF ACCUSED OF TORTURING PRISONERS IN PRESIDENTIAL PALACE

Rania has the head of the large table in the Chaos office for the general meeting. Dozens have responded to the call for new volunteers: filmmakers, journalists, translators, academics, photographers, and more. Every chair is taken, people sit on the wooden floors, lean against the walls, make coffees in the kitchen, smoke on the balcony.

"It's good to see so many people here," Rania says. "It shows how serious this crisis is. If you're here, you understand we can't just laugh this off. We only need to look at the history of Mussolini to see how this can spiral. Militias sent in to clear the streets, journalists killed. This is how it begins. We can laugh at them as much as we like but this is how it begins. We need to be producing content like never before. We need to dominate the media war. We have three enemies now: the Brotherhood, the army, and the police. Yes, each have differing interests—but we know for absolutely certain that there's one interest they all share completely and that's ending the revolution."

Their latest podcast, *Muslim Brotherhood Cadres Kidnap and Torture Protesters Inside the Presidential Palace*, is downloaded two hundred thousand times in a week.

DECEMBER 18: MARTYRS' FAMILIES STILL WAITING FOR JUSTICE. MORSI SILENT.

When the transistor finally arrives with a friend traveling from the States, Khalil and Hafez set to work on building a small analog transmitter. Capacitors, resistors, the transistor all carefully soldered into a circuit, attached to a battery and an inexpensive mp3 player preloaded with a one-hour program and set to loop. Late at night they attach it high up the trunk of a tree in front of a café in Bab al-Louq and walk away.

On Khalil's balcony Hafez trains a GoPro on the transmitter tree while Khalil scans the radio frequencies:

> . . . *what has been called a campaign characterized by misinformation supporters of the president mobilized enough votes to pass a new constitution that could significantly alter the character of the country in years to come and oversee an erosion of basic rights and dignities.*

"There it is," Hafez says.

The mp3 is a program made especially for their experiment, the narrator an older man—an actor uncle of Hafez's—speaking in the formal Arabic of the newscaster. There is no mention of Chaos, or even the revolution.

They say illegal radio transmissions get an automatic fifteen years. They sit back and wait. Hafez opens a beer.

"To bloody battles and bruised arms," he says.

> *Meanwhile, youth across the country continue to be detained in military prisons and prosecuted in military courts—a practice of the army now defended in the newly passed constitution.*

"Do you believe that stuff?" Hafez asks. "About the effect of the constitution?"

"It shows us what they're thinking. And it makes people angry."

"Not angry enough to vote it down."

After an hour the MP3 loops:

> *Hello, this is* Downtown Today *with the latest news. Egyptians have taken to the polls this week in what has been labeled the most divisive referendum in the country's long history.*

After fifteen hours and thirty-nine minutes, five commandos and a ranking officer arrive in a truck furnished with antennas and two satellite dishes. They find the transmitter without any problem. They ask questions of the people in the café but do not stay long.

"Well," Hafez says, "either we have to build a transmitter that can broadcast for at least a mile and still be both mobile and discreet—which might be beyond us—or it looks like we'll be sticking to the internet for now."

JANUARY 6: MORE ISLAMISTS APPOINTED IN CABINET RESHUFFLE

Just six months ago they were sitting in the Greek Club, counting the votes as they came in. The Greek was full, each table a collection of revolutionists and artists and journalists, a humming of excitement vibrating through the air around them.

Tonight is the first time in the history of the oldest civilization on earth that tomorrow's leader is being chosen by her people.

As night fell the numbers started coming in. He remembers Rania standing up with her phone in her hand, reading out the latest: "The Spare Tire is at thirty percent. Aboul Fotouh at twenty-three percent. Sabbahi is sitting pretty on eighteen percent. Shafiq is on seventeen percent and Amr Moussa is bringing up the rear with a measly eleven percent."

Results roll in from Ismailiya, Beheira, Marsa Matrouh, Suez for Morsi. Hamdeen scores wins in Alexandria, Port Said, and Damanhour. The night turned to focus on Hamdeen. Hamdeen can win Cairo. It will be Morsi versus Hamdeen. That's a fight we can win. Everyone will rally behind Hamdeen in the run-off.

And then Gharbeyya's results arrived, and Daqahleyya's, and Shafiq's numbers started to crawl up, and then Munoufeyya, Mubarak's hometown, lands with 55 percent of the vote going to Shafiq. Hamdeen falls behind but Morsi's numbers are relentless, and Shafiq keeps rising and then it was the worst-case scenario. Morsi versus Shafiq. The Brotherhood versus the military. The same story that's been played out for fifty years.

There was supposed to be something different. Something different was supposed to happen.

JANUARY 25: REVOLUTION ANNIVERSARY SPARKS MASS PROTESTS AGAINST MORSI REGIME

We were not ready for this.

Mariam is standing at the railings looking down at the sea of people beneath. Rania sits on a chair behind her, her head in her hands, not looking, not able to stop listening to the crowd below. Mariam's arm is raised, her hand pointing down into the yellow darkness.

"It's happening again. There."

Tahrir is full; thousands upon thousands of people fill the square to its concrete horizons, but there, in the middle, a shoal of people all twisting around a central point.

"It's happening again."

Khalil's running down the dark stairs, running down and out into the square, running toward the crush swirling around Mariam's shaking fingertip, hundreds of people all pushing and straining and shouting and reaching and Khalil forces his way past them, squeezing deeper into the crush; inch by inch he shoves past heaving shoulders and reaching arms until he sees a half-stripped body twisting in a sea of hands scratching and grabbing until it seems the woman will rip in half. *Make way! Make way! Get off me! Here, this way! Bring her this way!* A legion of voices screech words of help while more hands reach through the riot of bodies to grab at whatever flesh they can. *She's my sister*, a boy screams, *my sister, I swear she's my sister.* One man is bellowing and shoving at everyone around him—"Get away! Shame on you! Get back!"—and Khalil falls in next to him, heaving his body against the crush as a hand grabs at him and pulls at his waist and slaps hard at his face and slips into his pockets and another pulls choking at his shirt and an elbow lands in his side and a knife flashes in the streetlight. "Get away from the square!" someone shouts. "We need to get her away!" Inch by inch they push to get away, dragging the trailing crush, the young woman unconscious between them all, *she's my sister, I swear she's my sister.* There is a doorway. "Inside! Get her inside!" Push. Push. The crowd slowly grinds forward and the door hauls closed. "No one comes in! No one!" Khalil turns to face the crush, links arms with the men next to him as the crowd pushes and pulls at them but they keep their arms bound tight together against the shoving and shouting and the *what are you doing, who the fuck are you, make way she's my sister, my sister, I swear she's my sister* that calls out like a looping nightmare birdsong from the crowd. The boy, no older than fifteen, won't stop pushing and burrowing until Khalil knees him in the gut and he spins off back into the crowd. An arm flails and metal slices air and the line breaks as people scatter from a dirty switchblade and the flame arcing through the darkness and something clubs him on the back of his head and he falls and his shin crunches and his groin twists and something snaps and a sewage grate has given out and his leg is down in it and he's trying to haul himself out and now everyone is running because there's a man in a black balaclava—and he's pointing a gun at Khalil.

Khalil stops moving. The end of the pistol trembles. Trembles for long seconds of confusion. And then the balaclava's gone, running back into the crowd, bodies parting instantly before him and his swinging pistol.

Khalil hobbles quickly back toward the iron gate. The ambulance is coming. It must be. Just keep that door closed a little longer. That's all there is. Just a little longer. That's all now. Just keep the door closed.

JANUARY 26: BLOOD IN THE SQUARES ON REVOLUTION'S ANNIVERSARY

Mariam is in the dark bathroom, her body bent over the sink, her hands slowly rubbing over each other in the warm water. Her arms are covered in scratch marks, her scalp is raw from fistfuls of hair ripped out. The tissue pressed to her leg flowers red. The blood spirals.

There's a gentle knock.

"She's in critical," Rania says. "She's cut, badly, inside. A blade."

Mariam keeps her hands in the water, moving one over the other in slow self-hypnosis. The water constant, unquestioning. A blade. A blade. Her mind can't move past the word. She concentrates on the water running out of the rusted tap. What is this? What is happening? How can we go on from here?

A phone rings and Rania steps away. We were not prepared. Not for this. The blood swirls slowly down the sink.

JANUARY 26: 32 KILLED AND HUNDREDS WOUNDED IN FIERCE CLASHES IN PORT SAID

In the morning they take stock. Hundreds have been arrested, dozens killed, Port Said and Suez are in open revolt, Brotherhood headquarters are being sacked across the country and in Tahrir . . . what do we even call what happened in Tahrir? The hands, the knives, at least two dozen attacks.

Mariam is sitting cross-legged at the end of the bed, computer open. Khalil tries to sit up a little. His body is sore from the night and in the light he now sees the scratches ripping down her arm.

A string of messages wait on his phone for him.

OpAntiSH meeting today at midday. We need to be better prepared.

Should we go to Port Said today? At least 26 dead there last night.

Need more people in the intervention teams. Let's write a call today.

At least two hundred people arrested last night are still missing. We need to go out looking for them.

JANUARY 27: EMERGENCY LAW, CURFEW DECLARED IN THREE CITIES

Khalil and Hafez sit on the floor at the back of the Chaos office watching Morsi's speech on Hafez's laptop as the new volunteers arrive.

> *To the men of the police, I thank them for their great efforts in defending citizens and state institutions.*

The new president nervously looks down at his notes.

> *And I salute the men of the armed forces, for the immediate implementation of orders I gave them effecting their intervention to safeguard the security of this country and secure its buildings.*

He looks down, then remembers he is supposed to look authoritative and raises his finger in the air. He is building up an anger in himself. He shakes his finger at the country.

> *I have said before that I am against any extraordinary measures, but if I have to I will do it. So here I am doing it. To prevent blood being spilled and to maintain security against the rabble-rousers and those who operate outside the*

law and to protect the citizens I have decided—after
consulting the constitution—firstly: to declare a state of
emergency in the governorates of Suez, Port Said, and
Ismailiya for thirty days, as of midnight tonight. Second:
there will be curfew in the governorates of Suez, Port Said,
and Ismailiya from nine p.m.

"Emergency law . . ."

"We only just got rid of the emergency law."

"What is he doing?"

"People are going to be furious."

"It's as if he's actually trying to tell people that he's no different from Mubarak."

New arrest powers mean #Morsi gave army the powers to arrest him. As soon as MB card is burned and can't advance their interests anymore they'll arrest him.

@Moftasa

4:14 PM–28 Jan 2013

Ashraf stands on a chair at the front of the room, puts his hand in the air.

"All right, listen up! You've all volunteered to the intervention teams. Welcome. For those who don't know: the intervention team's job is to get into the crowd and get the women out of it as quickly as possible. I recognize some of you from the other night so you know how crazy it can be. The rest of you, listen up."

He pulls on three layers of T-shirts, pushes a ripped up piece of cardboard inside against his skin, and tucks them in. Better a kidney than your gut. He does his belt up as tight as it will go. He yanks at it, tries shoving his hand inside it. It's tight. A man two days ago had his anus scratched out to bleeding. Khalil's whole body clenches at the thought of a filthy fingernail probing. He takes his door key off the ring and pushes it down into his sock so it presses against the sole of his left foot, then takes his ID and fifty pounds and pushes them to the bottom of his right sock, ties his shoelaces as tight as he can. Nothing in pockets. Microphones? No. Not for this.

The sun has not yet set.

His phone vibrates with a message from Mariam.

Be careful today.

He takes a thick pen and starts to write Mariam's phone number high on his upper left arm under the sleeve of the inner-most shirt. Too much. Come on, this is too much. But, then again, no one will ever know. Unless the worst happens. He makes his bed and puts out a clean towel, checks he has soap, antiseptic, painkillers, and bandages in the bathroom. If we survive these nights, will we have anything left to hold on to?

He stands on the balcony, lights a cigarette. The last rays of the sun soak the tops of Downtown's buildings. The roof-tops piled high with rubble, the army of obedient satellite dishes pointed up into nothingness, the eternally shuttered windows, the city crumbling around him.

He joins his intervention team and takes position on the raised precipice opposite KFC, scanning the crowd for sharp movement, for panic, listening out for screams. They stand in their T-shirts—*Anti-Harassment Force*—ready to move, shout, fight when the call comes in. They watch the lookouts, climbed up high on lampposts, waiting for the signal, the point, the call to action. It will end in a single second. The silent blade, the grip you can't break, the last breaths crushed in a puddle of mud.

She turns on the phones in the Operations Room and places one of her lists on the table in front of her:

–~~organize packages for square teams~~
–check on safety packages
–backpack, T-shirt, bandages, scarf, flip-flops, tampons, loose pants
–confirm all safety houses
–confirm each safety house has basics
–antiseptic, bandages, clean towels, Wi-Fi passwords
–basic fridge supplies
–~~how many intervention teams?~~
–~~talk to captains~~
–~~check everyone has everyone else's phone numbers~~
–~~do we have enough T-shirts?~~
–~~have they been cleaned?~~
–Control Room
–who's in? who's on shift rota?
–supplies
–pens, paper, water, chips, Coke
–Valium

It is not long before the first phone call:
"Hello?"
"Hello. Hello? We need help. They're beating her. They're beating her! We need help, please."

"Okay, where are you?"

"We're in Suez. In the march. The main one."

"But we only have people in Cairo. Do you have friends in Suez you can call?"

"What do you mean? We need help! Please!"

"I'm so sorry we—"

"You need to find someone! They're going to kill her! Oh God, I couldn't stop them!"

"Okay"—she has to think quickly—"hang up, send me a location pin. I'll try to find someone."

"No, don't hang up! Oh God! You bastards! You bastards! Oh God."

She's sobbing now into the phone. Mariam reaches for another phone, tries calling someone in Suez, starts typing out a message on another. There must be someone in Suez who can help. She keeps the phone close to her ear, to keep the woman close.

"We'll get you someone. We'll work something out."

"Oh no. Oh no no. I couldn't stop them."

"Are you in a safe place? Just stay with me."

"I couldn't stop them . . ."

FEBRUARY 1: MORE INNOCENT VERDICTS FOR POLICE KILLING OF PROTESTERS

They sit on the bed in silence next to each other, Mariam's computer open between them. A young woman is speaking very carefully.

> *Luckily my friend was with me. She kept telling me it was going to be okay. She said into my ear that the most important thing is we hold on to each other, whatever happens. She kept telling me it's going to be okay. That we're going to get*

out of it. I held on to her as tight as I could while all those hands grabbed at my body.

The talk show host waits, his face pressed in theatrical concern.

"Do you know her?" Khalil asks.

"I met her that night," Mariam says.

I was yelling stop, stop, you animal, stuff like that, like an idiot, as though that would make a difference. I was hitting and pushing but there were so many of them.

She takes a breath. Mariam can see the map of thoughts running across her face. How much will she say?

And these men—they were members of the Muslim Brotherhood?

What?

The men who attacked you.

No. Well, I don't know. There's no way of knowing.

But you were in Tahrir protesting against the Brotherhood.

Yes.

So it would make sense that these are Brotherhood men.

It might.

She snaps into a new attention.

But we know the police have been raping people for years. And we know that in this society, in this world, rape is used as a weapon by men everywhere.

Well, thank God you're okay.

Khalil keeps thinking of that American journalist last winter. "How come there aren't more female candidates for the elections?" she'd asked. "Why is no one talking about this?" He keeps hearing his answer, vague words about how we must keep the revolutionary cause unified. *We.* Who is this *we* you speak for so easily? What were those easy words, appropriating, colonizing Mariam's language, her life, her answer that carries years of frustration and harassment and oppression and tension and sacrifice? Mariam's answer that you could never inhabit. Simply took it, claimed it, spoke it. Because it was easy. And, now, here we are.

She's not asleep. He can tell from her breathing. He looks at her and is repulsed by his base urges. His penis shrivels into itself—*she's my sister, I swear she's my sister.* I'm sorry, he wants to say. Sorry for everything, sorry for men, for all men, and the things they do, sorry for being one, for lying here thinking about the touch of your skin, for the weight of my body on yours, for every other woman I've ever looked at. It's not Egypt, it's not Egyptian men, it is simply: men. It is men who must be washed off the streets, men who start wars and fires and rape children and beat their partners, it is men who infect the air with testosterone and territory. Sure, Rania could club a baby seal to death, but it is men, always men, who are the problem. Remove men and maybe the world stands a chance. They say that scientists can create a baby from two eggs, so maybe that's the end of us. It's hard not to think it a good thing.

"Of course it's organized!" Nancy snaps as she packs safety bags full of emergency supplies. "Do I need to lay it out for you? The Brotherhood has come to power. They do a terrible job and everyone hates them. Good so far? They hate people protesting against them so now they're pushing a new strategy—one that only a secretive organization of *Brothers* could come up with—to end them."

"But they want to look stable," Mariam says. She's exhausted but she does her best to be polite with Nancy. "This shit makes them look totally out of control."

"For a month, maybe. And then they'll be completely *in* control."

"They don't take risks like that."

"So then the liberals are organizing these attacks?"

"Why does someone have to be organizing them? We get harassed every minute out there. Maybe this is just patriarchy's logical conclusion."

"There has to be some organization. It always starts with a big group forming a circle around a woman. That doesn't happen spontaneously. These men know one another."

"So they're just friends and this is their sick game. And every man who jumps in after—they *don't* know one another and that's the problem. And if someone *is* organizing this, then they understand that all you need is a spark to get a big fucking fire."

Nancy doesn't reply. She picks up an empty backpack and puts the safety items in: plain T-shirt, loose trousers, hoodie, abaya, underwear, flip-flops, tampons, sanitary pads, tissues, water, Valium. She looks up at Mariam: "We need to catch one next time. Interrogate him."

"Nancy, we're not vigilantes. We're there to protect the women."

"Well, maybe that's not enough. Maybe we need to send a signal."

FEBRUARY 4: AHMADINEJAD TO MEET WITH MORSI, SIGNALING REALIGNMENT

Mariam is walking the narrow road to the morgue, the trees above it struggle in the shadows of the Zeinhom halls of justice. A burned-out car sits filled with years of garbage, haggard cats pawing through it. They found one of the disappeared today. Mohamed El-Guindy. Mariam lowers her head as she makes her way past the women in black sitting in the coroner's courtyard. A dozen young men in hoodies stand in furious silence. Mohamed El-Guindy, another smiling face I never knew, another death in burning pain. She taps on the thick wire across the reception's cracked glass. The assistant begins to wave her away then looks up, recognizes her. For a moment he is unsure what to do, then gets up with a nervous sigh. The heavy metal door unbolts.

Khalil places the thick headphones over his ears, clicks through his download folder, and opens the video titled "Hamada Saber." The whole country has seen the video already, the poor man's name is on everyone's lips—but he feels sure he has to use it somehow for this week's podcast. He clicks play.

His name was Mohamed El-Guindy. He's been missing for days. He's laid out cold on the chromium table, as Mariam knew he would be. Rania has her arms around a woman's shoulders, his mother's. Mohamed's eyes are closed, his hair dry. Mariam gives the slightest nod and Rania leads the mother out of the room. The door closes and Mariam lifts the sheet covering him to check for a coroner's incisions but there are none. She walks to the small room at the end of the corridor. "Tell your boss to get down here," she says to the pallid receptionist. "Because those boys outside are not going home until they have an autopsy."

Hamada Saber's shirt is off, he is on the ground, he is rolling from side to side on the asphalt. Through the sulfuric purple hue his body stands out, alone amid the black riot gear, alone and naked and they are watching him writhe on the tarmac between them. He is old, he has no hair. He looks up, pleading with them as another kick lands on his back and his trousers are ripped off down to his ankles and Khalil feels the tarmac ripping at his naked body, clicks pause as the men in black drag him toward the waiting police truck.

"Did the coroner come?" Nadia, Mariam's mother, asks, as she pulls the door closed behind her.

"No," Mariam says.

"They must be working out their story. I'll do an exam myself. Can you lock the door?"

Nadia looks down at his face, purpled and swollen. She runs her hand through his hair. "He's young," she says, to herself.

There is no usable sound to Hamada Saber's video. A purely visual violence. There is a growing demand for videos from Chaos. People want to see the sources of their outrage. Khalil has always felt that there's something more cerebral and less exploitative about sound, a conversation rather than an authoritative statement of fact. But maybe the time for conversation is over. The kicks keep landing on Hamada Saber's body. The color of skin is startlingly clear through the pixels.

"He was tortured," Nadia says. "Badly. Clear signs of strangulation. And here: burn marks. Electrodes on his tongue. Photograph this."

"They're saying he died in a car accident."

"And photograph here as well. We can release these to the media if they keep denying it. Forceps."

Mariam passes them to her. She knows her mother's tools. Nadia works two shifts a week at a private hospital. The only way to pay the bills. And every Friday she runs a free clinic from their little apartment in Manial. Mariam used to go out in the morning and stay out of her way until the evening. She'd go kill time at the cinema or sit and work in the university library until one day she came home and found her mother with her head in her hands, crying. "What's the matter?" she'd asked, as she came around the desk to hug her. But Nadia insisted it was nothing.

The next weekend Mariam didn't go out. Their little living room filled with people from after prayer time, her mother greeted them, invited them into her office, all smiles. The last patient left around ten at night and Nadia went to her desk. She wrote a note on a piece of paper and stared at it, sat stone still for twenty, thirty seconds. Then quickly opened a drawer, dropped it in, and got up from the desk.

Mariam put her book down and got up from the sofa, walked around to the desk. She opened the drawer and inside were dozens, hundreds of slips of paper: notes and phone numbers and receipts and prescriptions. Months and months of overwhelming admin. Mariam pulled out the chair and got to work. Within three weeks she was running the follow-ups, the referrals, the phoned-in questions, the lost prescriptions, and the accounts.

"Photograph this, too."

An interview with El-Beltagy, one of the Brotherhood big shots, has Twitter alight. Khalil clicks on a link. El-Beltagy has a sincere expression on his face:

> *If we talk about the scene of Hamada Saber. If they showed you the other half of the story, you'd get the whole story. We turned a thug into a national hero. If you saw the first half you'd see him taking off his clothes so that he's ready when the cameras start filming.*

The crowd is growing angrier, louder.

> *Oh Lord, we will show them rage!*

Mariam dials the number of the man she knows with a hearse. She sends boys out to buy cotton for the shroud. Rania is sitting with the new martyr's mother. Mariam's phone feels heavy, rotten in her pocket. She taps on the wire-mesh window of reception.

"You'd better call an adult and tell them that there'll be a riot here if we don't have the autopsy report in half an hour."

FEBRUARY 5: THOUSANDS MARCH IN MARTYRS' FUNERALS

They sit together on the balcony. Her hand is in his and he hasn't stopped stroking it for as long as she can remember. The starless city beyond their balcony is many things to many people. A city of women and another of men stalking in dark parallel. A city of refugees living invisibly between restaurants, rooftops, and relief agencies. A city of hotel bars and street carts where the same plate of beans can cost a pound or a day's wages. A centralized city being slowly sucked out of itself, hollowed out by the satellite suburbs surrounding it. A city of thousands of years past piled high upon each moment of the living present. An underground city of police cells and hidden dungeons and transport trucks keeping its victims in secret circulation between its high-walled and watchtowered prisons.

Her hand is still in his and that's good, because if she just focuses on that, then everything else can fade out for a minute and she can just accept it and not question it or fight over it, it can just be, we can just breathe and not think about the dark underworld running beneath us and not think about January 25 and not think about the hospital, the phone calls, the morgue, and not think about what would happen if we stopped or what's coming or what we should have done different we can't stop there's no time, no time to think about ourselves or our mistakes or the morgue there's only today and there's only the work, there's only the lives and the crush that's all there is that's all that matters so we don't need to talk because with talking our hands will shake so, right now, his hand is enough, his thumb pressing down and circling back a little whirlpool of silent tenderness holding us frozen for a fragile moment.

FEBRUARY 8: POLICE BARRACKS STILL SITES OF TORTURE AFTER REVOLUTION

A huge message has been pinned to the bulletin board in the office.

TO BE FAIR, THE MAN IS ACTUALLY
THE ONE WHO STRIPPED HIMSELF NAKED.

He can hear Rania from the kitchen. "How did this happen?" she's saying. "How did we get these idiots? We *had* the fucking numbers. Seven million people voted for the revolution. If Aboul Fotouh and Hamdeen could have put their fucking egos aside for five fucking minutes things would have all been different." There are three people listening to her whom he doesn't recognize. She pours herself a coffee. "Anyway, fuck it. We'll take the Brotherhood apart and then finish dismantling the army. Anyone who gets in the way of the revolution's momentum will be destroyed."

FEBRUARY 10: FIRST COURT ORDER IN HISTORY TO SHUT DOWN YOUTUBE

In these pewter mornings you can hardly tell the difference between the death gray of the river and the smoke choking out of the tear-gas canisters sinking into its depths. A burned-out police truck lies smoldering in Tahrir. A crowd of teenagers throw rocks at the policemen. A dull cycle of violence has taken hold. The gas drifts from the street out over the water. Mariam, Khalil, and Hafez stand toward the back, watching, a gas mask in Mariam's hands.

We are fighting a slave army, she thinks: conscripts kidnapped from the countryside and forced to do battle in the capital. If they weren't here they'd be sweating in assembly lines in military factories or operating industrial deep fryers for the army's potato chips. But here they hurl rocks at children until they are locked back into their own prison trucks and driven back out to their supermax barracks in the desert. The officers don't get hurt, they don't even break a sweat.

Hafez has his camera around his neck but he is not taking any photos. It's all the same, he thinks: the same images are just repeating themselves. I'm just the middle man. I'm not dying, I'm not fighting, I'm not even asking these kids' permission. I take in their bravery—sometimes their death—and I'm the one who chooses how it's packaged and captioned and who sees it. Two photographs pay my bills for two months. We are all war profiteers.

With each shotgun cartridge unloaded Khalil sees the doctor, feels her hand gripping his, feels his chest snatching for her last breaths. He is not recording the sound today, he has hours of battle ambient already. And her recording still waits for him. Doctor_02022012.mp4. With each report he feels her spilling out of his arms.

They stand in silence. A cloud of tear gas wafts across the road. Mariam turns to Hafez: "Are you still working on the screenplay?"

"It's turned into a nightmare."

"Why?"

Hafez thinks for a moment before answering. Another volley of rocks is launched toward the police. "It's impossible to do the Eighteen Days without being clichéd. It's ruined already by its overtelling."

FEBRUARY 11: MORSI'S DRAFT NGO BILL "MORE REPRESSIVE" THAN MUBARAK-ERA LAW

She brings up cartons of juice without phoning ahead, places them down in front of Alia's parents, pulls the door quietly behind her. Alia is losing weight, her face is gaunt, yellowing in this shuttered ward. Mariam smiles softly at the parents.

"How is she today?"

"No change, dear." Alia's mother is young. Much younger than the father. They are formal with each other.

"God willing, she'll wake up soon," Mariam says.

"The doctors don't know anything." The father's voice is low and deep. "They don't know why she won't wake up."

"And we're going to have to start thinking about the expense soon."

"Don't worry about money," Mariam says. "I'll find you the money."

"God keep you, my dear."

With each day that passes their hearts are hardening. Alia, another friend I never knew. Trapped by the crush of men, clawed by twenty pairs of hands, raped with the blade of a dirty knife. Mariam takes Alia's hand and strokes it.

What can make you wake up after two weeks asleep? She strokes Alia's hand. We will get past this. We will get where we need to go. We've avoided looking it in the eye for too long. All this time working within a broken system, plastering a festering corpse from the inside. *The people demand the fall of the regime.* So we'll swap Mubarak for Tantawi for Morsi for Sharon for Obama for whoever, swapping them in one after another as we write long books and argue into the night about "the people" and what we think they want. We'll do it the few more times left to us before the world finally falls to the fever that will rid it forever of our bacterial civilization. Or we do the one thing we haven't tried yet, the one thing that might just change everything. The time is now, the people are ready: the only revolution left is a women's revolution. Tomorrow we say "enough." Every woman will stop working, managing, maintaining the world and we watch it crack at the seams. It's the only thing we haven't tried. We can all feel its potential, a static undercurrent crackling through the city, can see it in each other's eyes through the perilous streets, can feel our bones growing harder as the compromise drains from our bodies. The time is now: the conditions are perfect. It will be Egypt: the revolution flows through the country but its wave has yet to crest. From Mubarak to the army to the Brotherhood it subsumes one after another until there is nothing left but the final injustice of the patriarch. The time is now, the people are here, the flame has been lit: virginity tests, blue bra, mass assaults—we are the target, we are the oppressed, we are the front line, and while everyone else has shattered their political axes into impotent fragments, what more cohesive force is there than simply: women. Women suffering the same indignities from Alexandria to El-Arish to Alaska to Adelaide. The time is now and the people are here. We will not take this anymore. Your Arab Spring will be nothing compared to what's coming.

We will have justice for you, Alia. Just wake up and you'll see.

She should get back to the Corniche. Has there been any change? How many more children will the police have shot today? With the new walls dividing the city she is now closer to the morgue than to the battle—maybe she should go straight there.

"Do you need anything tonight?" she asks.

"Thank you, dear, get some rest," the mother replies.

"You don't have to come every day," the father says; then adds, softer, "we can see how busy you are."

"I know," Mariam replies. "But I like to."

She turns and makes her way down the dark corridor of the crumbling hospital, returns a missed call from Rania.

"Rania, what's up?"

"That twelve-year-old boy who's missing, remember?"

"Of course."

"We might have a lead. They've apparently got dozens of children locked up in the Red Mountain."

"The police barracks?"

"Yes."

"Oh, fuck."

In over a decade I have not seen as many cases of male activists
fully raped in police custody as in the past few weeks.

@HossamBahgat

9:23 PM–16 Feb 2013

FEBRUARY 17: CLASHES CONTINUE ALONG CORNICHE

How many days have we been out here? Khalil stands alone on
the bridge watching the children running to catch the skid-
ding gas canisters and throw them into the river. A boy laughs
as he launches a hissing gas canister back at the waiting police.
It's a game. Maybe it's a game for all of us, passing the time
until it's all over. Kids running away from their parents. Death
nothing more than sport for the police.

Words are sprayed on the river walls:

IF YOU DON'T LET US DREAM, WE WON'T LET YOU SLEEP.

You need discipline to win a war. You need chaos to win an
insurgency. So which are we?

Young boys are pulled away one after another, asphyxiated,
the gas clinging to their feet as their friends drag them away.
Once, not long ago, a night of tear gas would bring out crowds
in the thousands, the streets would be filled with disenfranchised youth, old leftists, new anarchists, photojournalists, foreign correspondents, doctors, police narcs, street kids, and riot
tourists. But there is no glamour to these long, painful afternoons. No one to watch the withering spectacle.

A motorcycle screams toward them with a new injury. He

sees a face savaged by buckshot, a trail of blood. Then the bike is gone and a young boy is on his knees, scooping something up from the asphalt.

"We have to bury it," he says, holding up the brains and flecks of skull.

FEBRUARY 18: MORSI COURTS EXILED
MUBARAK TYCOONS FOR FUNDS

Hafez is sitting alone in the dark of the office. Everyone else went home hours ago. Messages from Nancy sit unanswered on his phone. He didn't know if he'd got the shot. He didn't think about it at the time. Run, point, shoot. A war photographer works on instinct. He ran, he pointed, he shot. But he couldn't bring himself to check if he'd got it. The motorcycle tore away, the young boys ran after their friend, the poor do the dying.

Alone, in front of his computer, he can look at it. And it's there. The frame is alive with the panic of death, the burning tires, the flailing arm, the last goodbye. There is a holiness in the tableau of sacrifice. A sanctity that he has violated. He works gently on the colors and contrast, but with each tinting a cancer of doubt grows in him. How many waves of outrage must we spark to reignite the revolution? How many last breaths will we auction off to the breathless internet? If a revolution's fuel is death, then what will be its end?

FEBRUARY 23: EGYPT ORDERS $2.5M WORTH
OF TEAR GAS FROM USA

In the nights Khalil meets her. The doctor. In his dreams she is holding his hand, her legs lie over his while they watch television. He dreams of her touch, gentle and loving, stroking his hand. They are in a house of warmth and soft furniture and they are in love and his hand is on her knee. Their happiness at having found each other glows, fills the room: they do not need to speak. She holds his hand. His heart is electric with love, the metal pellets in his back burn with happiness. She gets up, pulling him with her. He follows and sees she has something strapped to her head and when she turns it is not her face he sees but the black of the gas mask, the long darkness within it. I still love you, he says, I still love you. The mask moves toward him, moves in for the kiss, the darkness swirling now into a cosmos of bullet holes and breathing and bleeding. I still love you. I'm here. I still love you. I'm here with you. And then flick, something lands on his chest and a red flower begins to bloom and he wakes with a start and a burning back and a grief cut with a silent guilt that racks him until the dawn.

FEBRUARY 24: POUND IN FREE FALL AGAINST THE DOLLAR

Nelly's voice erupts out of the opening door: "Mariam, darling! How are you? And yes, you must be Khalil, oh how nice to finally *meet* you! We've put this off for far far *far* too long! Mariam, I can't tell you how awful you've been keeping him hidden away to yourself. So *handsome*. Isn't he, Honey Bear?"

Honey Bear, looming large behind her in the doorway, grumbles in assent. His arms are huge, hairy, and crossed over his chest. His wrist is weighed down by an enormous silver watch.

Nelly releases Khalil from her squeeze and beams a big smile at him. He wonders if his clothes smell of tear gas.

"There just hasn't been a good time," Mariam says.

"In a year?"

"Well, come in then." The father's hand is thrust out. "What would you like to drink?"

"Whatever you're having, thanks," Khalil says.

"I'm having whiskey."

"That's just fine."

"You speak Arabic," the father says.

"Yes."

"That's good. Mariam said you're American?"

"I was just born there."

Nelly ushers them inside and they take their places on the large couches overlooking the garden. When was the last time you saw grass? He wants to get up and touch it, to take his shoes off and feel the soft blades on his feet. It's been a long time.

"You've lost weight, darling! You must make sure you eat! I know you're out running around all the time but you have to eat! Khalil, is she eating? You have to make sure she eats!"

She's right, Khalil thinks. Mariam is getting thinner. In the rare moments they have at home together she never eats more than a piece of toast. She fell ill a few days ago but refuses to rest.

"So . . ." The father leans forward. "Khalil, can you please explain precisely what it is you and my daughter *do* together."

"Um. Of course," Khalil says, stalling. "What exactly do you—"

"Well, I know none of you believe in earning money. I'm not talking about that. But this *activism* business. When I ask her what she does she says she's an activist—"

"I never say I'm an activist," Mariam says.

"Well, your mother does."

"And," Nelly offers, sunnily, "they always say it on the Face."

"It's just Face, Nelly," Mariam says, curt, "for Facebook."

"We earn what we need," Khalil says. "We don't have many expenses."

When no one picks up the conversation Khalil half clears his throat. "I heard a little about your desalination project."

"Yes?"

"It sounds very interesting."

"Yes." The father rouses himself. "Desalination is the key. Get the salt out of it and we've got enough water here to plant the whole desert. Enough water to produce as many fruits and vegetables as *your* fine country."

What does it take to become a fucking Egyptian? Do I have to staple my passport to my forehead? Get Nasser tattooed on my left arm and Amr Diab on my right?

"Yes," Khalil says, "the produce in Palestine is excellent."

"Palestine?" The father is taken aback. "Ah yes, Mariam mentioned something about that. Not many *Egyptians* called Khalil, I suppose. Do you go? I'm sure my daughter is desperate to throw herself in an Israeli prison."

"Not enough. As soon as things calm down here I will."

"The Israelis want our water, of course. See all this business funding the Ethiopians' wretched dam?"

"Yes. Morsi's handled it badly."

"You're damn right he has! The fool's risking war!"

The father takes a slug of his drink and sits back in his chair.

Khalil can see Mariam's hand is shaking a little. She doesn't sleep enough. She spends each day between the Corniche and the field clinic and pharmacies and hospitals and donors and the morgue. She feels him watching her. Last night she was feverish.

Don't come too close, she'd told him, *don't waste your time. Don't pity me. It's so hot in here. Medicine is pointless.* But when the first drop of cool water landed on her forehead her skin sighed in relief and she relaxed and waited for him to press the wet towel against her burning forehead again but then she was alone and the room was dark and they were driving through a valley, dark mountains on either side. Her father was driving. Her little cousins next to her. The car wound down, deeper and deeper into the valley. The boy shouted: "Guess again! Guess again! What am I?" and his little sister shouted words back at him. They'd been playing the game for hours, on a loop. Guess again. Guess again. The car dropped deeper into the valley. Her father didn't speak, didn't play the radio. The mountains crept higher, darker, sharper. A light shone against them, a horn sounded, a car swerved and screamed and everything stopped. She looked out the back window and there it was, for the thousandth time, the coach down on its side across the road like a beached whale, a field of emerald glass between them, glinting blue in the hot sun, and in the middle of the highway a movement, a man dragging himself along the tarmac through the cutting glass toward her. She opened the car door, like she does every time. There are never any words to say. She stood there, the sun fierce on her head. More are coming. Falling out of the bus. Dozens of people crawling toward her. *Mariam!* her father shouts. *Get back in the car!* "But—" The man was close. Close enough to look at her. *Mariam! In the car!* Close enough to watch her turn, to watch the car pull away. "But—," she said, for the thousandth time. *Mariam*, her father shouted. *You can't change anything.*

"So," the father is saying, "are you gonna get married and give us some grandchildren?"

Mariam puts her drink down. "We've talked about this before," she says. "I'm not having children." Who would bring a child into this world? Who would have a girl and send her out onto these streets of men?

"Still with this nonsense?" her father growls. "Your mother

said the same thing for two years. Would you have preferred it if we didn't have you?"

Nelly turns to Khalil. "What about you, Khalil, do *you* want children?"

"I'm . . . not against the *idea*."

"Well, if neither of you can tell me how you're ever going to earn any money it's probably for the best. Those little mouths are expensive."

"Was *that* why you went private, Father?"

"Everyone goes private, sweetie. You'd know that if you'd ever worked a real job in this country."

"Well," Nelly cuts in quickly, "are you two not thinking about marriage?"

"We don't need to get married," Mariam says.

The father leans forward: "Are you sure?"

"Yes," Mariam replies coolly.

The father turns to Khalil and fixes him with a raised eyebrow and a dread look: "Are you *sure*?"

"Yes," Mariam steps in, "I'm sure. We've had this conversation before."

"And it never gives me any answers."

"And it won't today, either."

Mariam turns decisively to look at the garden. The lawn is a deep and tempting green leading to thick bushes of red flowers. She remembers the boy, his hands open, we have to bury it, a shallow grave, a single red flower to mark it.

"Khalil, dear, tell me something." Nelly is leaning forward, pouring herself another glass of water. "You have an American passport, yes?"

"Yes."

"Oh." Nelly shoots Mariam an unsubtle wink of faux female solidarity. "How useful." But Mariam's eyes are fixed on the garden.

"So if you're not having children, what are you going to do with yourselves?" the father says. "Do you have a plan for your lives? I respect you kids. I do. Maybe I don't say it, but I do. But I don't see a plan, not for your lives and not for your revolution. I was against Mubarak, sure. Everyone was. Then you go and drag the army through the mud and what have we got now? The Brothers. The *Brothers*! What are you doing about them?"

"Don't you watch the news?"

"Sure, I see a hundred kids throwing rocks at nothing! What's the point in that? They're not gonna storm the palace like that."

"No, but it stops Morsi from being president as long as they're out there. It's a message, it's saying he has to *earn* his authority."

"But why *violence*?" Nelly says. "Why not sit outside peacefully?"

"We *were*! *They* attacked *us*!"

"I just think the message is so much stronger when it's peaceful."

"In the end it's only violence that does anything," Mariam says. "Without battling in Mohamed Mahmoud the army would never have set the date for the transfer of power."

"No," the father says definitively. "Don't think that. You were lucky. The day the army decides to open fire you won't be able to stop them."

"We stopped them at Maspero."

"Maspero was a mistake. Believe me. If they get the order . . ."

"I thought you said they would never get the order."

"God willing."

FEBRUARY 26: DEADLIEST BALLOON CRASH IN DECADES
KILLS 19 IN EGYPT

The days are folding into each other. The emerald glass cuts at her tired hands, blue and red, bleeding out slowly in the desert. The man crawls toward her. The riot is unchanging. The protests are unending. Knives flash in the yellow dark.

She takes a bottle of water and sits alone on the grass in front of the Mogamma3, gently watering the earth around the single red flower. Bodies rot hidden in the morgue. Electrodes are clasped to young boys' tongues. Blades are taken to genitals. The president thanks the police for their hard work.

MARCH 3: PLAGUE OF LOCUSTS HEADED FOR EGYPT

He stands in the shadow of the ancient mountain of rock and rubble and watches the sun fall behind its silhouette. The waves are still, the water is a silver patience. The sun is setting, slowly, and he's standing in the Sinai shallows, the eastern wind breathing in off the sea bathes him in calm, the ripples racing away from his legs are stunning in their mathematical beauty but there, always, the voice from the scratching dark— *she's my sister, I swear she's my sister*—he is alone, his arms full of a body but he can't see the face, the shallows are long and flat and unmoving as glass until the reef and the drop, and he is walking out through the stillness to the edge, to lay it down and watch it sink and mark the spot with tears and say that she has been properly buried.

MARCH 5: EGYPT TO START RATIONING FUEL SUBSIDIES

No time for artistry. Production is up to two podcasts a week. The Brotherhood spent the weekend torturing protesters in a mosque. The police are arresting and torturing children by the dozen. The economy is collapsing. The new constitution is medieval. Record, splice, upload. No time for artistry. And no need either. Everything Chaos puts out is downloaded in the tens of thousands.

MARCH 9: POLICE ABUSE DEEPENING UNDER MORSI REGIME

The door to his apartment is a patchwork of stickers of political initiatives and protest slogans—and proud in the center is Nefertiti in a gas mask, her eyes fierce and angry and full of power, his favorite of them all. Nefertiti, always alert, always angry, a constant reminder not to stay comfortable inside for too long.

The apartment is dark. Mariam is not home. She will slip into bed next to him when he is asleep and he will wake up and find her at her computer. She can't be sleeping more than four hours a night.

The locusts did not come. Not to the city. And in their absence he had felt a perverse anticipation. He had wanted them to come. You wished a plague upon yourself. For what? A metaphor?

MARCH 11: KILLING OF ANTI-BROTHERHOOD FACEBOOK ADMINS RAISES FEARS OF TARGETED ASSASSINATIONS

Mariam stands in the wings of the Dream TV studio in Media City watching Ashira. She looks strong, almost godlike, the bright lights reflecting off her as she speaks:

"This is what they bring us? This is the revolution they promised us? Tantawi the war criminal is honored and Mubarak's police chiefs are free on the streets and not a single feloul minister arrested? And now this? Now they're killing people on the streets. They're arresting children by the hundred and assaulting women in the square. What *is* this? This is not what we were promised by the Muslim Brotherhood when they swore to continue the revolution."

Mariam loves watching Ashira in action. She is powerful without being aggressive, she is always exactly the right level of angry.

"No, of course not." The TV host grins. "And let's not forget that they said they wouldn't even field a presidential candidate."

"That's correct."

"And then they fielded two."

"Exactly. They've been lying from day one, and now they've ridden the revolution into power."

"Yes. We will take some phone calls now. I know that our Christian neighbors are very concerned and we'll be hearing from them—after the break."

The Brotherhood does not have many friends in Media City, and they are making their displeasure known. Dozens of men are in angry encampment outside the gates, complete with toilets and a butcher and an open fire. A "medieval siege," the media is calling it.

"Welcome back," says the host, beaming. "I want to pick up where we left off. Miss Mohsen, you were talking about the electoral promises of the Muslim Brotherhood."

"Well, let's start with prosecutions. The police who killed our families must be prosecuted."

"There must be trials, certainly."

"There must be trials. And when we put our evidence before the judges they will be jailed. We have two years' worth of work. Evidence collected. Names. Some of the families, they know the names of the police officers who killed their children. They see them in their neighborhoods. Can you imagine—"

Ashira pauses, something catches in her throat.

> Ashira waits. She is always waiting. She can't stop
> herself from waiting. She never changed the locks.
> She knows, she knows, but what if—
> She used to call his phone. Every hour, on the
> first day. Praying, first, for the mobile network to
> come back up. Then every day. Then every two
> days . . .

"—Can you imagine what that feels like?"

"And does the prosecutor general know this?"

"Of course. I've spoken to him myself. Look, the Muslim Brotherhood made electoral promises to the Egyptian people that they have not kept. When they were running the campaign for Mohamed Morsi they approached me."

"Directly?"

"Yes, directly. They asked me to stand onstage with Morsi at rallies and say that I want him to be president. Because I'm one of the families of the martyrs."

"And what did you say?"

"I asked why I should do that. They said that Mohamed Morsi was the only way that we would get justice. That when he came to power he would carry out the will of the revolution, that he would make sure that there were investigations and trials. That he was better than Shafiq. They said—"

> One day it rang. Her heart nearly burst out of her
> chest. It rang and rang and a man answered, a voice
> she didn't know. He said he'd bought the line, but

there was a tremor in his voice. She called again. She called again and he knew why she was calling and he told her. A neighbor was selling sim cards he found in the garbage near his house. And where do you live? Near the Red Mountain, he said.

The Red Mountain. A barracks within a fortress out into the desert. We all know its name, have heard it repeated on the lips of shivering children arrested and left fighting over buckets of rotten slop in its dungeons. Can you survive the Red Mountain for two years? Could Michael be shackled deep in its darkness? She talked to the children released, showed them photographs, photographs with and photographs without a beard, but nothing. You can't knock on the door of the Red Mountain.

Spilled blood dries and cracks unpaid for. A thirst is rising. Our killers roam free. Our need grows sharper. The months of talking are over, one word clings to her like sweat: *al-qasas*. It was bread, freedom, social justice when all this began. Words to die for. But the new word now: justice, vengeance, retribution. Call it a blood debt. Whatever it is. It must be paid.

"How will we be in touch?"

It was the last thing she asked him, her severed phone useless in her hand, the crowds brewing outside, his feet pushing into his shoes.

"I'll be home by sunset. Whatever happens."

She sat on the balcony and watched him walk away.

In the not knowing all you're left with is waiting. Waiting. For anything. For you to see Horreya.

For you to see the little woman she's turning into. Waiting and not waiting. Living and not living. I am forgetting what it felt like to close my arms around you, are you forgetting me? Are you in a place that lets you forget? Or is your world like ours, a gray mirror of longing?

The talk show host is watching her, nervous in her silence. "What did they say?" he prompts.

Ashira looks up again, clears her throat. "They said that they would honor what my husband, what Michael, died for."

MARCH 11: MILITARY COURT ACQUITS VIRGINITY-TEST DOCTOR

The sunlight catches generations of dust floating aimlessly in the air.

"How long's it been closed?" Khalil asks.

"Long time," the doorman replies. "Ten years at least."

Does the dust drift through empty air forever, animated by the vibrations of the city alone? The sunlight eases through his body to cut its perfect lines into the darkness and the warmth on his back floods him with a memory, the inner sanctum at Abu Simbel, his mother's voice in his ear. He can still feel the teenage awe: the grandeur, the theatricality, the perfect alignment with nature.

A fluorescent light cricks into life and the sunlight is vanquished.

"The children don't want anything," Tariq says. "Just want to sell the place and be done."

Ancient furniture buried in the dust, mirrors whose glint is long extinguished, bookcases heavy with volumes in Arabic and English, and in the corner, an old record player and shelves upon shelves of LPs.

"When did he die?" Khalil asks.

"Last week."

"The children don't want *anything*?"

"Nothing."

"I'll take the records."

"Okay . . . but you won't forget me?"

"How could I forget you, Tariq?" Khalil says, and feels in his pocket for a note.

Hafez is sitting in his regular chair, reading the newspaper, while Khalil sorts through the records, reading out some of the names: "Johnny Cash, Dalida in Arabic and in French—"

"Do your Johnny Cash impression," Hafez interrupts.

"Why do the impression when we have the real thing?"

"Come on. Do it."

"Maybe later. For now we've got some Neil Diamond, the Doors, looks like all of Fairuz, Abdel Halim, Umm Kulthum, Ennio Morricone, Charles Aznavour, Dionne Warwick, Serge Gainsbourg, Françoise Hardy. And loads I've never heard of: Dora Bandaly . . . Hoda Haddad . . . Joseph Sakr . . . Jacqueline."

Hundreds of records. A lifetime of music. This is what you've always needed. No more digital distractions, no more parental excuses—now you can sit down, record to record, and listen to all of Umm Kulthum and you'll finally get it, you'll understand the Lady. Wait till you tell the old man. As he flicks through the remaining records he almost expects to see the Reverend Franklin among them.

He pulls out a Fairuz album, slips off the sleeve. "Whoa," he says, and holds it up so Hafez can see.

COLUMBIA RECORDS, 24 SOLIMAN BASHA, RADIO CINEMA
ALLEYWAY, TELEPHONE: 43784.

"Shit," Khalil says. "Imagine having a Columbia Records in Cairo."

"You'll be lucky if you have a single record store in New York in a couple more years," Hafez says without looking up from his paper.

A Columbia Records in Cairo. We walk past the ruined Radio Cinema alleyway every day. When people talk about the Cairo of the past he can never truly believe the picture they paint. Cairo University was all miniskirts and Vespas and cycling down clean, wide streets in black-and-white movies. Cinema Odeon was for Russian films and Qasr al-Nil for French, the Italianate buildings of Downtown were a brilliant white and there was a ballet or an opera once a week that they claim was world-class.

A church bell sounds and Ennio Morricone's piano ripples into the room—"The Ecstasy of Gold."

Khalil sits down, opens a beer. "Your photo is everywhere," he says.

"Yeah," Hafez mumbles, without looking up.

"You're not happy?"

"Happy I photographed a child dying?"

"You know what I meant."

"No. I know. I don't know. We've done it to ourselves. Each scene has to be more shocking than the last. Then they care for fifteen minutes until the next horror horrifies them. And how many horrors until people have to just switch off?"

Hafez stubs out his cigarette.

"Do you think they're assassinating people?"

"The Facebook admins? They've killed three?"

"And at least six more beaten or stabbed."

"Maybe they are. I mean, why not?" Hafez takes another gulp of his drink. "We're in the great game now."

Each of them is alone in the music, the vast cemetery, the

dance of death spiraling into it, and as it crescendos Hafez raises his glass a little: "To bloody battles and bruised arms. To *glory*. Glory in a good death."

There is a silence.

When did the music stop playing?

"There are no good deaths," Khalil says. "Only deaths."

"There have to be good deaths. Or what's the point in anything?"

The silence hangs between them.

Hafez looks up from his drink. "Wouldn't *you* have been happy to die in the Eighteen Days?"

Khalil is quiet for a moment—"*Happy* is a strong word."

MARCH 20: RATIONING ANNOUNCED, BREAD PROTESTS BEGIN

He's woken by his doorbell. Mariam isn't there.

"Good morning," the neighbor from upstairs says. "I'm sorry to disturb you."

"It's all right," Khalil says, though he doesn't invite him inside.

"I just . . . it's the news and, well . . . where's our country *going*?" the little man says, wringing his hands. "What are you all going to *do* about the Brotherhood?"

"You've seen the protests?"

"But they have a *stranglehold* on the country. And they have America and Qatar. *This* is what the revolution was for? To deliver Egypt to the Brotherhood?"

MARCH 25: MORSI BURIES HUMAN RIGHTS INVESTIGATION INTO ARMY KILLINGS

New investigation from Chaos Collective: Muslim Brotherhood kidnaps and tortures people in Moqattam Mosque.

@ChaosCollective: Great job! We'll see these Brotherhood bastards in prison for what they did!

@ChaosCollective: How can men of God behave like this in a mosque?

@ChaosCollective: You don't mention who started it. Brotherhood HQ came under attack. They merely defended themselves.

@ChaosCollective: Heartbreaking to see what's happening to Egypt.

@ChaosCollective: Weren't you all the same side? Please explain what happened???

@ChaosCollective: Fuck those Brotherhood motherfuckers! Egypt will never accept Islamo-fascism.

@ChaosCollective: Stop your Mubarak propaganda. The Brotherhood came under attack, defended themselves.

@ChaosCollective: Where were the police through all this? Letting their new partners work in peace?

@ChaosCollective: Police withdrew, leaving civilians exposed to mob of thugs. Brotherhood members defended themselves.

@ChaosCollective: God save Egypt. Once the Brotherhood cements their grip on power we'll never be able to shake them.

MARCH 26: ALAA ABD EL-FATTAH ARREST ORDERED FOR INSTIGATING VIOLENCE

Ali looks about ten years old, though his father says he's thirteen. Mariam sits opposite him. Ali's mother has put a plate of sweets out and she nearly reaches for one but stops herself. She feels guilty when she eats, feels guilty in her body for any moment of indulgence when so much is left undone.

"It's okay. Take your time, Ali."

Khalil checks again that the recorder is running.

"They made me watch. They threw me in the truck and there were so many people in there and they made us watch."

"Who?"

"The government. The police. They made us all watch. Two men. They made them touch each other. They said if I didn't watch they'd slit my throat. Then they took us to a prison. It was underground. Once a day they threw in a bucket of dirty beans for us to fight over."

No time for artistry. Soon we will be up to three episodes a week.

APRIL 5: MASS ARREST AND TORTURE OF CHILDREN EXPOSED

The light cuts through the shutters, stretching itself long over the wooden floor, widening out as it lands on the far wall, a shadowed fanning across Mariam's VISIT PALESTINE poster. He has a book open, a Hobsbawm, and a passage highlighted with a black star in the margin. He reads it again:

The main shape of the French and all subsequent bourgeois revolutionary politics were by now clearly visible. This dramatic dialectical dance was to dominate the future generations. Time and again we shall see moderate middle-class reformers mobilizing the masses against die-hard resistance or counterrevolution. We shall see the masses pushing beyond the moderates' aims to their own social revolutions, and the moderates in turn splitting into a conservative group henceforth making common cause with the reactionaries, and a left-wing group determined to pursue the rest of the as-yet-unachieved moderate aims with the help of the masses, even at the risk of losing control over them. And so on through repetitions and variations of the pattern of resistance—mass mobilization—shift to the left—split-among-moderates-and-shift-to-the-right—until either the bulk of the middle class passed into the henceforth conservative camp or was defeated by social revolution.

Is it all so straightforward? Are we all doomed to the certainties of the historical materialist? Or is that a deflection of responsibility? When Mariam comes back to the bedroom, her coffee in her hands, he reads it to her.

"Well, that's depressing," she says.

"It doesn't have to be."

"Why not?"

"Maybe it's a pattern to be broken."

"But you can see the same happening here."

"Maybe it's different here. There are no Islamists in Hobsbawm's universe. We're not liberals versus conservatives here. We have the Brotherhood *and* the army: two extreme rights. And us."

"Well, thank God for that, then," she says.

APRIL 7: SECURITY SOURCE: FOREIGN INFILTRATORS AT ALL-TIME HIGH

The organ is low and strong and dangerous as Khalil puts his hood up and slips into the crowd. Above him banners and slogans march in time. His headphones are in, a church organ pulling at his tired muscles. Dark bodies move at his sides, touching, pushing slightly, unlooking. Fists punch at the night. *Down, down with every president!* The balconies above are empty. The choir begins its chant, *Koyaanisqatsi.* This is life now. Constant protest. We will not be cowed by the army or the Islamists or the police or global capital. Maybe we *are* the endless march. *Bread, freedom, social justice.* We are the opposition. Is this our role? Round and round the same streets again and again in permanent check against whoever is in power? *Koyaanisqatsi.* The organ climbs higher. You are in a church, a cathedral, walking down Talaat Harb Street to the altar. Prophecies. Maybe Hobsbawm is right. We've been doing the same thing for hundreds of years. Marching, fighting, chanting, dying, changing, winning, losing, marching, fighting, chanting, dying, marching, chanting, planning, failing, fighting, marching, marching, fighting, fighting. *Koyaanisqatsi. Koyaanisqatsi. Bread, freedom, social justice.* The march carries on. He looks up. The city doesn't watch us anymore. Doesn't cheer. Doesn't jeer. And above? Beyond? Is anyone still watching? Does anyone care about this dogfight with the Brotherhood? The old lines of communication with Athens and America have dried up. And Syria, Libya, Bahrain, Yemen—we can only bleed so much. And Palestine. When will Egypt release me to you? How many times can we march through downtown? *Down, down with every president!* Truly. Yes, yes, remember it is us. We are the vanguard keeping the flame alive. *Koyaanisqatsi.* Sheikh Emad, Gika, Bassem, Mina, Michael, Ayman—we march behind you. Our banners of war. It's for you that we can't stop. You who have given everything and all we can do is fall in step behind you until you can rest. This time will be different. This time the future can still be made new. The organ plays on unrelenting. *Koyaanisqatsi.* On and on behind you. On and on behind you.

Angry mobs roam the street. Her father calls. *Please come and see me.* So she's sitting in his living room, waiting for him to appear. *There are rooms for you girls.* She remembers how he kept repeating it. As if that was all it took to make it all right. *There are rooms for you girls.* And then he was gone. She's probably spent a total of two weeks in her room upstairs, each careful detail of Nelly's—the tight undersheet, the scented soap, the color-coordinated towels—fermenting the annoyance in her.

"Mariam," her father says, formal almost. "Thank you for coming."

She stands up and he bends down to kiss her on each cheek. "You're well?"

"Fine, thank you."

"Are you eating?"

"Yes."

"Did you talk to your sister recently?"

"Not so recently," she says. "But I'll call her."

"Do. She's worried about you."

"She's in Germany. All there is to do there is worry."

He pours himself a glass of water from the pitcher between them.

"Here," he says, holding out an envelope for her to take.

She takes it, almost suspiciously, opens it. Inside is a plastic ID card. With her name on it and an old photo: *Visiting Consultant, New Dawn Cancer Center.*

She looks up at him, questioning.

"Your mother says you spend a lot of time at hospitals. And at the morgue. I thought this might help . . . keep you safe. If the police start asking questions, you're registered in the system there."

"But how—"

"Best not to ask."

"Okay . . . well . . . thank you."

She's hugging him. It's been such a long time.

"You're doing good. For our country," he says. "We're proud of you. You'll get rid of these bastards too, God willing."

APRIL 16: MUSLIM BROTHERHOOD PUBLISHES BOOK OF MORSI'S ACHIEVEMENTS

Khalil glances over his shoulder, the slightest movement—but undeniable. He feels his back and its metal, moments of a frozen chaos suddenly superheating with a need for attention. A glance in the mirror is all he'll give it. A glance is all it takes, all he needs to remember her, to feel her last warmth dissipating through his fingers, hear her last breaths whispering out of her body, see her—no, not her face. He can't see her face, can't see anything beyond the mask. He tries, alone, at night sometimes, to remember his footsteps faltering heavy with her body limp in his arms lurching forward through the gas to the doctors, each moment until the mask is pulled off. And then: nothing. She's there, on your computer. Doctor_02022012.mp4. Will you ever listen to the recording? He sees the dark of her mask before him, sees a city burning in its reflection as the steel in his skin begins to burn. Our bond. Our metal mined from the same Minnesotan mountain, an ancient unity splintered and smelted into a million pellets for a hundred thousand shotgun cartridges to be ignited into our flesh to divide us, to forever bind us.

APRIL 17: MORSI LOSES CONTROL OF SINAI AS ROCKETS LAUNCHED AT ISRAEL

"Get rid of this for me. Hide it." She's pressing her phone into his hand. "Let's do something fun today," she says. "Something normal!"

"Sure. What do you want to do?"

"Let's go to the cinema. Let's walk to Galaxy and watch every film that's on."

"I've been waiting two years for this day."

"Great. Get dressed."

Their route is determined by the army's new walls cross-hatching the city, a cement hamster-run on a city scale to keep the constant protests away from the government's buildings. First, though, they turn down Mohamed Mahmoud Street and a silence envelops them as memories return of the long nights on patrol, the knives, the red flares burning through the howling crowd. They walk quickly past the long murals, through the dark memories, aiming for the open expanse of Tahrir. But then there is the red flower.

"Can we sit for a minute?" she says. The flower lives still, looks healthy. She sits carefully down next to it and pulls a bottle of water out of her bag. They sit in silence, the flower, the young boy's final offering to the living between them. He can feel her falling into a place into which he cannot follow.

APRIL 19: POLARIZATION GROWS OVER MORSI'S PRESIDENCY

Battalions of Hamas operatives are currently active in the country disguised as police officers. Morsi has made a deal to sell Hamas Sinai in exchange! We've seen maps. There are *maps*!

Paid agents of chaos are at work day
and night to discredit the government
and undermine democracy.

The plan has been in the works for decades. Sinai will
be sold!

Egypt will be divided!

Egypt is a prize! The whole world wants to see Egypt on
its knees!

Christians are burning
the Brotherhood
headquarters and come
disguised as Salafis, or
as the Black Bloc or
even as the police.

A new crusade against Islam is afoot, being
waged by a secular alliance of the Coptic
media and El-Baradei and the Americans.

Obama the secret Muslim is part of the Brotherhood's
conspiracy and is defending the Morsi government.

Obama the warmonger
is in Israel's pocket and
is working full strength
to bring down the
Morsi government.

The Coptic Church is busing armed fighters to lay siege to the presidential palace.

The Brotherhood isn't even Egyptian, they think they're above the nation, their loyalty is not to Egypt.

It's an occupation. Yes, they're occupying Egypt.

Egypt!

They will sell the Suez Canal, they would sell the pyramids if they could. They've leased out Karnak to the Gulf.

The forces of chaos and the Mubarak regime and the British and the Iranians are lobbying together to undermine democracy and agitate against an elected president.

MAY 4: MUBARAK CRONIES BUYING THEIR WAY OUT OF JAIL

"Smurfberries! Oh my God, oh my God. Shut up and listen all of you. Whew . . ." Rania can hardly contain her laughter. "*Dr. Smurf* prescribes cakes, pies, ahaha, ahahaha, cakes, pies, and smurfberries as part of a healthy diet! Oh my God! Ahahahahah!! Hashtag smurfvillage!!!"

"Why are you talking about the Smurf village?"

Rania's heaving with laughter, she can't speak. She hands Khalil her phone.

"This is their prime minister?! Who *are* these people?" Rania's still laughing. "Can someone put them in a time machine and give them five years to get ready to be in government? It's all just too *embarrassing*! My God. We don't even need to write articles or make videos anymore, we just need to make one long list. Who has a pen? A pen for the whiteboard! Come on, people, what kind of office is this? Okay. Number one: They make the Harlem Shake illegal."

"That's how you start?" Malik asks. "Not with their fucking *militias*? Not police reform?"

"Oh, you and your police reform," Rania says, waving him away. "The police can't be reformed, the wretched cunts have to all be killed."

"But the Brotherhood didn't even look at the report," Malik insists. "Didn't even do us the fucking courtesy of *pretending* to look at it!"

"Fine. Number two: They ignored your report. And the report about the army killings in the Eighteen Days. And the report about torture at Ettehadeyya. Then you have burning down churches and torturing children and destroying the economy and ramming through their backward constitution and honoring Tantawi and reinstating the emergency law and taking the IMF loan and—we're gonna need a bigger board."

She sees Nancy isn't even smiling, let alone laughing. "What's the matter with you?"

"This isn't a joke, you know," she says sternly. "We won't be laughing when we're all in jail."

MAY 7: MORSI RESHUFFLES EGYPT'S CABINET.
THREE MORE POSTS TO THE BROTHERHOOD.

One word is on everyone's lips: Tamarrod. Rebel.

Nancy has a sheaf of petition papers pressed to her chest. She has pinned one up and is arranging a stack next to the office door. She moves hurriedly. "We should all be out working the streets, I'm going to go down to Talaat Harb, who's coming with me, where's Hafez? Hafez! Let's go get signatories downstairs!"

Tamarrod is a petition, a movement, a moment—a vote of no confidence in the government, a demand for early elections. The sign-up sheets have proliferated around the city as concerned citizens distribute and collect signatures.

Within an hour Nancy is back upstairs. "I have to print more." She beams. "Everybody wants to sign! I need at least five hundred. Rania, is the printer working?"

"Huh?" Rania looks up from her computer. "Yes, I think so."

"Okay, great. At least five hundred. Everyone's signing. Everyone *hates* him!"

Nancy, invigorated with optimistic possibility, hurries back downstairs.

JUNE 19: POLICE PREPARE FOR VIOLENT PROTESTS ON JUNE 30

There is a screaming made harsher by the hissing microphone. The video is grainy, brown. There is a mob, men, sticks, rising and falling, lifting and smashing down on bodies. There are hands held up to try to shield their faces. There is a snap of red in the middle, distinct from everything else, brighter, more terrible. The sticks keep falling. Hundreds of them. Falling. Again and again. No mercy. No doubt. The sticks keep falling. Is this now Egypt? The people demand the fall of the regime.

She is talking again. Her lips move in the night. He lies next to her, watching as her face slips in strained and silent conversation, a name on her lips. "Toussi," she says. "We're going to be late, Toussi." Khalil pulls her close to him, puts his arm over her. "Toussi," she says, "don't keep me waiting."

Morsi is ten days away from his first anniversary as president and the broadcasters are feverish with news of the new petitioners' rebellion. June 30 will see the protest to end all protests. No one knows what's coming. How many people will take to the streets against the Brotherhood? How many will be for him? What will happen when the two crowds meet?

He dresses without waking her.

Walking to the office, he can feel the anticipation in snatches of conversation and shuttered shops.

Nancy is already in the office.

"Khalil, good. Hi. I think we need to have a meeting. I've been getting a lot of messages about Chaos and how come we haven't announced that we're part of Tamarrod."

"But we're not part of Tamarrod."

"Aren't you going to protest on June thirtieth? Isn't everybody?"

"That doesn't make us part of Tamarrod. We've never officially taken those positions. We didn't for the elections."

"I just think we should endorse it officially. For the momentum."

"The momentum's doing just fine without us."

"But you *are* going down on the thirtieth?"

"Ah. Come in," the landlord's lawyer says. "Take a seat. Will we be renewing today?"

"Yes. Another year."

"Certainly."

The lawyer pulls out a file, leafs through the papers. Then, without looking up, asks: "Will you be protesting on the thirtieth?"

"I'm undecided."

"Undecided? I wouldn't have picked you for Brotherhood."

"I'm not Brotherhood."

"I see," he says, though Khalil is sure he doesn't.

"And you?" Khalil asks. "You'll be marching then?"

"Me? Heavens no. I'm taking my family out of the city. Who knows what will happen. The Brotherhood is ruthless."

Khalil doesn't say anything.

"They're a threat to our entire society, you know," the lawyer continues. "Did you know half of them aren't even Egyptian?"

Khalil doesn't say anything. The lawyer returns to the papers, tutting to himself, "And then such a horrible business with those Shia."

"Yes. Awful."

Khalil wishes he hadn't watched the video. The sticks, the crowd, the lifeless bodies dragged through the streets in merciless ecstasy. His mind replays the nights patrolling Tahrir with Opantish the polar flare burning a path through the crowd, the heaving of hundreds of bodies all reaching, reaching . . . He doesn't see faces, can't feel one night from another, but he can hear the shouts and screams and the *sister, she's my sister* following him through his dreams.

"Of course"—the lawyer looks up from his papers—"the Shia's beliefs *are* alien to our society."

Every day a piece of the country falls into the sea, washes into the desert. A train crashes into a microbus full of school-children. A building collapses onto the poor families who called it home. A factory burns down. The river is poisoned. Khalil stands at the edge of the elevator, prepares—like every day— for its floor to fall out, rehearses his last thoughts on the long climb up.

The irony of our one and only sure
victory being both pyrrhic and
compromising.
@Alaa
5:39 AM–26 June 2013

Morsi berates the nation for two and a half hours, his voice following Mariam around as she walks through Downtown.

Every revolution has enemies.

It will be terrible, the thirtieth, and all she can think about is her eyes. Everything else is out of her hands, but she can at least try to keep the buckshot out of her eyes.

The twenty-fifth of January revolution belongs to its people. It was a single revolution.

She counts her friends, trying to work out how many sets of goggles she needs. She walks up Talaat Harb toward the old Opera and on every screen she passes is Morsi.

We have to operate to remove the worm from the nation's body.

Twenty. She needs twenty sets of goggles. She counts again. When she finds the shop Morsi is still speaking, shouting now, shaking his finger at his impertinent subjects.

Some people are abusing some of the freedom we're giving them!

Industrial goggles are expensive. She digs into the bottom of her bag for the envelope with the month's rent and hands it over.

The armed forces deserve the respect of all Egypt's citizens for choosing to side with the revolution.

She leaves and walks back into Downtown. Morsi is still shouting. With the goggles in her bag her heart rate relaxes a little and she stands with a crowd gathered around a kiosk to watch.

My last message is to the corrupt troublemakers among us: Choose sides, you crooks. Your days are over.

A young man walks out into the middle of the street and chants at the top of his lungs:

"Down, down with the Morshid's rule!"

His chant echoes back from a dozen more voices. Enraged, the cafés of downtown empty into the streets.

"Not a single concession, the motherfucker. Nothing!"

"He calls himself a Muslim and not a word about the Shia men murdered."

"I'll break that finger of his and shove it up him if he doesn't stop shaking it at me."

"The nerve!"

"You heard how he addressed the police? He's giving them the green light."

"Everyone who's against him is a thug? Really? That's the best he's got?"

"He's finished! He knows it! You can see he's terrified!"

"Looks like June thirtieth is going ahead as planned . . ."

JUNE 29: ARMY DEPLOYS TO SECURE GOVERNMENT MINISTRIES

Six half-drunk Stella bottles sit on the table, cigarettes burn in the ashtrays, counting down the minutes. Anticipation hangs over the whole city. Morsi is on the television above them. Highlights of his speech being looped and dissected by talk-show panelists. Sixteen hours to go.

The waiter comes over. "Hello, Mariam. What can I get you?"

"How bad is the whiskey?" Rania cuts in.

"It's not bad at all, Rania," the waiter says.

"We'll have seven."

"Fucking hell," Mariam says.

"Well, we can't sit here just waiting to *die* all night! And if we're checking out tomorrow, then what's one last hangover?"

She was expecting a laugh but everyone is too nervous.

"Do you actually think it will be that bad?" Nancy asks.

"I don't know," Rania says. "I have no idea."

"We'll be fine," Hafez says, coming alive again from one of his introspections. "It's going to be big. Too big to attack."

When the drinks come Rania holds up her glass: "To the inevitable."

Mariam sees the same scenes playing out in her mind. It will start with a bomb. Shotgun pellets will rip through the air, into eyes. They are coming, through the gas and the chaos, they are coming. Snipers will start picking us off. The police will plant a bomb to turn everyone against one another. The Brotherhood will plant a bomb to scare off the next protests. The army will plant a bomb so they can restore order. The feloul will plant a bomb to force the army to intervene. The Israelis will plant a bomb to start a civil war. The police will plant a bomb for the bloodsport. There will be panic and stampedes crashing into new walls built to block the escape routes. There will be kill lists and men stalking through the mayhem with photographs of targets. We will be trapped between the new walls, we will be drowning under the crush. Can you hide under a dead body? Can you close your eyes and lie still for hours while the last life bleeds out of the stranger on top of you? You will hold your breath in the silence of the dead street and listen as they walk through the wreckage, grinding their boots into open wounds, closer, closer, executing the flesh that flinches. It will start with a bomb and the survivors will march on the Brotherhood camp to take their vengeance and the civil war will begin. It will start with a bomb and there will be no escape. Rania slams her shot glass down on the table: *"Again!"*

JUNE 30: ZERO HOUR: EGYPT AWAITS HER FATE

They dress in silence, the morning sun bright through the window, the street outside quiet as winter. He steps onto the balcony. There is a momentum long out of our control. Can't we not go? Just say it. Can't we be sick or tired or scared and just stay home?

"If Morsi would just . . . I don't know—a single concession is all it needed," Khalil says.

Mariam puts two pairs of goggles aside for them, starts packing her usual bag. "He's not going to budge," she says. Spare clothes, bandages, antiseptic spray, scissors, newspaper, money, lighter, phone charger, gas mask, pepper spray, switchblade. "Whatever's coming today: they have a plan."

"So we're walking into a trap," he says.

"It's too late to do anything about it," she says.

"They all have plans and we don't."

"We never have plans."

"Yeah. Our great strength."

"It *is* our strength," she says.

He doesn't reply.

"What would you prefer? Planning for more elections supervised by the army?"

"No, I'm happy to spend my life marching and protesting

against each shitty government that comes in because I'm too pure to take a shot at actually governing."

"If what you want is to play politics, why don't you go pick a party?"

"I just want to know *what* I'm risking my life for. What the plan is. Since when is that an absurd question?"

"Dying for a plan is called being in the army. Dying for something new is a revolution."

"You sound seriously nuts right now."

"So stay home. No one's forcing you out."

"I'm not going to stay home and watch you all get killed on television."

She's silent.

Then, softer, she says, "Look—you're marching for early elections. You're marching against the next dictator. You're marching to bring down a fascist. What more is there?"

"And the army?"

"They got burned so badly last time they were in charge. There's no way they want the spotlight again."

"But isn't it better just to vote Morsi out?"

"Well, that's the demand, isn't it? More of your elections. We're just not going to give them three more years to prepare. Look at just one year. Look at their Renaissance project, look at what's happening to the country. People are being *lynched*. We are being dragged to a very fucking dark place."

JUNE 30: MORSI: I REFUSE TO CALL EARLY ELECTIONS. THERE WILL BE NO SECOND REVOLUTION.

Khalil scans the rooftops, tries to see beyond the march to whatever is waiting ahead. Mariam is in the middle of the crowd. He hangs to the side, keeps one eye on her.

The drumbeat pulls up the familiar words, the old strength.

The people!
Demand!
The fall of the regime!

A group of Ultras chant with anger, their drum pushing the march forward. A large sign held high between several people reads:

**NO TO THE BROTHERHOOD, THE ARMY, & THE POLICE.
THE REVOLUTION CONTINUES.**

Khalil searches across the rooftops for the glint of a sniper's rifle. When it begins, will we all just run, alone, or will we still stand together?

Then he sees Hafez. "Where the fuck were you?" Khalil says.

"Huh? Me?"

"Yes, fucking *you*. We said we'd meet at one. I've been looking for you."

"I was working. What's your problem?"

"We said we'd meet at one. We have to all stick together today."

"Fine. Calm down. We're all fine. Have you been to the palace yet?"

"No. Because we said we'd meet here."

"Well, there's a fuckload of people over there."

At the turn into Khalifa Ma'moun the street widens and Khalil can see in the distance, brilliant in billowing white, the banners of the martyrs waiting to greet him and he feels his heart slow down. Maybe there is no attack. Maybe Hafez is right, it's just too big. He walks through the garden of white, the names we have followed for so long. Each flag a symbol of a hundred more fallen behind it.

Omar Salah, whose face caught the sunlight perfectly as

we marched in his funeral through Downtown. Mohamed al-Shafei, whose bravery will live forever in a thousand photographs. Gika, who waved in the wind at the gates of the presidential palace. Mina, who flew high through every minute of every battle since Maspero, pulling us long through winters of gas and bullets. Sheikh Emad, whose hands bless Mohamed Mahmoud Street, the heart of our urban necropolis. Khaled Said, to whose life we owe everything.

He sees Rania and Rosa standing in the shadows of the flags, enclosed in a rare garden of calm, the white cloth, the faces fluttering in the wind, looking down at them. Hundreds of people are flowing quietly through, the moment of transition between the energy of the revolutionists' march and the crowd massing around the palace.

These are, without a doubt, the biggest protests in the history of Egypt, possibly even the entire region. #June30
@Bassem_Sabry

At the palace Mariam finds herself alone in a flutter of Prada sunglasses and fake Louis Vuitton bags and children screaming in American accents and signs saying SISI: SAVE EGYPT FROM THE BROTHERHOOD and THE ARMY, THE PEOPLE, ONE HAND. She shouldn't be, but she is surprised by how many they are. Where did these people all come from? Where have they been hiding for the last two years? Where were you all when the Brotherhood attacked us along this very street?

She takes a deep breath and chants:

The pigs!
Are thugs!
The pigs—

"Stop that! Stop that!" A shout comes from the crowd. "This isn't the time!"

"The pigs!" Mariam shouts. "Are thugs!"

      "Hey! Cut that out! Don't be so rude!"

A woman with bright blond highlights is screaming. "The police are our brothers! Who do you think is keeping you safe today!?"

"You should focus!" another sunglassed pair of lips is shouting. "Enough of your chaos!"

    "She's a paid infiltrator! Take your filth
    somewhere else!"

            "There's no room for you in
            the revolution!"

      "It's time someone taught some
      of you kids some manners."

"She's paid for by the Americans! Tell your
Obama we say no to fascism!"

            "The revolution
            continues! Bread,
            freedom, and human
            dignity!"

A man claps his hands together: "The police, the people, and the army: one hand!"

And everyone joins him in happy unison: "The police, the people, and the army: one hand!"

They clap aggressively at Mariam, a circle of sunglasses and bangled wrists starts closing around her, chanting into her face—

      "The police, the people, and the army:
      one hand!"

There are too many of them. She pushes out from among them and hurries away from the crowd.

Nancy's apartment is full of people Mariam doesn't know. She squeezes through them to the bathroom to wash the street off her hands, her face. It's a fiesta. She recognizes Nancy's father in the kitchen, pulling a carton of juice out of the fridge. "You kids have really done something magnificent here today. Really impressive." He looks around at the few young people politely standing with him, his face beaming with touchdown pride. "So how many of you are in Tamarrod?"

If the MB wishes to survive even a bit, Morsi should announce early elections, and a new leadership should take over the MB. #June30
@Bassem_Sabry

The Salah Salem Highway is a carnival of car horns and flags and fireworks. The traffic is unmoving. Khalil is driving, everyone sits in silence. He turns on the radio.

> *Across the country Egypt has today witnessed a historic day that the BBC is calling the largest protests in the history of mankind. Today, the first anniversary of President Mohamed Morsi's election has seen what many are calling a new revolution . . .*

He turns it off.

"So, my dear friend Malik," Hafez says. "It seems both you *and* the Brotherhood both fell into the same trap."

"Oh, shut it, Hafez. What do you mean?"

"Consent, my friend. You forgot that, even if the battle is only between the five percent at the top, you're not running the show unless you have consent."

"Unless you can fucking *manufacture* consent, you mean."

"Sure: manufacture, maintain, whatever. But if you can't do it, you're out. That's the new world, my friend. Your two and a half percent have to watch out."

"So what now?"

"It's down to Morsi," Hafez says. "Call early elections and this ends now. Or he wants some kind of dogfight."

"And what about all these people calling for the army to step in?"

"No, the army isn't that stupid. This Sisi guy's meant to be smart. He won't make the same mistake Tantawi did. They need a civilian front."

In the tunnel ahead men with flares and Egyptian flags dance in hysterical celebration:

The people! The army! One hand!

Mariam winds up her window. "Do you have your stuff, guys?"

"Yes," Khalil says. "We got everything."

They are headed for Tahrir. It will be full tonight. Opantish is back on. Khalil has their nightsticks and flares in the trunk and cardboard boxes to cut up and stuff in their shirts.

Mariam's phone rings. "Yes, we're on our way. I know . . . The streets are totally jammed . . . We're on our way."

She hangs up. "It's started," she says, without looking at any of them. "Three attacks already."

JULY 1: DEFENSE MINISTER SISI SETS 48-HOUR ULTIMATUM FOR MORSI TO REACH POLITICAL COMPROMISE BEFORE MILITARY INTERVENES

The flare burns for nights, burns the hands, the faces, burns the road through the crowd. She waits for the next phone call, he waits for the captain's fist to signal into the air. Fireworks flood the night sky, each report a shockwave shivering through their bodies, a beaten dog flinching. The fireworks do not stop. The calls do not stop. The fist is raised and he falls into line and pushes out into the crush, into the men scratching and the helicopters circling and the flags raining down onto the grasping drove. *The people, the army, one hand.* She answers the hotline in the Operations Room, they coordinate a hundred people across ten locations and map the teams and the emergency drivers and buy supplies and field media requests and calm nerves and dress wounds and she doesn't cry in front of anyone but alone in the bathroom and alone in the dark she always thinks of Alia and her parents in the green darkness of the hospital waiting, waiting, and waiting.

Fireworks in the street celebrating the end of the democracy experiment.
@SarahCarr
4:24 PM–1 July 2013

Tahrir is lit by four huge spotlights hanging from hotel balconies, illuminating the flag-waving adorations of Sisi, pulling them like fish toward the cameras.

"Tahrir!" the state TV correspondent screams. "Tahrir, we can tell you, is not the drug-fueled, sex-swamped, Islamist-controlled progenitor of all our political, economic, and vehicular woes we thought it was. We were mistaken! Tahrir, we are pleased to tell you, dear viewer, is the manifestation of the beautiful and indomitable Egyptian spirit once again, it is the common man taking control of his own destiny and placing his faith in General Sisi and the army, it is the corrective revolution to restore us to the path of January twenty-

fifth. Therefore we have floodlit it for your viewing pleasure. From the same balconies we used to hurl journalists'
cameras off."

They have been watching, learning, they have mastered the
Egyptian spectacle.

JULY 3: MILITARY MORSI PLACES UNDER HOUSE ARREST

The roar of a helicopter grows louder, louder, louder and a cheer
rises up from the square and the machine waits, its mighty noise
thundering down on the masses beneath, to receive their ho-
sannas, its body revealed to them through the light of a thousand green lasers irradiating up from the lowly crowd, each a
monochromatic pledge of fealty to the metal god in the sky
above them, dazzling the mortals below.

At last! Egypt has not one living
ex-president but two!

Whatever protesters' grievances there
can be no alternative to constitutional
and electoral #legitimacy.

The Army will never allow democracy
again if President Morsi is couped.

This is no coup. 14 million people asked the
army to protect them from terrorism.

The people have once again shown their power.
They've shown they can change the regime,
and they know they can do it again if necessary.

Prez Morsi enjoys huge support but
protests are being distorted and amplified
by elite-owned media.

Brotherhood supporters launching violent
protest marches daily.

JULY 8: 51 KILLED OUTSIDE REPUBLICAN GUARDS HQ

The kitchen sink is full of coffee cups, plates, improvised ash-trays. The fridge is empty. No one has cleaned the office for weeks. Mariam is looking for a clean spoon when she hears the front door open and Nancy's voice coming through it.

"Well, who do *you* think is behind the attacks?" Her tone is sharp, bullying.

"I don't know," someone mumbles. Hafez? "I don't think they're entirely organized."

"Well, let's apply some *logic*, shall we?" Nancy is angry. "Who *benefits* from protests ending? Who are the protests in Tahrir *against*?"

"It's not that simple."

Mariam steps out of the kitchen to say hello, but Nancy is in full swing and ignores her: "Maybe it *is*. You always said you thought the police were involved. All you Opantish people kept saying that. But why would the police be attacking *this* crowd? These are their people. So this is proof—it's *always* been the Brotherhood."

"It's not that simple." Hafez is tired, harried. His beard is long, scruffy. His hair, too. He looks unslept.

"You can think what you like but the logic is there."

"Fine," Hafez says. "Let's drop it."

"I don't understand. You were against Morsi. You wanted

him gone. Now he's gone and he's, he's started a terrorist *insurrection* and—what?—you feel *sorry* for him? They're throwing children off *rooftops*! They're *terrorists*!"

Christian militias spark violence while 30 million
Egyptians gather in support of Morsi today.

In photographs: Empty tents at Morsi rallies.

In photographs: Record numbers turn out
for President Morsi.

Islamist mob kills teenager by throwing
him off a rooftop.

Revolt against #Military_Coup across all Egypt.
Reports of whole governorates now engaged
in civil disobedience.

At least five civilians in Manial dead after
Brotherhood march attacks residents.

JULY 14: 18 DEAD IN CLASHES AT BEIN AL-SARAYAT

The nights fold into each other. They dress for another night on patrol and he's putting his ID into his sock and his door key into the other and she stops and holds him and tells him to be careful and then she's gone to the Operations Room, where she switches on the three hotlines and waits for the first call before the flare ignites through the red teeth and shadow blacks of the crush and the helicopters dip over the shrieking crowd drowning out the cries for help from the circles of men and knives.

Mariam finds Khalil sitting on a muddy stairwell behind Hardee's, his head in his hands, his intervention team waiting to be called out into the square. "I brought you a sandwich," she says, knowing he won't have eaten for hours. "I brought for the whole team."

"Thank you," he says, touching her hand. He puts his nightstick down. His shirt is ripped open at the neck, his hands are covered in mud, maybe blood. Who have we become?

JULY 15: 7 DEAD IN CLASHES ON OCTOBER BRIDGE

He opens the washing machine and shovels the Opantish T-shirts in. His phone sits waiting for him on the kitchen counter but he doesn't pick it up. Just five minutes more before it's time to breathe in the toxic fumes of the Internet.

He runs the tap, flicks on the radio, starts the dishes.

> *More news has surfaced of violence emanating from the terrorist Brotherhood's illegal occupation of two major city squares at Nahda and Rabaa . . .*

He flicks it off.

They call it polarization. Two ends of the country pulling away from each other toward the extreme, leaving the middle clinging on above the gulf.

He picks up his phone, heavy and inevitable as Pandora's box. Soon he is knee-deep in a new dawn of the pro-military's bullying triumphalism and the Brotherhood's sanctimonious hypocrisy. And the hectoring paternalism of the international commentariat.

JULY 24: SISI TO THE NATION: GIVE ME A MANDATE
TO END THE BLOODSHED

Hafez hands him a cigarette. Tens of thousands have flooded the square to give Sisi his "mandate." There is nothing to do but smoke and watch.

"You know the ridiculous thing," Hafez says. "The thing I find ridiculous is that no one mentions, you know, the people. Why is Morsi out"—*BANG!*—a firework sends a shudder through them both. Hafez looks ill, like he hasn't slept for days. He's talking quickly, his mouth tripping to keep up with his overwired brain. "Why's Morsi out? Because more people marched against him than have ever marched against anything in the history of"—*BANG!*—"in the history of marches and, yes, we'll go back into some kind of dance with the army now, but we know that the army can't take power directly again"—*BANG!*—Khalil lights a cigarette and it cuts at his throat, bone dry from the long dehydrations of patrol nights. He is too tired to speak. "Even if Sisi feels the hand of history on his shoulder, SCAF wouldn't let him put himself in as president. It makes them too vulnerable in the long run."

Death toll from clashes between security forces and Morsi supporters rises to 72.

Evidence surfaces of MB killing protesters AND police during the 18 Days.

Morsi in good health, says EU's Ashton.

Minister of the Interior coordinating with armed forces to disperse sit-ins at Rabaa al-Adawiya and Nahda Square.

Feeling in #Rabaa is that of #Tahrir in #Jan25,
but police retaliation more brutal & protesters
more determined.

Let us say it courageously and honestly:
"No to free elections in Egypt."

More bodies surface near Brotherhood sit-ins.

Sweet little girl now singing on #Rabaa
#AntiCoup stage. Click for pictures from largest
rally Cairo has ever seen.

Anti-Morsi protestors told Amnesty International
how they were captured, beaten, subjected to
electric shocks, or stabbed by individuals loyal
to the former president.

#Egypt's first & only democratically elected
President #Morsi is the only one who can
speak for all #Egyptians. #Morsi is a symbol of
Egypt's struggle for freedom & liberty.

Rania is in the kitchen. No one else is in the office.

"We have to do a podcast," Khalil says.

"Okay."

"We have to clarify our position. I'm sick to death of all the assholes on Twitter and *Time* and the rest of them. I'm going mad."

"So let's write something down. Where's Mariam?"

"Where do you think?"

Mariam hardly leaves the Operations Room. He doesn't say

anything more. He knows Rania hasn't been back in the Operations Room since January.

"So we'll write it ourselves," Khalil says. "It's all simple: we're not with the army or the Brotherhood and everyone who says they're the only options has no idea what they're talking about. The revolution is still the strongest force in the country. This is just another wave of the same political process that's been going on for two years, and if they think that Sisi or any of them are strong enough to stop it they're not paying attention."

"You're right," Rania says. "We should say it. But I don't think anyone's listening."

The Brotherhood has rejected al-Azhar's efforts
to resolve the political crisis through a national
reconciliation initiative involving all parties.

The Minister of the Interior says plans are in
place for the peaceful dispersal of the sit-ins.

The Brotherhood calls on all supporters to take
pilgrimage to sit-ins at Nahda and Rabaa.

Brotherhood snipers killed 10 people
protesting in front of MB HQ.

#Democracy #Freedom #Dignity
#Social_Justice are ideas.
You can't kill an idea when its time
has come.

The Minister of the Interior
says plans are in place for the peaceful
dispersal of the sit-ins.

Repeat: our safety is in numbers.
If you care about democracy
Go to Rabaa or Nahda now!

AUGUST 14: POLICE OPERATION TO CLEANSE
BROTHERHOOD SIT-INS HAS BEGUN

Go to your brothers in the hospital! The crackling speakers rever-
berate between the buildings. *Go to your brothers on the front lines!*
Mariam and Hafez move quickly through the side streets. The
guns are still for now. Rabaa is a tent city of tarpaulins and
broken bottles and cooking gas and posters of Morsi and men
racing to the front with blankets full of rocks, bricks, sandbags,
water, and unshakable groups of women marching through the
acrid smoke, chanting battle cries for their president. *Prepare
the barricades! There is no god but God! There is no god but God!
The martyr is the beloved of God!* Something big is on fire in the
distance.

Hafez is on one knee, taking photographs, when a booming
recording floods over the street:

*This is the Ministry of the Interior. You are ordered to
vacate this area. This is the Ministry of the Interior. You
are ordered—*

"Come on, Hafez!" Mariam is pulling at him. "We need to
get to the field hospital."

With a great thud the gunfire begins. A heavy artillery
sound followed by an automatic. *Thud. Tktktktktktk.* People

are running in all directions. *Thud. Tktktktktktktk.* A bulldozer is slowly chewing its way through the encampment, crushing the tents and fragile barricades before it, men push a refrigerator toward the front and hide behind it and pop up from their hiding places and throw rocks, but they bounce off it harmlessly. Behind the bulldozer comes an APC and the guns. *This is the Ministry of the Interior. You are ordered to vacate this area. Thud. Tktktktktktktk.* They are running, away from the guns and deeper into the camp, through the alleyways, and a man falls and another and *thud. Tktktktktktktktktktktktktktktktktktktktktktk.* They're coming fast. A car siren is sounding, the bulldozer is inching closer, the wooden tent poles crunching underneath it. Get to the hospital don't look back don't hesitate breathe just run stick to the sides don't listen just run oh fuck just run you'll know when you're shot so just run.

The hospital is all burning and weeping. Bodies being carried bleeding and moaning, the index finger of a right hand up, blood trailing thick and shining behind them, the high voice screeching out of the speakers on the stage again and again. *Don't run! There is no god but God. The martyr is the beloved of God. Hold your ground! The revolution continues! Hold your ground!* The smell in the field hospital suffocating her, clinging to her mouth and skin, climbing up into her nose, breathing over the sweat on her chest, dried blood and Dettol and mud and smoke and terror and sweat and the windows all closed and the doctors with gas masks on and there's blood everywhere and every inch is a dying in this room of soaking blankets and blood-sodden shirts and the air is all last breaths wept out of lungs ripped open with buckshot and a baby, two babies, are crying and it's the only sound that makes any sense. The yellow light streams in hot through the closed windows and suddenly Mariam is so hot she's sure she will pass out. The gunfire draws closer. This is the end. No one is coming, no one is stopping this, no one is saving us. They are coming, the guns and the trucks are coming.

A bullet hole can be so small. A body can hold so much blood. A baby can cry for so long.

Get to work. Concentrate. She looks quickly for Hafez. Stick together. He's filming. He won't leave without you. You can help. Tourniquets, basic dressings, stop the bleeding. That's all anyone can do. She looks around at the doctors, dressing the wounds. That's all anyone can do here. Stem the bleeding, dress the wound. Save an arm, a leg. Stem the bleeding, dress the wound. *Crack*. A new gun. *Crack*. A different gun now, stronger. *Crack*. Its echo lasts through you. *Crack*. One sure death at a time. People running, pushing, picking up bleeding brothers and lost sons and doctors with their arms raised, pleading with people to wait and—*crack*—they're coming closer—*crack*—people are pushing out through the door and everything is the thrashing of a body drowning and straining for a last breath, for a chance and then there are more bodies, new bleedings being pulled back into the room and the door is a portal of white light and wind and people pressed against the wall to either side of it. *Crack. Crack*. So many people pressing against each other, keeping out of the corridor, breathing and crying and praying, all corralled together, pressed against a wall with a man lying bleeding just beyond the doorway, his arms spread out, his shirt thick with blood and no one can reach him to pull him inside—*crack*—blood is flowing out of his gut and coagulating around him in the debris of cardboard boxes and medical gloves and tissues and syringes and masks and plastic bags and water bottles. Toussi, you're here again. You're killed again. *Crack*. We're coming for you, we're coming, you're wet with sweat. And blood? Don't look. There's nowhere to run. We're coming for you and there's nowhere to go, nowhere to go, nowhere to run. Stay here, with the injured, where you can help. They will give the injured passage. What are you talking about? They're attacking the hospital, you can't get out and the man on the floor isn't breathing anymore, the pool of blood has stopped growing and someone reaches out into the hallway and hooks the tips of his fingers into the dead man's trousers and tries to pull him closer and his body starts sliding across the hot slick of thick, dark blood pulled behind him, congealing around his trousers heavy with blood slipping down to his hips and down beneath his bloodied pubic hairs and penis. Please don't let me die here, where no one knows me and no one will find me and no one will call my mother and I'll be pulled into a pile with all the other bodies buried and burned. Please don't let it be here without even a rock in my hand, facedown in medical waste, please don't let it be now. Who will call my mother? She'll hear the words and won't believe them but she'll know it's true. I can't do this to her, she can't take it, she can't, I can't do it. Don't think about her. We'll get out. Don't think about her or your friends all in black and holding back their tears and choosing their highlights of how they'll remember you. They'll remember you. Oh Khalil we should have done things differently, I should have been different. How will you remember me? My mother will be all alone with no one left. She'll know. As soon as the phone rings she'll know. An unknown number and her heart will stop and from the first breath of the voice down the line she'll know before the words come and the ruin begins and the apartment is filled with black and aunts and uncles and friends and patients and everyone who ever shared two words with her each in a barren procession of formality and distraction and a bottling of rage and there'll be no one she can ever talk to. Will Khalil look after you, Mama? Will he come and sit with you day after day? Will you take strength from each other? You can look after each other. Everyone who dies today will be named a terrorist. This isn't helping. This isn't you. Stop. Stem the bleeding, dress the wound. You can keep some people alive. Stem the bleeding, dress the wound.

Wait.

How long has the stage been silent? When did the baby stop crying?

An electronic voice booms through the room. *"This is the Ministry of the Interior."* Machines. They've sent machines to kill us. *"You are ordered to vacate this area."* The air is so hot with smoke and gas and blood that she can hardly breathe and the bullets, the bullets, just keep your head down, just grab Hafez's hand and try to keep breathing and pray and breathe and say thank you, God, and please let it be quick.

PART 3
YESTERDAY

Tomorrow, we will die the same death.
@mahmoud_hakem
2:23 AM–15 Aug 2013

I'm sitting, smoking alone in the heat on the balcony.

Cars pass, honking their horns in celebratory rhythms. Happy, sweaty families shout *Long live Egypt.*

Dalida's voice wafts up, relentless, from a shop downstairs:

> *My hope, always was, my country*
> *That I'd come back here, my country*
> *Staying close to you fore-e-ver!*

Shut up shut up shut up.

◆ ◆ ◆

Someone has ripped the eyes off the Nefertiti sticker on my door, scraped off the "No" and scrawled *Yes* to the Military Trial of Civilians.

◆ ◆ ◆

In the night, the city is silent. Nobody moves through the hot darkness of the curfew. The streets are still.

◆ ◆ ◆

You talk in your sleep. Not to me. "Run," you say. "Run." I lie in silence next to you, listening for clues about the things we don't talk about. I should have gone with you. I should have been there. "We're going to be late, Toussi," you say through the dream. "Everyone's waiting for us." I listen for the words I can't ask for. I've forgotten how to sleep.

◆ ◆ ◆

The room is shaking. Your eyes open as an army helicopter passes low overhead.

◆ ◆ ◆

The daylit world is worse.

Sisi is everywhere. On posters on every street, on car windshields, on necklaces and key rings and cupcakes the Great Savior's saccharine smile beams out at us, his sweating underlings. Downtown Cairo has become a military-themed fairground of Sisi sandwiches and fridge magnets and posters and cooking oil relabeled with his name and cupcakes iced with his face and women in camouflage pants posing for selfies, flashing their vampiric smiles and CC claws. No talk show dares air without a paean to his virtues of manhood and charisma, no storefront is safe from the burning mob without his Apollonian gaze staring down at you, there will be blood, blood, and more blood. Nine hundred killed in a day. Egypt has never been more glorious. We'll kill nine thousand for our homeland. Are you not relieved? Are you not Egyptian? Do you not love your country? Are you trying to keep her on her knees? Now we see your true colors, now we know who to come for in the night. We are free of the terrorists, at last, we have been delivered. The country was crumbling, Egypt was on her knees, the Brotherhood was an occupying force and we now have been liberated by the great Sisi. Free at last, free at last, thank God almighty we are free at last. Sisi, did you know, was the true name of Ramses III? Sisi the lion and the lionhearted. Our eagle and our beret and our flag are one in you, Sisi, and the victory you have led us to. Oh Sisi, my Sisi, you have returned Egypt to the Egyptians, you have led us out of the desert. Women grow weak in the knees and men rise firm at the sound of your name. We will face down the terrorists together. Oh Sisi, my Sisi, the last three years have been so very, very hard. Oh Sisi, my Sisi, you are the answer to my crossword puzzle. Your name, in its perfect and eternal symmetry, can sell my potatoes.

"Masks! Get your Sisi masks! IDs! Sisi IDs!"

I stand before a street vendor's collection: Sisi posing proud on posters before a photoshopped lion, Sisi masks with their eyes hollowed out, Sisi ID cards. *Name*: Abdel Fattah el-Sisi. *Address*: Ministry of Defense. *Job*: Savior of Egypt.

At least fascists are never funny.

The new pop hymn to El General echoes through the street—

> *This is the hero who gave up his life*
> *Who carried your name, my country*

Speakers tower in front of a shop, a bored tough sits with his hand on the volume. The music vibrates through me, violates me.

> *The one who protects our land*
> *The one who protects our honor*

I pick up the Sisi mask and hold it close to my face and I'm holding my breath, afraid, I think, to look through the eyes. "Five pounds!" barks the hawker.

The one who Egypt
Proudly calls her son

I hand him the money and walk toward Tahrir and its daily demonstration of love for Sisi. It is hot. I do not take the mask off.

Bless these hands
Bless my country's army

There are no cars on the streets, children fondle balloons, young women eat ice cream and older ones blow kisses at soldiers on tanks and pose for photographs and shout into the air.
"Long live Egypt!"
"Sisi yes! Sisi yes!
Morsi no! Morsi no!"
"Pay attention, Obama!
Pay attention! Don't
stand against the
Egyptian people!"
"The people!
The army!
One hand!"

There's no escaping the electromagnetic swamp of sound trash.
Are we in some sick laboratory? Can you take this man, this black hole of charisma, this oozing miasma of featurelessness and turn him into a leader? Can you follow the simplest play-

book of power and morph this Quasimodean combination of bureaucrat's paunch, jowled cheeks, and balding scalp into a demagogue of the month to be washed down with your Coke? Identify existential enemy, mobilize killing forces, pump hysterical nationalism onto the airwaves, pose for photos with lions, use basic fonts, invoke mythological pasts, have choirs of children sing your name and voilà: sit back and look upon your works. Frankensisi. A man who came from nothing, who is nothing more than a collage of outdated ideas bolstered by a brute strength. A man born of crisis and fear and shortsightedness, the product of peak mediocrity. At least Mussolini had a chin you could hang your laundry off but Sisi, this tubby bureaucrat whose speaking voice belongs in a bingo hall, this is what we get?

The fascists are smiling at me. I am safe behind Sisi's death mask. I walk silently among them, toward Tahrir. All around me are men shaking vigorous thumbs-up—*nine hundred killed in one day!*—and rattling bangles of victory signs scratching at the sky—*martial law reinstated!*—and I keep walking and Botoxed lips and trousers pulled high over paunches and posters of meaningless words and a rising noise above of the thousands in Tahrir, the swarm, the nest. We will be there soon. I am part of this new world now.

> *Bless these hands*
> *Bless my country's army*

And how long before they discover the traitor in their midst? On every street around Downtown are men dressed in thick black fatigues, balaclavas pulled over their faces, fingers ready on the trigger, each cartridge primed with a million consequences. One hundred potential deaths unleashed into a world in chaos. I try not to think of my back, how it's sweating, itching, pulsing, the old wounds reopening slowly as I prepare for the warm rivulets of blood to congeal and bind to the fabric of my shirt, each bleeding hole an unexpelled sphere of steel pulling out of me, pulling me toward the mouth of the gun, toward the beginning and the end and all we need is the bark of a dog or an engine to backfire for a twitching trigger finger to rip stinging flesh out across the hot asphalt with another name to scratch onto our never-ending list.

Bless these hands
Bless my country's army

In Tahrir the moist crowd coagulates and eddies into itself with the obligatory roars in happy supplication to the helicopters overhead. A woman clutches a poster to her face, presses her diaphoretic lips to Sisi's unblinking eyes, shouting: "We're behind you, Sisi! Don't hold back!" And standing on the central circle, I see Nancy, a poster held high above her head:

SISI, CLEANSE EGYPT OF TERRORISM

I stand and watch her, invisible behind my mask. The sun presses down, I feel the sweat collecting on my upper lip, on my forehead. I think about taking it off to look her in the eye but I can see her hand raising and her mouth yawning open and the word *traitor* silencing all others. I see a limp body swinging from the lamppost we once used for Mubarak's effigy.

Bless these hands
Bless my country's army

◆ ◆ ◆

The bag of dirty Opantish shirts sits untouched at the end of my bed. I can feel them rotting with the sweat of those nights but I don't wash them. I push the sheets off myself and open my book to the same passage I keep reading:

> When I first reached Barcelona I had thought it a town where class distinctions and great differences of wealth hardly existed. Certainly that was what it looked like. "Smart" clothes were an abnormality, nobody cringed or took tips, waiters and flower-women and bootblacks looked you in the eye and called you "comrade." I had not grasped that this was mainly a mixture of hope and camouflage. The working class believed in a revolution that had been begun but never consolidated, and the bourgeoisie were scared and temporarily disguising themselves as workers. Now things were returning to normal.
> —George Orwell, April 1937

◆ ◆ ◆

Mariam says she smells the morgue everywhere. She can't get away from it. It drips off her hair like cigarette smoke in the shower. She dreams of it. She doesn't see the bodies, can't see their faces, but their smell sticks to her. She dreams, she says, like an animal, in dark smells and twitched traumas, in confusions and instincts and terrors from a place before language.

"It was like machines," she says one night in bed, in the dark. "Like machines coming for us. They didn't flinch."

I don't say anything.

"When we got out," she says, "they were cheering. Hundreds dead. And they were cheering."

She doesn't say anything more. I don't know what she sees when she looks at me. Just someone who wasn't there.

◆ ◆ ◆

My hope, always was, my country
That I'd come back here, my country
Staying close to you fore-e-ver!

The sounds climb through my walls, stand over me in the bedroom dark. In my dreams I grind my teeth now. I grip them close together and my sleeping jaw squeezes through the night. A part of my brain beyond reason or rationality takes hold, breaking the bones in my mouth, puncturing my gums with pressure and pain that carries through to the waking hours and the lonely sadness that even I, now, mean harm to myself.

◆ ◆ ◆

We're sitting on the balcony at the Chaos office. It's empty. Hafez lights a cigarette. Our silence is long, the city's is not. I can't bear the sound of it, the normality of the car horns, the unkillable ambient noise of daily life.

He flicks the ash of the cigarette onto the floor.

There is no breeze tonight.

"I saw Nancy in Tahrir," I say.

"Yeah?"

"Do you talk much?"

"No," he says. "Not a word."

I didn't need to see Nancy standing in the crowd in Tahrir. Her toxic Twitter feed is enough.

I'm tired of these phony revolutionist Brotherhood lovers destroying Egypt . . . Hasn't Egypt been through enough without her own

218

citizens working to corrupt her? . . . If we don't stand behind Sisi now we are endorsing terrorism . . . Enough is enough. Standing with the Brotherhood is treason and traitors must be dealt with to the full power of the law.

How could this happen? How many nights did we spend working and fighting together? When did everyone become a fascist? Nearly every supposed liberal intellectual with a newspaper column or a TV talk show is lining up to kiss Sisi's ring in a feverish media orgy of millenarian nationalism.

"You couldn't have known," I say later, "that Nancy would flip."

"That's not true."

"People have gone nuts."

"Mariam always disliked her . . ."

I don't say anything.

"So no photos for now?" I say, and he gives me a cold look.

"And no podcasts either?" he says.

"No, no podcasts. But why aren't you putting the Rabaa photos up?"

"There's no point. Everyone knows what happened and they're fine with it."

After a minute of silence he turns to me. "It's more than that, actually. I'm not putting them up because that's what *they* want. Rabaa was a spectacle. They want us to see it, to be afraid, to understand how far they can go."

◆ ◆ ◆

Nefertiti.

I'm sorry, Nefertiti. I loved that sticker, her fierce eyes, the gas mask, the high crown. We would greet each other every day, she would watch as I found my keys, she would welcome me home. And now her eyes have been torn out. By a neighbor, by someone who walks past my door every day, someone watching us.

Maybe it was the older man upstairs? The one who was always friendly until the last time we talked in the elevator. "Good morning," he had said cheerily, "and a thousand congratulations for us all."

"Excuse me?"

"The army stood with the people again."

". . ."

He fixed me with a look of grandfatherly affection. "You were part of Tamarrod, right?"

"No. Not at all."

"But all the stickers on your door."

"None say Tamarrod."

"Well," he said, crestfallen, "you must still be pleased."

"I'm not pleased at all. Most of those stickers are campaigns against the army."

"You're *Brotherhood*?"

"No, of course not."

"So how can you not be pleased?"

"Did you not see what they did at Rabaa?"

"Who?"

"The army."

"I saw that the Brotherhood were armed."

"They killed a thousand people in a day."

"A thousand terrorists, maybe."

"A thousand terrorists . . . ?"

"The Egyptian Army would never knowingly spill a drop of innocent blood."

◆ ◆ ◆

Four men sitting on the street corner turn to look at me. They have small plates of food in front of them, but they're not eating. Across the road a taxi waits with its engine running. "Where you going?" the driver shouts. I don't answer. Never get into a waiting cab. The old woman who sells vegetables is watching me, the blunt knife in her hand hollowing out a white eggplant. A hawker laden with posters bellows out to the street, "Bless these hands! Get your Sisi posters! Bless these hands!" Two men in sunglasses and leather jackets loiter under a tree, not talking, just watching.

"Basha!" someone shouts. The new doorman is lying on his cot by the front door. He pulls himself up, rubs his bloodshot eyes. "Basha!"

"What?" I say.

"I have to tell you. The police came around. Said they wanted to know if any foreigners live in the building."

"And?"

"I said no, of course not."

"Fine . . ."

"That's what I figured."

"You figured right."

"So . . . ?"

"So what?"

"So I don't get a reward for being right?"

"What?"

"You wouldn't want me to get it wrong . . ."

I give him twenty pounds. The men on the corner are still watching. I put my headphones in, but I don't press play. There's no escape. It is coming for us all. The knock on the door, the quick silencing needle, the electrodes fastened onto your tongue, the first shovel of sand choking you in your shallow grave, bodies dropping out of planes into the sea, blunt machetes going house to house. Argentina, Chile, Algeria, Indonesia. It is our turn now and they will cheer in the streets as you're dragged into the police truck, they will wave as you're driven out into the desert night, they will grow hard watching the plastic bag sucking desperately into your mouth. It's coming for us all. There is no one who will be safe from Mohamed Ibrahim's vengeance, from Gamal Mubarak, from every pig who ran for his life out into the fields on the twenty-eighth. They will go house to house and in the urinous light of an underground cell we will see each other, stripped and shivering, one final time.

A truck with speakers attached to it drives past and the street shakes with the music:

> *Bless these hands*
> *Bless my country's army.*

A hand grabs me on the shoulder—"Hey!"—and I spin around—*this is it*—my body tense, ready to be dragged into a waiting van, ribs alive and alert and waiting for the blade to slide in. I see the scarecrow frame, the jutting cheekbones, the quick eyes and I'm searching for a name. Fuck. My heart is racing. "Hey," I say, heart still quick. I can't remember his name but I remember the last I heard he was in prison. Drugs. Assault. Something bad. Something we believed. So what's he doing out so quickly? "Welcome back," I say.

"Thanks."

He's standing in front of me and he's not walking on and so I have to stop, too. He's thin as ever, his clothes are cut up, his skin is Dalmatian with dark patches and scars and he keeps shifting his weight from one foot to the other. After a pause I ask him how he's been.

"Fine," he replies, "fine. Keeping on the straight and narrow, you know."

"That's good."

"Yeah. And you?" he says. "You're here? In Egypt?"

"I'm here."

"Oh yeah? You live here?"

We're only a few meters from my building. Did he see me come out the door?

"No. Over in Abdeen."

He's going to ask for money, I'm sure of it. How much do I have in my pocket? A hundred? Two fifties? Too much.

"Got a cigarette?" he asks, and we each light one. After a while he says, "They asked me things," looking off into the middle distance, "on the inside. Questions. You know?" Don't say anything. Let him talk. "'Who do you know from April sixth,' they kept asking. 'Where do they hang out?' That kind of thing." He takes a slow drag. "I didn't tell them anything, of course. But you guys should be careful."

"Everyone needs to be careful now," I say.

"I tried to call Mariam but she doesn't answer my calls."

"You know why."

"Tell her I'm in treatment. I swear to God."

"I'll tell her."

He squeezes the last drag out of his cigarette, drops it to the ground. "See you around," he says, and is gone and I'm the asshole with a hundred sodden pounds in my back pocket.

◆◆◆

I go out into the crowd again. I leave the Sisi mask by the door. When the heavy knock comes I'll prop it up to throw them off the scent. I'll put it over my face as they pull me through the spitting mob crowded around the police truck.

My headphones are in my ears. My pockets are empty. Just ID and an old mp3 player. Too risky to take a phone out. No recorder. There's nothing to record. It will be cold soon. The *Solaris* soundtrack is playing. I walk through the crowd, their eyes scanning the skies for a helicopter to cheer, a falling plastic flag to catch. We are not of the same world. The posters, the cheering, the adulation, the bloodlust. The world is as distant as cinema: the faces in the setting light stream past, each the same, each now dark and sharp and forever untouchable.

◆ ◆ ◆

In the emptiness of the Greek Club Mariam sits talking to Rania and Rosa. I can tell that she's planning something.

"We're not planning anything," she says when we're walking home. "Just a protest."

"About the new protest law?"

Sisi wants to make protesting illegal now that he's ridden a protest into power. Smart man.

"Yes, against the protest law," she says.

"When will it be?"

"We're not sure. Depends when they pass it."

"Where?"

"On the street somewhere. We don't have any details yet."

She's avoiding my questions. Why won't she tell me more?

◆ ◆ ◆

It takes six men to bring Ashraf down, all pulling and kicking and tripping at him until his legs buckled and he fell, like an elephant, to his knees and the hyenas kicked and bit and slapped at him until his face was ground down into the asphalt under their boots and their knees kept landing into his gut, again and again until he finally gave up and his body was still

and his eyes stopped straining to see if they had caught Mariam
or if she'd got away.

◆ ◆ ◆

When I stopped running I was on my own. I thought Mariam
was ahead of me. I turned back to the gas cloud behind me.
The police had stopped chasing, people were gathering themselves again.

I can't find her. No one's seen her. Calls go straight to voice
mail. WhatsApp yields a single gray tick. My phone vibrates,
but it's a message from Hafez.

You OK? Everyone's arrested.

I drive while Nadia, Mariam's mother, makes phone calls.
"No, we don't know which station. We've got lawyers at as
many as we can. We'll find them, I promise. I'll call you when
I know anything. There's too many arrests to keep them hidden
for long. Just let me know if you hear anything, we've got to
work quickly. I'd rather spend a year in prison than a night in
a police station."

I drive faster. We've been to four police stations already and
no sign of them. Mariam, Rania, Rosa, Ashraf, and dozens
more. All arrested.

A crowd has gathered outside the police station in Tagamo3
al-Khames. I've never been here before. Why did they bring
them here? To get the prisoners away from Downtown?
Two, maybe three hundred people are here. The usual chants.
Mariam's mother argues with the policemen. Someone, looking
through a window, spots Rosa being led into a room inside.

At midnight a fight breaks out and a crowd of testosterone
chases a man away, slapping and kicking at him as he runs.

225

"Who's that?" I ask Hafez.

"That?" he says, straining to see. "Looks like one of the founders of Tamarrod."

I look back toward the police station. It was a beautiful setup.

The gate opens. An officer with a toothpick in his mouth and a gun clipped to his belt strolls out and steps close to Nadia, who stands at the front of the crowd.

"Your daughter will be released soon. Go home. Enough of this."

"We're not going anywhere until they're all out on the asphalt," Nadia says loudly but calmly. "And we demand a list of names. How many people are you holding? Either release them all or hand me a list immediately."

"Look," the officer says, smiling. "Nothing's going to happen tonight. We have to wait for the prosecutor to call. They're all asleep inside. So why don't you all go home."

"We're not going anywhere until they're—"

"Hey!" a young voice shouts, and everyone turns. "They've taken them out the back! They're gone!"

Nadia turns to look at the officer, who gives a half shrug of smug guilt. She spits on the ground and turns away.

Two cars speed off in pursuit.

"Where do you think they'll take them?" Hafez asks Nadia.

"I have no idea."

My phone vibrates and I hear Hafez's beep, too.

Rosa shared their location with you

"They've driven south," I say, handing my phone to Nadia as we run to the car.

Five minutes later and another location pin.

"They're driving out into the desert," Nadia says.

I press down on the gas. I don't think about what the police are planning to do out in the desert. I keep my eyes fixed on the road.

It is a heavy dark in the desert, our headlights a bright violence on the eight women shivering at the side of the road.

They are fine. Rosa is bruised up. Mariam is fine. She gets into the car with a woman I don't recognize.

"Did they let the boys out?" she asks.

"No."

"Then we have to go back to the police station."

◆ ◆ ◆

An overweight child runs around the glass table in the waiting room, I have a bottle of cold water in my hand, for the pain, the child's brother is playing a video game, the television is on loud, the receptionist's phone rings at an aggressive pitch, I close my eyes and try to block out the pain in my teeth, I close my eyes and see it falling, closer, we all watch it, the Molotov, falling closer, waiting until the last second to move, the television switches pitch, I open my eyes, the receptionist shouts down the line—*What!? What!? Well, when was the last time you fed him!??*—the boy runs round the table, Ashraf is still in prison, Ashraf and two dozen more, I ran, of course I ran, everybody runs. Nearly everybody. The boy runs around the table, car horns sound from the street, the television crackles to news—*political activist Alaa Abd El-Fattah has been arrested at his house on suspicion of organizing the recent disturbances outside the Shoura Council*—my jaw clenches shut and a stabbing pain shoots into my mouth and the boy runs around the table and I couldn't have known, no one could have known, but the fact is I left her, I ran and I left her, it doesn't matter, she doesn't need you, she never has and you've always known it—*Youssef! Stop that!*—the boy keeps running around the table and I'm wishing he would fall and smash through it and the TV gets louder with each thought and the tinnitus of the Game Boy and the boy's panting but there are no sounds anymore, no pure sounds, nothing indistinguishable from the crowd, nothing but static attacking the world around it, a flood of sonic waves all broken and ugly and bonding with each other into mutant monstrosities until there's nothing to breathe but carbon monoxide and dust and we're all doing it and no one cares they're all living and shopping and shitting and it's you, you're the anomaly, you're the problem, crouching in the corner with your eyes closed and pressing at your burning jaw and holding your breath and counting to ten.

"Tell me where it hurts."

The cold metal of the dentist's instruments presses at my burning gums. It hurts everywhere. His light blinds me, I close my eyes and try to ignore the pain. The radio is on.

The Minister of the Interior, Mohamed Ibrahim, today announced a successful operation against an armed militia of Hamas fighters under the supervision of the terrorist Brotherhood.

I try not to listen to it. Listen to the drill, the scraping of metal on bone instead.

"Terrible, isn't it?" the dentist says. "What the Brotherhood is doing?"

Don't listen.

"How can they kill their own countrymen? Egyptians!"

He forces my mouth wider with his sharp metals. Mariam sleeps on her back, looking up at the night like the figure on a sarcophagus. Last night I woke up and looked at her and for

228

a minute I was sure she was dead. The long untouching night in the tomb begins now.

"The Brotherhood would destroy the country before letting it prosper—" the dentist says as something pierces the raw flesh in my mouth with sudden burning pain. *Is it safe?*

> *President Vladimir Putin has promised Russia is available with whatever military aid Minister of Defense Abdel Fattah el-Sisi requires to fight the terrorist threat in Egypt.*

"Egyptians! They're killing Egyptians! A curse on Morsi and all the traitors." The probe presses harder and harder, the light is blinding—"the blood of an Egyptian is a precious thing"—is it safe? Is it safe? Oh God, *is it safe!?* "You can rinse." A precious thing.

I spit out a mouthful of dark, bloody water. And another. He passes me a tissue. I manage to mutter a word: "Rabaa."

"What's that, son?"

"The army spilled more of Egyptians' precious blood there than anyone ever has."

"No," the dentist says, ice calm, pulling his gloves off on the other side of the room. "That's all Photoshop."

"And Maspero?" I spit another mouthful of blood out. This isn't smart. He knows your name, has a copy of your ID, can make a phone call. *I have a foreigner in my office talking about Rabaa.*

"You saw what they did at Maspero."

"I saw the Brotherhood's lies, certainly. They were discrediting the army to win the elections. Who else would kill Christians?"

"I was there. It was the army."

"My boy—," the dentist says, looking over my file. "If you hit a kitten, what does it do?"

I don't say anything.

"If you hit a kitten," the dentist repeats slowly, "what does it do?"

I don't say anything.

". . . It scratches you."

◆ ◆ ◆

Ashraf,

How are you doing in there? I hope the food and supplies are all getting through okay, that your cell is not too bad. We're getting all the things we can together, and I'm setting up a book system to make sure you all have stuff to read. Mariam says she's going to try to get you a radio.

She's working really hard to get you out. We all are, but her most of all. She blames herself. I tell her not to, but she does. I'm sure you can imagine.

There have been some big protests and lots of media coverage. Hopefully we can keep the pressure up and get you guys out of there. Having Alaa as a codefendant could be good—it will certainly mean the pressure stays up. Is he in the cells with you or on his own somewhere?

Let us know about any specific books you'd like or if you have any new ideas—or new material—for podcasts. We will try to get Chaos back in action properly again now.

See you soon man

K

◆ ◆ ◆

There is a black hole in the center of our lives. A silence, an unsaid lurking, a word, a place, dark matter slowly pulling all else into its nothingness. A thousand deaths live on television. And none of them us. And who are we, if not the ones fight-

230

ing, not the ones dying? Should we have been ready to die for our enemies? Did we do this?

◆ ◆ ◆

Black open-backed jeeps with men in SWAT gear drive around the streets. The air is filled with the white noise of helicopters, circling forever over Downtown. Bombs go off every other day and yet the city swells, its waveform growing denser, lazier, with each new life that flows in through the petroarterial highways into Cairo's choking heart.

At a checkpoint we wait in silence. Fifteen policemen with assault rifles stand scanning the traffic jam. ID check. Hafez is behind the wheel, keeping his eyes straight ahead. We're all thinking of the same night, I'm sure of it, driving too fast, passing a bottle of duty-free sauce between us, driving up to a party in Moqattam, my hand out in the night air feeling the current pressing down on it when we came to a traffic light and there were two police sitting in front of their truck looking at us and Malik wound down his window and without warning us shouted—

"Hey! Fuck you, you son of a motherless cunt!"

Hafez hit the gas and skidded off and we all stuck our middle fingers out the windows like a bunch of stupid kids but the pigs didn't even *move*.

2011. We owned the streets.

The police drops Hafez's ID on the dashboard and we look blankly ahead and no one says anything and we drive on in silence.

◆ ◆ ◆

We were being hunted. From the very start. Tracked and harried by professionals with nothing to do but wait. Stalked through the thicket and we didn't even know we were lost. The July sit-in. The sleepless nights punctuated by the looping Casio piano and 1980s drum machine of Mohamed Mounir crunching over and over again until the dawn and the coming heat. The worst days of 2011.

One morning a group of men shambled through the square, pulling a battered teenager between them, slapping their prisoner again and again, shouting out to the crowd—*He's a thief! A thief!*

Mariam stood up and without a word trailed that spectacle of frontier justice. I followed behind her. The crowd moved into the shantytown erected in the Soviet shadow of the Mogamma3. They dragged the teenager into a large tent and without a second thought Mariam opened it and followed inside to reveal an interrogation. Hands tied behind a young man's back, two older men towering over him, cigarettes dangling out of their mouths, sweat spreading down their backs and out from their armpits. In the corner a boy was on the ground, hands bound before him, a dried trail of blood cracking down from his nose around his mouth.

"Who the fuck are you?" a sweating interrogator demanded.

"Who is *he*?" Mariam replied, sharp and firm. "And who are *you*?"

"I'm head of security."

"Since when does Tahrir have a head of security?"

"Since it's been compromised by infiltrators."

"What are you doing to this boy?"

"We're questioning him."

"You're torturing him."

"We're asking him questions."

"You're letting him go. Now."

The head of security took half a step closer to her, his chest out, eyes fixed down on her. "We'll let him go when we have our answers."

"You can ask your questions outside." She held up her phone. "I've just sent our location out and the lawyers and journalists are on their way."

A small tick became evident as his mouth curled up to the right and the eye above it snapped shut, moved half an inch to the side.

Should we have known then? Were we already compromised beyond repair?

◆ ◆ ◆

The cold has set in. The police are on the rampage, the jails are full, the judges are more craven than we could have possibly imagined, and Sisi is devoid of an original thought. Everyone knows this. The streets are empty. Posts are unshared. The airwaves have been cleansed.

"You should call Rania," Mariam says. "You could see about working. Put something new out on the Shoura case."

"We did two episodes about the Shoura case already. Did you see our stats? The first one got 214 downloads; 42 of them were from Denmark. We need to think of something new."

"No, we need to keep doing what we do," she says. "We had a medium, we *have* a website, followers. We have to be consistent. When we stop talking, then what does it do to everyone else?"

"But we can't just keep saying the same thing."

"If that's what there is—then that's what we do."

"And then what? We work people up so they rise up against the army and then the army falls and then? Then the Islamists take over? The police? The Americans send a peacekeeping force? We can't just keep saying everything is shit. We need a new answer. The whole world needs a new answer."

"Well, is that what you're working on?"

"You want me to come up with a new ideology?"

"I want you to do *something*. You have a brain. That's your thing. So use it."

I sit quietly. I can't think here. Every time I try the inescapable sound of the street trips the needle of my thoughts into a pointless anger. She zips her hoodie up and sits on the chair next to me.

After a while, I say, "Don't you think you should have told me?"

"Told you what?" she says.

"About your plan?"

"What plan?"

"*What plan?* Your Shoura Council plan to get arrested."

"What do you mean, *plan*?"

"We're standing out there together in the street and you *know* that you're going to be arrested. You *plan* on being arrested and you don't tell me. How is that possible?"

"If I'd told you, you'd be in prison now."

After a moment I have another question: "Did you tell Ashraf?"

"No," she says. "He just didn't run."

◆ ◆ ◆

The taxi driver lights a cigarette and the car fills with toxic smoke. Open the window, let the smog in. There is no escaping it.

The radio, as always, is playing.

> *And look at this piece of news. Egypt stands tall today. A cure for AIDS. America, China, France—they've all been working on this for decades. But it's Egypt that shows the world the road forward. The army has developed a cure. And it's not only AIDS that they've cured but hepatitis C, too."*

I wish we had taken Maspero.

The driver is sizing me up out the side of his eye and I'm waiting for the inevitable, it will come, any second now we'll open with the light, entry-level suspicions of the upstanding citizen, and, if everything goes to plan, move on swiftly to open accusations of espionage. *You're not Egyptian, are you? Where are you from?* Sixty-seven seconds, a new record, ladies and gentlemen, a high-water mark of patience and acceptance, a gold standard set by you, sir. Yes, thank the Lord, I am Egyptian. Birthplace of it all, from the beginning to myself and beyond. And you? Are *you* Egyptian? Oh, a son of the Nile! My! And how many non-Egyptians have you caught this month? Excellent. General beratements handed out? Unveiled women, you say? Christians? Homosexuals? All in a day's work. Israelis! Heavens. No, I hadn't heard the news about their commandos working with Hamas to infiltrate the country through Sinai. No, my radio is temporarily out of service.

> *Look, the fact is there's a lot to celebrate. And we can talk about human rights and all such things when we live in a country like Switzerland. But until then we have to roll our sleeves up and we have to fight. Just look at our enemies! America, Qatar, Israel, Turkey. Egypt is a country the whole world would have back on its knees!*

Yes, they're doing a fine job, our boys. Yes, Egypt is a country that many others would relish lying low. Yes, we must. We must be vigilant. Vigilant in the face of our great country's enemies! Or maybe we won't talk at all. Maybe you should get a fucking grip. No, it's inevitable. Any second now it will start up. *Are you Egyptian?* Yes. *But you don't look Egyptian.* I'm only half. *Ah, well one drop is enough to make any man Egyptian.* That would be nice. *Are you Egyptian?* Yes. *You don't look Egyptian. Can I*

ask what you're doing in Egypt? Why do you speak Arabic?
Christ. Let's get it over with already. *Are you Egyptian?* Yes.
*Where are you really from? Oh. You're not really Egyptian then. It's
not your culture.* Did I ask for it to be my fucking culture? Am
I going around wearing a fucking I-heart-pyramids T-shirt?
You can keep your fucking culture to yourself.

> *There probably isn't a more important country—
> strategically—in the whole world right now. Look at us,
> Egypt is at the center of everything. You only have to look
> at a map. Look at it! Go on.*

Egypt has become an island floating away from reality. A
madhouse, and we're all locked in together.

> *Let's not waste each other's time with facts. Anyone can come
> up with facts. The only real truth now is in how you feel.*

◆◆◆

The pain in my mouth is inescapable. I try to counter it with
painkillers, with ibuprofens and aspirins and acetaminophens
and codeine, I coat my gums with anesthetic gels and clove oil
and ice cubes, with effervescent pills and fingers dabbed in
whiskey, but any progress made in numbing the pain is undone
as soon as I'm asleep. I lie in bed waiting for it to start, I lie
awake in the heavy, yellow dark of this city that is never silent
and never still, the dark that fills itself with the names and the
faces and the last breaths of the dead and is spent now waiting,
waiting, waiting for what's coming as my teeth start their pri-
mordial cracking and crunching against each other. I am here
with you. I still love you. When the dream comes the pain

hides. In the dream the ceilings are low, the sounds are muted, the light is dark. I walk, slowly, through the mosque's silent antechamber into a room with a high, vaulted ceiling. I am slick with sweat, my hand aches from being clenched in my pocket. Breathe. You're inside. In the middle of the room are two ornate carved rocks: Ishaq and Refqa. Isaac and Rebekah. Side by side but not touching, each eternally alone in the vast dark of the cave beneath. A cool wind rises to greet me. A hand closes around my heart. My neck aches and my skin burns. The walls are cracked. Bullet holes. How many bullets, Baruch, did you unleash here? How many before you had a moment of doubt? I am pulled toward one, the wind breathing me in toward its emptiness, my back is burning, the metal splinters want their freedom, and then I know it's her. It's you, isn't it? Is it now? The bullet hole is breathing, sighing, and I'm touching it and it is not cool to the touch but warm and it is not breathing but bleeding and when I pull my hand away it is dripping red and all the other bullet holes are sighing out little breaths of blood and the green paint above me is fracturing and dripping and a flood is gathering, spreading out like a thunderstorm across the mosque's vaulted sky above. This is the place. This is my name. This is the end. It has happened, at last. When I turn she's behind me: the doctor, the darkness, her hand outstretched. I follow her out into the streets but the road ahead is dark and she is far ahead and then everything is illuminated by a cloud of white fire by spreading in the sky and from it burning white tentacles are falling and a man is on fire. This was all for you, Bouazizi. *Is* all for you. We will finish it for you. The doctor turns back and with a great voice like a mountain says: "There are more than can ever be named and you shall name them."

◆ ◆ ◆

The street outside is silent. There are two tanks stationed in two pools of silent yellow streetlight and I think of the bats and the river trees and walking with Mariam and the silence of the 18 Days and how I'd stretch my hand out over the river and I feel my rib cage straining to open itself to let an old and warm and lost part of the world into it, to let the bats and the night and the silence into it, to become not alone for a moment. Rania, Rosa, Hafez—we all live minutes apart from one another. Mosquitoes flit effortlessly between our private worlds but we sit alone in our crumbling apartments and plug instead into our cyberpsyche of chats and kisses and matching opinions and block and like and report buttons, retreating from the world that is cold and hard and dark into our digital city of filtered control and clarity.

"Sisi posters!" a lone voice echoes up from the street. "Sisi IDs! Sisi everything! The Revolution continues!"

I close the balcony door but the words still shiver through.

◆ ◆ ◆

The African wild dog has the highest kill rate of any animal. The wild dog hunts antelope in broad daylight. It is not faster or stronger than the antelope. It can't run farther. But it has a plan and doesn't question it. The pack fans out—quickly— flanking the deer, forcing it left, then right, then left again, wearing it down with a deadly geometry. Soon the antelope is exhausted. Soon it is dead. The wild dog hunts mathematically. It has a plan. It doesn't question it.

We could have seen. The July sit-in. The 2011 heat of summer. The bituminous barrens of Tahrir soaking up the July sun and steaming it back out through the day and through the night and there was nowhere the heat couldn't get to. The days melting into one another, nerves fraying and fights flaring up.

On the fringes of the square were rumors of constant attacks, men with knives and rocks, and Molotov cocktails biting at the borderlands. Inside, Tahrir swarmed with narcs and plain-clothes officers circling around us with their mobile phone cameras while state television barked day and night about the swamp of immorality festering in the middle of the city. We tried to end it, to withdraw on our terms, but the men on security refused to leave their posts and we, the nice revolutionists, wouldn't leave anyone to stand alone.

Two days later those same men were wearing military-grade body armor and pulling people out of their tents. I watched from the sides as our ex-comrades tore down the camp, watched them laugh as they beat and arrested everyone they could grab hold of.

The wild dog hunts mathematically, it hunts with a system. If the deer could hold a straight line, it would get away. The deer is faster. But it is hard—impossible, maybe—in the thicket.

◆ ◆ ◆

Across the landing a neighbor now leaves his door open, his television blaring out for all to hear:

> *We must be aware of infiltrators! We must be vigilant! Constant vigilance! Spies are among us. British spies look like Arabs but they have military training! American spies pose as tourists and take photographs of sensitive buildings! Palestinian spies survey our prisons constantly, looking for weak spots to spring their leaders! If you see something, say something!*

I wish we'd taken Maspero.

Everything is buried so deep the old man can't even cry. His boy is dead and he can't go home and fall into his wife's arms, pull his children onto his lap. He can't sit quietly with his friends until it all comes pouring out. He can never feel the break. He'll never let himself. Ramadan Ali's father's tie is knotted and his suit is clean and he's here.

"You know, of course, sir, we're gathering testimonies about what happened at Abu Zaabal. The government must be held to account," Mariam says.

I have two microphones set up. One on his lapel and one on the table. I wait for her signal to start recording. I will get back in the game. Ramadan Ali's story has to be told. It doesn't matter if no one downloads it, it will be there, a testament, and one day it will be needed. I'm getting back in the game.

The old man is hesitant. Mariam pulls her chair a little closer to his and says gently, "We want to bring your son's killers to justice."

"Yes, I understand."

"Where would you like to begin?" Mariam asks.

He clears his throat.

"Let me get you some water first."

She moves quickly into the kitchen. The Chaos office is all but abandoned, though the water's still connected. Maybe we can build from this.

She places the glass in front of him. "Take your time: if you could please tell me what happened."

"Yes. My son was on his way to work. He works close to Rabaa al-Adawiya Square. He was on his way there when the sit-in was dispersed. We live close by. He was arrested. At random. There's a video of his arrest that I think you've seen. We visited with him in the police station, his mother and I. He was fine. And then we got a phone call. When I . . . when I went to the morgue. They tell me it's my boy. They tell me it's Ramadan. I don't know. They gassed them. They threw a gas canister into the truck. The police. They burned them. He looked burned."

A new banner is strung across the street below. In bold red lettering read the words MARTYRS OF THE REVOLUTION above photographs of dozens of policemen.

Afterward, I hold her hand in the cold and I realize how long it's been since we touched each other.

◆ ◆ ◆

ABU RAMADAN

It's not that he's scared. He just thinks he'll be sick. How can you walk out there? How can you breathe? When he thinks about the heat, the horns, the sunlight shining off the hood of a car as you cross the road in front of it, the shouting, the fumes. The fumes. He can feel them creeping into his throat, pulling into his lungs, stealing his last breaths. The fumes. My son. My beloved son. Did you know it was over? Did you have a chance to say a last word, think a last thought? Did you fight the other men, did you try, did you come close? Or was it over from the start? My boy. The city is gas and heat and fighting and suffocation. How long did it take? Did they hear you, the men outside? The police. Did the man who threw the canister into the truck—did he stay to listen to you dying inside? My boy. My boy.

How do you take your last breath when there is no breath to be had? My boy. The whole world is your death.

◆ ◆ ◆

Mariam's phone rings and I see her body freeze, as it does every time now. It is never good news.

"Hello, Tante," she says, and I know that it is Umm Ayman. "How are you? No, I'm not doing anything. You saw the email? Yes, we're going to do a human chain on the bridge. Yes, we have to focus on small things for now. I know. What? I don't understand? But, Tante . . ." Mariam gets up so she can pace, walks to the kitchen.

When she comes back she almost doubles over herself with tears.

◆ ◆ ◆

UMM AYMAN

She can't stand on another stage or talk to another camera and declare eternal revolution. So many have died, she can't have another life on her conscience. She can't send any more young men to their deaths.

What would Ayman have had her do?

Every time she joined a protest, every time she joined a call for disobedience, every time she used her son's name to push his revolution forward she cut short a young life. She can't do it anymore. She can't speak for him, she can't tell people what to believe, or what she believes Ayman would have done, or what might lead us to justice. She can't sit with another young mother returned from the morgue. She can't carry the names of all the dead anymore. There is no stopping them. They will kill them all. We have to find a new way. Every protest, every human chain, every time we set foot outside they shoot to kill. She can't send any more young people to their deaths.

◆ ◆ ◆

We stand in cold silence along 6th October Bridge. I hold up a poster. FREEDOM FOR ALAA, it says. Hafez and Mariam's says FREEDOM FOR ASHRAF. Each of the Shoura Council detainees has a poster. We hold them in silence.

The cars drive past, unlooking, hundreds, thousands of them keep their eyes firmly fixed ahead.

Alaa, it was only yesterday that all of Cairo shook with your name and your face flew on banners from Oakland to Manila. Only yesterday that you marched into the military court to denounce it before the captivated audiences of the world. You had so many friends once. We were prime time once.

We stand outside a courthouse. We stand on a bridge. We run from the tear gas and the plainclothes and the shotguns and the informants. We stand on a bridge. Fifty, sixty people where once there were ten thousand.

◆ ◆ ◆

There was an old man. Years ago now. We were having one of the first Chaos meetings in a café. He was sitting at the table next to ours. He kept glancing up at Rania as she was holding

243

forth about all the earth-shattering things we were going to do. "Something the matter?" she said.

"No. Sorry. No, nothing," he said, and turned back to his coffee, his paper. How cowed, I thought, these old bourgeois are. But he couldn't stop listening to us. After a minute he got up the courage. "It's just—I wanted to say . . . I'm sorry but I heard a little of your conversation. And . . . we're all behind you, you kids, so, please, don't stop what you're doing."

I keep thinking of that man, that reflex of shallow pride burning in my throat.

◆◆◆

I can't remember the last time I saw the horizon. Sitting up here in the Virginian, its sprawling terrace overlooking the city lost in smog, the waiters hiding inside, the furniture unchanged since 1970. I gather my collar up. I was unprepared for this winter's cold.

"Fucking fascists." Hafez is talking to his phone. I don't read Twitter anymore. Egypt. Terrorism. Security. Stability. There are only four words left. Hafez has cut his hair off. I'm sure my own is starting to fall out. I leave him to read his bad news. The city simmers beyond. Through the graying green cloud of pollution a few higher buildings mark themselves out around Downtown, and beyond them like an eternal middle finger rises the Tower of Shame, looming above the skyline, empty, vast, forever unfinished, reaching up through the fumes like a sci-fi signal to our future of ruin. Our Chrysler Building, our expression of our own age in steel.

There are no birds in the sky.

"What do you do when nobody looks anymore?" Hafez says. "What's the point in taking photographs or making podcasts when everybody already knows what you're saying? They don't just know it—they like it."

"Mariam thinks we shouldn't stop. She thinks what matters is consistency, just saying we're still here."

"No, you need to be shocking. Each time has to be more shocking than the last. Which is impossible."

We fall into a silence.

Were we not supposed to be the new New York? It was supposed to be unstoppable. We were the future. But the same guys always win. *New York.* You think all that beautiful progress of yours, all that music of your father's, didn't come with a price? The same price as always. War. Always war. There can be no peace without war. The modern world was birthed by the machine gun. Don't forget it, it wasn't music, wasn't your father's jazz, wasn't Ulysses who did shit. It was the Maxim gun. Modernism was born in the trenches. It's the same playbook every time. War and peace. War and reconstruction contracts. Destroy the South and charge for the Reconstruction. Say you liberated a people and build New York from the spoils. Destroy Iraq and charge for reconstruction. Say you liberated a people. Burn it down and send in Bechtel, Halliburton, BP. Play it smart like the Israelis. Sell the bullet *and* the cement. Again and again. So don't whine about progress. Don't talk about *change* unless you want to pay the price. Progress means destruction and you have to choose which side you're with: the steam engine or the men laying the track.

After a while Hafez turns to me and says, "You know I was there—"

"Where?"

"When that doctor . . . the one you . . . in Mohamed Mahmoud."

Suddenly the setting sun is hitting my face directly. "I didn't see you."

"I know," Hafez says. "I was filming. When I saw you, I stopped. I don't know why. My thumb just pressed the button and I stopped. It felt wrong. But now, I don't know. Maybe it was more wrong not to film it. Back then it used to make a difference. A pretty woman dying on film—"

"Stop."

◆◆◆

I don't remember it being so cold in the 18 Days. The days were bright and clear and cheering us on. And the nights? The Camel Battle was hot with flame and energy but the later nights, those dark middle nights, they must have been cold. I can still see Tahrir as it was. At least I think I can. Men from the countryside, their heads wrapped in scarves, their thicker wraps around their shoulders. It had rained. The burning remains of the Camel Battle had been cleared away and the paranoia of the state was worming in: foreigners, spies, Zionists, terrorists—all are hard at work bringing the country to her knees. People huddled in groups around small fires, sharing what spaces of blanket there are, waiting for the next attack. A low mist hung over the gray morning. Will they come with guns again? We will struggle, with these numbers. Delegations from the other revolutionary cities—Suez, Alexandria, Fayoum, Mansoura, Luxor, Aswan—have made camp and are in conversation. They are ambassadors, they come with a mandate. What is decided in Tahrir will be followed throughout the country.

Alexandria, they say, has become autonomous. The government has disappeared entirely from its streets and civilian brigades are running the city. From Luxor one man jokes how his brother has kept a unit of policemen under siege for four days. Four days! He howls with laughter. They sent them in some water and said they'll let them go when Mubarak falls. Everyone bursts into hysterics. I was an engineer, a taxi driver, a teacher, a carpenter, a soldier, a civil servant. My life was not as it should be. My children's lives . . . So here I am.

But my memories are slipping, fading at the edges.

◆ ◆ ◆

There's a piece of paper in the trash. I can't help but pick it out. It's one of Mariam's lists.

> Collect letters for prison
> Food rota for prison
> Books for Ashraf

◆ ◆ ◆

She dresses quickly in the morning.

"I'm going to help Ashraf's mother with her shopping," she says.

Mariam has become close with Ashraf's mother, helps her coordinate the food schedule with the other families.

"You should take a short break," I say. She hasn't stopped for a day since Rabaa. I can see her hand trembling when she eats.

"I'm fine."

"Ashraf has a big family. You don't have to take this on."

"I know. I want to."

"But you can't do it forever."

"No. Not forever. Just until he's out."

Then she's gone and I'm alone again in the emptiness of the apartment. How long will we carry on like this? Do we still see anything in each other beyond the memory of our failures?

◆ ◆ ◆

I sit on a plastic chair outside the prison wall. My phone is dead and I didn't bring a book. Ashraf's case is being heard in an emergency terrorism court inside Tora Prison. They don't let us in to watch the proceedings. So we sit outside. I watch four egrets picking through the pile of trash that no one even sees anymore. They are supposed to be white. A brilliant and proud white, but these wading birds are long grayed by the trash they hunt through. I see the bats flitting through the trees on the Corniche during the silent nights of the 18 Days. Adapt or die. The egrets have made a choice, given up on grace and beauty in exchange for survival here.

Mariam sits next to the mother of one of the Shoura Council prisoners, pen and paper in hand. She moves from one parent to another, she knows them all, has a respectful rapport with each.

◆ ◆ ◆

Mariam's phone rings. It's early. Very early. The sun is still a gray idea through the curtains.

"Hello?"

"Hello." The voice is deep, male, and unfamiliar.

"Who is this?"

"Mariam?"

"Who is this?"

"It's better if you stop, Mariam."

"Who is this?"

"You know who this is."

"What do you want?"

"I want you to be careful. You have a reputation to protect. You're living with a foreigner. You're making people agitated. You need to be careful."

"I'm helping the families of the prisoners."

"You're giving them false hope. You cannot change anything. Not you and not your mother. Okay? This is the friendly call. There won't be another."

The line dies.

They will torture her. She knows it. They will come for her mother first. They will torture her. They will come to the house or the clinic, all men in leather jackets and she'll open the door wide how she always does, never afraid, and a giant hand will be on it and push its way in and the apartment will be filled with them in every corner ripping open mattresses and tipping out drawers and stubbing cigarettes out on the wooden floor before they drag her away to a dungeon, a basement, a place that's cold and damp and has one swinging lightbulb, and they will torture her. They will torture her in a dark room far away from where any sound can reach her and she will be alone and telling herself she's not scared and telling the men that she will never be scared even as they pull the electric wires between her toes, even as they rip off her top, she will tell them to go to hell, she will scream it as they burn their cigarettes out on her nipples, she will spit in their faces not knowing if tonight's the end but if it's the end let it come quickly, spit to end it faster, there is nothing to tell, there is no way out and we will never know, never find her, never see her body, her face, her wounds, her ripped back and bound wrists and we will not find her in the desert or floating in the river though you'll be looking for the rest of your life, waiting, every phone ring a stab of unsilenceable hope, now and forever. They will torture her. And there will be nothing you can do. You will sit in silence and rage in the darkness and there will be nothing you can do to protect her. They will come for her. They will come for all of us. The finger on the trigger. It pulled. Didn't hesitate. One by one, a bullet in the brain for each of the injured. The trigger. They pulled it. The yellow heat streaming all around her, the smell of disinfectant and rotting blood filling her mouth and the men executing the injured, one by one. The trigger. They pulled it. There will be no mercy. They will torture her, they will kill us all, they will burn the world, the trigger, they pulled it.

◆ ◆ ◆

There are days, minutes, moments I will circle around forever. The late-afternoon sun dipping over a shimmering lake of people and banners and babies on shoulders and I'm up on the balcony at the One's. The One, whose apartment was always overflowing with people. People on computers, charging cameras, smoking cigarettes, lining up for the toilet, making plans, preparing sandwiches, changing clothes, breaking down, doing interviews, taking naps, calling home. Everything still so new in those first eighteen days. In the dining room a group of people are gathered around a table, voices indecipherable from one another:

> "No! We have to put the Israeli
> gas deal in the first five. The top
> half. This is a global moment, it's
> not just about Egypt."
>
> "Okay, okay. Hang on. *Number one*: The fall
> of the president."

"Let's just call him Mubarak."

"*Two*: The dissolution of both houses
of parliament."

"Fine."

"Yes, next."

"*Three*: The end of the emergency law."

"Of course."

"Agreed."

The sun streams beautifully into the room. People and faces and voices I would come to know pressed against each other over the long wooden table.

"What do we have next? *Four*: Establish a
national salvation group."

"You all know how I feel about this one.
Call it a salvation government. Better yet,
call it a revolutionary council."

"That sounds like we're going to start executing people in the street."

"And who's supposed to choose
this group? Who is this
addressed to?"

"Everybody. We take Maspero, then we're the ones
creating reality."

Yes. We will take Maspero. I can still taste the feeling. We will win it all.

"*Five*: Immediate parliamentary and
presidential elections."

"Immediate?"

"When did we all become fucking liberals? We have
no idea where this is going, why are we going to start
calling for elections right away? This is the chance to
do something different."

"We should be talking big picture, not electoral politics. This is a message to the world."

"We need demands that the people can understand. We can't stand up and say we offer you the exciting unknowns of anarchism."

"*Six*: The trial of those responsible for the killing of revolutionaries."

"Shouldn't that be higher?"

"The end of the gas deal with Israel should be in by now."

"*Seven*: The immediate trial of those who corrupted and sold the country."

How beautiful it was, when the words finally came streaming down from the balcony for the whole world to see, the wind gently moving through the thick cloth and the painted words.

◆ ◆ ◆

A group of men, all sunken cheeks and three-day stubble, stand in silence under Tahrir's winter sun holding up ragged posters of Sisi. I want to stand and watch them for a minute. Do they talk to each other, do they check their watches to see when they can go home, do they compare rates?

I don't stay in Tahrir for long. I'm walking. I'm standing at Tak3eeba and lingering. I don't want to be out in public, to be among people slamming down checkers and laughing at bad jokes through swallowed cigarette smoke. I don't want to be alone, I don't want to be with people. Call Mariam. We can pretend we're a couple of kids and sit at the back of the big Odeon auditorium. What was it meant to play back in the sixties? Russian cinema? Italian? Mariam's mother told me all about her old Downtown, Nadia's city. Imagine, watching that world die into this one. Seeing your streets fill with dust and trash and watching old beauties slowly crumble and these brute brown towers clamoring up into our yellowed sky. Imagine watching the spaces of your world turn ever more uncaring until there was nothing left anyone could think or do or say except to shrug and cast their eyes down to the ground. There is nowhere to turn. Cinema Miami isn't Cinema Miami but a shotgun shattering Sayed Wezza's body and Akher Sa3a isn't a sandwich shop, it's standing on the street eating egg sandwiches with Malik and Hafez and arguing through the dawn and Mansour Street is running in the dark and the lashing of buckshot and the Estoril alleyway is you reaching over and buttoning up my jacket against the cold and my heart crashing against my chest and Champollion is Hafez throwing up from tear gas and laughing about it and Qasr al-Aini is my hand reaching for yours and cigarettes on Osama's balcony and Qasr al-Nil is Qasr al-Nil and Mohamed Mahmoud is our holy of holies where the two cities of the dead and the living meet. There is nowhere to turn. You are alone. There is nowhere left to go.

◆ ◆ ◆

The air tastes of iron and mold. A large atrium opens, the walls a dark gray, a single fluorescent tube above a solitary desk. A policeman, his face obscured by shadow, sits smoking. He doesn't look up. Behind him an enormous banner: THE MARTYRS OF THE REVOLUTION. Face after face of dead police in their black uniforms. The room is silent. The cells are underneath us. I listen carefully for any sign but hear nothing.

Mariam steps up to the policeman. "I'm looking for someone," she says forcefully.

He doesn't look up from his newspaper as he mutters "Uh-huh."

"Hafez Mansour. A photographer. Is he here?"

"Nope."

"We've been to all the other stations," she lies. "So he must be here."

"If he was here"—he looks up at her for the first time—"I'd tell ya."

"We believe he was arrested photographing a Brotherhood protest today."

"So he's Brotherhood?"

"No."

"Then he's not here."

"I'll look in the cells, then," Mariam says provocatively. I try to stand taller.

"Can't do that," the cop says.

"Why not? If no one's here . . ."

"Not gonna happen."

"Get your commanding officer, please."

"This isn't the army, girl."

"I know my colleague is here," she says, cold.

He pushes his chair back with a deep grunt of annoyance, walks off to a back office. He pokes his head through the door and mutters a few words. He turns back to them. "You wanna talk to someone?" he says, and gestures toward an open door at the end of the dark corridor. "Be my guest."

Mariam turns to look at me and a moment of doubt passes between us that fills me with dread. I follow behind her.

Inside, a large man sits at a cluttered desk. An ashtray spills itself out onto yellowing files. Two walkie-talkies and three mobile phones. His paunch stretches the limits of his white uniform, a patina of sweat clings permanently to his upper lip.

His gun sits clipped to his side. "What is it?" he says, without looking up.

"You're holding a journalist," Mariam says, and her complete absence of formality makes him look up and he sees us two revolution kids and half a smile creeps onto his face.

"What did he do, this journalist?" he says.

"Nothing," Mariam says.

"Then we can't be holding him."

"He's a photographer," Mariam says.

"Brotherhood?"

"No."

"Is he a member of the syndicate?"

"No."

"Does he have any accreditation?"

"I don't know."

"Huh." The sweating officer sits back, lights a new cigarette. "Your friend: are his employers in Egypt?"

Mariam hesitates for the first time. ". . . He's freelance."

"Freelance . . . he earns money from his photographs?"

"I don't know the details of his work. I just know he's missing."

"But you know we have a security situation in the country? Foreign powers interfering in our affairs?"

"Everyone wants to bring Egypt to her knees."

"Precisely. We have foreign agents gathering information. Photographing sites of national security."

"Fine, but not this one. He's a journalist. He has a right to—"

"Don't start up on that rights stuff."

"Look, we just want our colleague."

"*We?* So who's this guy?" He points his cigarette fingers at me. "He doesn't speak?"

"Only when there's a reason," I say.

"Oh." The policeman looks at Mariam: "He your *friend*, is he?"

"He's a colleague."

"Not your boyfriend? You're not married, are you?"

Mariam shoots me a look: Be cool. But the cop is staring at me, I have to speak again: "Look, our colleague has been missing for two days and—"

He sits forward, he's heard the flaws in my accent. "Where you *from*, boy?"

"Egypt," I say simply.

"You don't sound it," he says through narrowed eyes. "Or look it."

I keep silent.

"I want to look in the cells," Mariam says.

"What?" he hisses.

"I want to check in the cells for our colleague."

"Who the fuck do you think you are, girl?"

"I'm looking for a missing person."

"The cells are closed."

We should leave.

But Mariam isn't moving. Her body is coiled tight next to me.

"If he isn't here, then let me look in the cells."

"You want to go in the cells?"

"Yes."

The policeman stubs out his cigarette and slowly looks her up and down.

"Tell your boyfriend he can wait outside. I'd like to talk to you alone."

"No," Mariam says, crossing her arms. "He stays here."

"Okay," the policeman says, a yellow smile cracking across

his face. "He stays here. You want information? Well, we want information, too. Boys!"

There's a movement from outside and two more cops come over and block the door. The officer leans forward, his paunch pressing into the filthy desk before him. "So . . . is it miss, or is it madam."

"You can call me doctor," she says.

"You're looking for a strange man. Is he your husband?"

"No."

"Do you have a husband?"

"What?" Mariam says, with venom.

"You're a pretty girl. It's a normal question. You're out with this foreigner in the middle of the night looking for another man who's not your husband. What would your father think?"

"We're here for a journalist—"

"So you married or not?"

"We're here for a—"

"Did you come here looking for a fuck, girl?"

Mariam doesn't say anything. I can feel her controlling her rage. My shoulders wait for the men to grab me, pull me away, to force her down on the desk.

"You say you want to see the cells? You want to see the cell we keep the Cockroach in?"

The men are breathing harder behind us, getting ready.

"You want to spend an hour with the Cockroach? And you, boy, you'll watch. What do you say?"

Mariam does not take her eyes off him. Then she starts speaking, slowly, deliberately.

"We came here looking for a prisoner," she says. "We notified lawyers and journalists who are on their way here now. We'll carry on this conversation when they get here." She turns and without hesitating steps toward the door and—faced with Mariam's unflinching stride—the men step aside.

◆ ◆ ◆

At dawn I'm running and a phone is ringing and the land is watery, industrial somehow with billboards, train cars, and steel girders bridging swamplands and I'm running from something, there are men coming through the trees and waiting in corridors, there's a gun in my hand—maybe I shoot at them—all I know is I'm running. Don't stop. All that matters is one thing: Always leave one bullet for yourself. The men are chasing me, they've fanned out and slip between the rusted trains and the reeds and the phone is ringing louder and louder but how can I answer my phone now? We're in New Jersey. The trains, a Jersey train yard. I don't know my way around Jersey. They're gaining on me and I know what I have to do and the phone won't stop ringing so I turn around to face them and put the gun in my mouth and pull the trigger. But I don't die. My mouth explodes in pain and blood is bubbling down my throat and they're coming closer and the phone is ringing louder and louder and I'm hearing Rania's voice.

"Say that again?"

I shake Mariam awake next to me as I speak down the phone: "What did you say? Hafez? What about him?"

Minutes later and we're at the hospital and Rania's saying they found him an hour ago and Mariam asks her how bad it is and I only hear the word *coma*.

I sit on a chair outside Hafez's room. I wait. We all wait. Mariam slips silently in and out of his room. We need O-negative blood, she says to the waiting corridor. A flurry of tweets fly out. Within half an hour the first donor arrives.

We wait. We wait. The sun rises.

Blunt-force trauma. Deep bruising and abrasions across the back and head. Rectal lacerations. Three fractured ribs. Shearing scars across the legs. Electrical burns. Dozens of whip marks. Broken fingers. Multiple cigarette burns.

We don't talk because if we talk we'll have to think and if we think it can only be about what happened deep in the cells, about Hafez alone in the freezing silence, about each cut, each cigarette burned out on his skin, about each voice he might have heard from underground and each desperate hope and each minute more we could have been looking for him and each moment he prayed for it to end.

People arrive with food and water and people leave and come back the next day but I stay fixed on my seat in the corridor. There are no windows, no indication if it is day or night. A place without time where all that matters is the next beat of your heart. Men shuffle along with their catheters excruciating out of their gowns and bags of sulfuric liquid hanging from their hands and when I look at them I feel my penis retract into my body.

There is a dead cat on the street outside. Freshly run over. Its eyes still glinting. Four men with mustaches and the loose leather jackets of the state sit smoking next to it, unbothered.

The city doesn't show mercy or respect. It races on around us and our silent island of dread.

The sun rises. There is no change.

I don't want to go inside. I watch the corridor. Cockroaches scatter over the chairs. The cat rots outside. There is infection everywhere. On the floor, in the air, in the food, in the breath of a cigarette. It is inescapable. The walls are covered in graffiti. DOWN WITH MILITARY RULE. MOHAMED IS GOD'S PROPHET. MORSI WILL RETURN. THE REVOLUTION CONTINUES.

Everyone searches for answers somewhere.

We must prepare ourselves, someone says.

Malik arrives from London and we hug and don't talk about

the world outside, about his new job, his new life away from Egypt. We sit next to each other in silence. Mariam is reading Hafez the newspapers, talking to him about whatever she can, hoping for a sign. Nancy paces up and down the corridor. She is not sleeping. When did they last talk? The sun sets again.

When Mariam comes outside she takes the seat next to mine and though our hands are only inches away from each other they never touch.

◆ ◆ ◆

I'm woken with a gentle pull on my arm. Mariam pulling me up and awake, leading me through a heavy yellow door. You should talk to him, she says. He'd like to hear your voice. For a second I think he's awake but she tells me no. But he can hear us.

She points at the blue plastic shoe covers scrunched up together in a black bag hanging on the wall. Next the face mask, a flimsy plastic gown, and a Dettol wipe for the hands. We walk through the ward and I try not to look around at the rows of rising chests and open mouths, I keep my eyes down until Hafez is in front of us, lying flat under a white sheet, feet bare. Tubes. Dozens of plastic tubes, all racing into his body, into his nose, his mouth, his arms, and farther down where I cannot think about. His eyes are open but not seeing. A tube plunges deep into his mouth. It is a hard thing being kept alive. We can only hope it is a merciful one.

I sit down next to him and we sit together in silence and when the nurse leaves I come a little closer. "Can you hear me?" I'm sure his hand twitches slightly. Is this the one that was burned on the twenty-eighth? No, it was his right hand, his throwing hand. The hand he led with while we all stood frozen and stunned.

There are the craters of extinguished cigarettes all over your skin. Three, four, five blistering lesions on your left hand alone and I'm holding it and I don't know what to say. What is there to say? How often have I thought of my mother's room, those wasted hours sitting outside, leaving her alone at the end. I've always sat outside.

You must be missing music. I see you in the armchair in my apartment, see the LPs, feel the needle and hear the words pushing at my throat and I'm singing, soft as I can,

> *I've been in the storm*
> *So long*

Your skin feels so loose, so weak to the touch. When I move my fingers they leave behind an impression. I keep stroking your arm, real gentle. There are spots of sweat on the fragile skin. Hardly any hairs.

> *I've been in the storm*
> *So long, chil-dren*

Where are you, Hafez? Are you here with me or trapped in an in-between world? What do you want us to do? Everyone should make a list for if they come to this. I know I'd only want the people very closest to be allowed in. I'd want to be touched. I'd want the ventilator to be on the left-hand side so my right was where people sat, because if you could move anything it would be your right hand. I'd not want my feet touched. Or visible. I'd want my nails cut. I'd want to listen to music for two hours a day, classical music. Nothing with words. I'd like a woman's hand to press on my forehead, to stroke my hair occasionally. I'd like to not feel alone.

If only I'd sat like this with my mother. If only I'd been older. I should have brought a chair into that vast blue spotlit room and just sat with her, taken up residence next to her bed and read to her and stroked her hair and shown her I knew how to be the thing she wanted me to be. I could have given her that moment's rest as her body shut itself down.

Can you learn responsibility without betraying it in youth?

I've been in the storm
So long

I started crying at some point and I'm trying to keep my voice low and I'm sure a finger flinches and then three fingers are weakly squeezing my hand for the fleetingest of moments.

This is a test. A test from an old god.

Lord, give me little time
to drift

An old god and a cruel one.

◆ ◆ ◆

And on the twelfth day, Hafez gives it up.

◆ ◆ ◆

A metal casing is placed on top of the body and Hafez is wheeled out of the room and out into the long hospital corridor. Silently his friends and family fall in behind, all the people who kept vigil outside, men reach to place their hands on the casket. The corridor is lined on either side with waiting families. A silence falls as we move through. We emerge out onto the arcaded walkway of an old courtyard, the sun is low and warm and the Italian pillars cast their elegant shadows across the wall while swallows dart between them. The whole world, it seems, has fallen silent and Egypt has somehow summoned a moment of unbearable grace to help us on our way to the morgue.

◆ ◆ ◆

> Oh Lord, I wish I had of died
> In Egypt land.
> —Exodus 16:3

◆ ◆ ◆

I stand alone on Qasr al-Nil Bridge, looking out at the dark river. The party boats light up the Nile like a neon vision, each enveloped in its own echoing of scratching speakers.

> *Bless these hands*
> *Bless my country's army*
> *Bless bless these hands*
> *Bless these country's hands army*

This song will never go away. Nothing will ever change again. We will all grow deaf together in a deadly spiral of rising volumes and battered eardrums. Maybe we really are all stuck in the Matrix. I see the record on my shelf, hear Hafez laughing as the first notes of Wendy Carlos's Moog hit. Was it a good death, Hafez? Did you die alone, or did you hear us all around you? You heard us. Your fingers told me. You told me. The raw blistering of your hand on that first canister. The people surging forward over Qasr al-Nil Bridge and the bodies carried back and the eyes lost and the flesh punctured over and over again by the merciless steel of power. People racing forward while I froze, while I watched you grab the burning metal like a hero in a movie. Did you die for these people, Hafez, who will never know your name? For your perfect photograph that they will never see?

January 28. Nothing more, now, than a dark puddle of blood spreading around a young man's head; a scraped trail of cerebral darkness as he was dragged away, the blood reaching, grasping back for the moment when it was last alive. The fall was silent. Right next to me. You didn't know, brother, that that was your last moment. Didn't have a chance to stand up to it. The bullet didn't even come with a sound.

◆ ◆ ◆

Mariam's not home. She spends her days between courthouses and prisons. I don't send her a message. What would it say? *How are you doing? Do you want to have dinner?* What normal people's language could I imitate? Anyway, I don't do it. I try not to open my computer. Sit in an armchair and read a book. Remember that? I sit down with my edition of Hobsbawm. I know the passage I need to avoid. The one I thought could never happen to us. The electricity cuts and the apartment is plunged into darkness.

I stand on the balcony. The streets are black except for one billboard glowing atop a distant building. A perfect green lawn, an angular new house beneath a picture-book sky with a happy family of shining teeth and the words YOU LOVE CAIRO, BUT YOU LOVE THEM MORE. The building shakes, a military helicopter buzzes past. My jaw is clenched. I find another codeine and wash it down. Were we nothing more than a salve on the wounds cut by power, white blood cells in a cancerous body? Was it us keeping it alive those few heartbeats longer? If we removed ourselves from this ecology of suffering, would nature not revolt? Or would the flood of violence simply end us all? There are no birds in the sky. No birds in the city. Only helicopters and the lingering chemtrails of fighter jets painting aerial hearts in the wretched red, black, and white of the flag. You shall not pass, the borders are closed, there are no more birds. Good riddance to them and the pigs and their influenzas, we don't need them, we don't anything but Egypt. A rotten carcass of a donkey floats down the river. Close the land, the land is radioactive, come back in a hundred years. There's no music here, not anymore, there is only noise, the whispers of conspiracy and raspings of harassment and the trumpet of fascism. All informants, watching. I remember some shadow of a time when I would walk down a street with my eyes ecstatic over every detail, every possibility for the future, but all I see now are soulless strip lights and dying animals and cracked windows in crumbling buildings and inescapable memories that make up this sulfuric city of our dead, our metrocropolis of failure.

A snowstorm on Mount Catherine. A botched operation. A police bullet. A barrel bomb. A fall from a balcony. Once a month, every month, someone is taken from us.

> I'd like this to be played at my funeral. Hopefully after a long and happy life.
> @Bassem_Sabry

Yes—it's beautiful, the soundtrack to *Lost*. Bassem Sabry has good taste. Giacchino's best work. A touching, innocent piano, the gentle violins rising up and carrying the picture. Beautiful. And then it actually happened. And then it was being played, midday on Gramafoon and the world froze. A shoal of sorrow came together in tears and then was gone again and Bassem Sabry was still dead.

Ali Mustafa is dead. A death on Facebook. I read it once,

twice. There must be hundreds of Ali Mustafas. It can't be him. It can't be the Ali you know, the Ali you met on those nights out on Mohamed Mahmoud. The Ali you know was in Egypt, not Syria. And then there's a picture, a white sheet, a bloodied face, and your stomach and chest are pulling away from the screen. Ali. An Assad barrel bomb. His sister is commenting on his page, she's heard the rumor, is searching desperately for information. Don't let her see the picture. Please don't let her see the picture. Take it down. Please. Take it down. Oh Ali . . .

We are surrounded by the conversations we didn't have. Names to hold close. Little knives in permanent orbit around the heart.

"Did you know Nadine?" No. I should have. We were on the same side. Can I still miss you now you're gone? Can I still hate the doctor who cut you open and left your body to poison itself? The hospital that tried to cover it up? I didn't know you, Nadine, but I think of you. I didn't know you, Mohamed, or the people you lost your way with on Mount Sinai, or what your last thoughts were, trapped in the snowstorm, hoping for a help that would never come, listening for the army helicopter that only rescues tourists. I didn't know you, but I knew we were together in this, that we have stood together, night after night, regime after regime. We stood together, we failed together. We die apart.

◆ ◆ ◆

"I remember my dream," Mariam says. I'm awake. Lying next to her.

"What was it?"

"I dreamt we're all dead. And we're living in hell. We just don't know it yet."

◆ ◆ ◆

I spend my days alone, walking with my head down through the crumbling city. The office sits empty. Rania does not leave her house. Malik has gone back to London. Mariam shuttles between prisoners and their families and police stations and prisons. Every day food and clean clothes and letters and medicines go in; plastic containers, laundry, and instructions come out. I walk the streets, through our city and theirs, the city of the dead and the living, the city of the living and their overlords, the city of the state that cuts through us without regard, its shadow network of prisons and dungeons and police barracks connected through the constant invisible motion of opaque vehicles and watchful patriots and radio waves. Down every street a life is being wasted shivering in the back of a police truck, an order is being given, a fear is being played on as thousands of prisoners rotate between police stations, prisons, and courthouses in a perpetual citywide motion. The lower world has swallowed the upper. Now the honorable citizens of the city spray-paint out the eyes of our dead. We walk each day among their desecrated memorials. Our lives are a desecrated memorial.

I'm standing before the reaching wreckage of the NDP headquarters. This is all we truly have left. How much longer will they leave it to us? I can still feel the heat of it, January 28, the taste of the smoke filling the night sky, a dictatorship of burning papers fluttering down into the river.

The river didn't blink.

Did we stand and talk in front of it? Hafez is taking grainy pictures on his cell phone as the flames lick up at the upper floors. "Look at this," Hafez keeps saying, "fucking look at this! What is going on?" An ant stream of furniture and computer parts makes its way out of the building and down into the waiting boats below. An army soldier standing in front of an APC transfixed, like everyone else, by the silhouetting flames. "Is this a coup?" Hafez says. "What's going on? Where the fuck did the police go? Have they run? Are they gone?"

There was another fire that night. There were hundreds. But there was one at the heart of it all. An army truck ablaze in the center of Tahrir. The first army vehicle to enter the square. Kids standing near it said it was full of ammo for the police, so they lit it up. But what happened to the second truck? Was someone standing ready with a Molotov? Was there a moment of doubt? Of mercy? What consequence was carried in that hesitation, what history was lost?

◆ ◆ ◆

"I haven't seen you in so long," Rosa says as she hugs me. I don't say it's because Rania stopped replying to my texts. Maybe we only ever had the work. We have to pack up the office. We can't keep paying rent on an empty space.

"Did you see this?" Rosa says, handing me a video on her phone. I'd been sent the link a dozen times but hadn't opened it. I press play:

Chaos. What kind of an organization is called Chaos?

A fiery state televangelist talks to the camera.

You think that gives them some kind of cover? Well, what's Mossad called? And the CIA? Names matter. So they call themselves Chaos and they've been laughing at us. For years now. They've been out in the open and people were too innocent to say anything. They've been working to

*undermine the country. To undermine our security. To
spread lies and misinformation that deliberately target the
public morale. Any foreign infiltrator has long known that
the best way to weaken Egypt is to weaken the bond
between the army and the people. And this is exactly what
they've been doing. You should see the houses they live in.
Suites in Zamalek. Swimming in the Marriott every day.
You should see their bank statements! The British. The
Israelis. Hamas. Iran. There isn't an enemy of Egypt that
they're not taking from. And us? We just let this carry on?
Open borders to our enemies to fund whatever they like to
hurt us however they can? Egypt is a prize! The whole
world would see her on her knees. Egypt is a prize! And she
is riddled with traitors.*

"Just as well we're getting out of here," I say.

When everything is packed Rosa is hugging me again. I try
to avoid her eyes. When we look at each other it's like we're old
lovers, our limits and secrets and failures all open between us.

◆ ◆ ◆

"I made these T-shirts," Mariam says, opening her tattered
backpack, pulling out a white cotton shirt, taking off its plastic
before she hands it to me.

Mina Daniel's sketched face smiles out at me, a yellow sun
disc behind his head, the words underneath: *Who'll Be Next?*
I fold it carefully and put it on my desk. She is focused as she
counts out her remaining stock. Is this life now? A T-shirt, a
bag, a constant vigil in clothing? I feel the sudden dark hope-
lessness of the lunatic, of the mental asylum: *Here, I made this
for you.* Same time, same place, every week. Take the drawing,
thank you, it's lovely, fold it, put it away. She knows that the

T-shirts aren't bringing anyone back. She still knows that, right? Of course. We're just paying our respects to the dead.

When Mariam looks at me does she imagine my body cold and still and laid out on the metal of the coroner's table? Everyone looking to her for an answer. He's been shot. An autopsy, we must have an autopsy. Everyone is staring at her. Will she fight for it or will she just run, just need to get me out of there, take me somewhere, somewhere private where we can be together, just for a minute, just to say goodbye? But she knows that moment will never come. We will never be alone together again. We will leave the morgue to the cemetery and our last hours will be spent with the weeping of family and the anger of friends and there'll never be another chance for her even to squeeze my hand or run her hands through my hair or kiss my cold lips. Never again. They can take it all from us in a second, whole lifetimes of things we should have said. Words calcifying, tendernesses curdling in guilt. The morgue, the morgue, the house of ungraceful death. The Rabaa heat will never wash away, the refrigerator trucks lined up outside, each heavy with uncounted bodies, each burdened with a family's son, each the center of a new and incomparable grief, the corpses will never be washed away, nothing will ever be washed away.

◆ ◆ ◆

You can hear the music, the party, the laughing from the street. Like a swarm of locusts, all mercilessly communicating with one another, assaulting one another with ideas abundantly un-surprising. The same words again and again and again.

I push open the door. The lights are low and the air is preg-nant with smoke that burns my eyes through the darkness of bodies, random, pushing, pulsing in a neon blue light catching shadowed faces lit for a blazing moment by the glow of a cigarette before slipping back into darkness. Who are these women shrieking with laughter and these seedy men lining up their new objects of harassment and these bros throwing high fives in the kitchen and rubbing at their gums? What is this place? How did we get here? We, the unjailed, the unkilled pass the bottle, light a joint, fuck the pain away all faces warped and animal and older, desperate, lonelier now, now *we* are the zombies, the failures, the ones who grow fat on the land and send kids to die at the front and cry tears for the cameras while we drink on their graves. We are the ones who can choose when to play and when to quit. The ones who said it could all be so easy. Us. We are the ones.

◆ ◆ ◆

"The Dantons of history are always defeated by the Robespierres because hard, narrow dedication can succeed where bohemianism cannot."

Words read long ago, on a morning when the light that cut through my window was still beautiful. A million becomes a thousand becomes a hundred becomes one. This is the way of things. This is the long end of the extraordinary.

◆ ◆ ◆

Umm Kulthum crackles from the little radio in Stella. There's still a twinge of bitterness every time I hear the Lady and don't feel anything. It's your failure now. I pull my phone out of my pocket. I remember how Mariam would pull up a chair and put her hand on my knee and every man in here would be watching. What stupid things I felt proud of. What terrible things I couldn't see. My phone is in my hand and when I look I see it: Doctor_02022012.mp4. No. There is nowhere to go, no memory to take shelter in. I put the phone down and light a cigarette. We used to fill this place. Dozens of people pushing tables together every night creating infinite combinations of jokes and conversations and ideas. And now? What do you do when the world stops moving forward? When there is no difference between the days? When time stops and your story doesn't have a glorious end to race toward? When there is nothing, not a single thing in the world within your power to change? When your artifices of autonomy and agency collapse? What do you do when time stops meaning anything other than a countdown to your last breath? It's like watching yourself drown. Knowing the end, knowing what's coming and that there's nothing you can do about it. Nothing changes. Everything is drowning. All of time and all of experience is one whirlpool and we're all being sucked down it, each passing that same low-hanging branch and grabbing for it and missing, being pulled down and down, each cycle coiling tighter in on itself as the branch slips tantalizingly out of reach until the only question left is: When do you give up? When is it easier to drown?

A voice rises from a table in the corner. An old man with a pipe and a scarf is holding forth to a young acolyte. "What do I think of Bashar? To tell you the truth I'm with Bashar. Why? I'll tell you why. Bashar al-Assad is the only one who can save Syria. He's the only one. The only one. No one else has the strength. And here's what else: Bashar is Alawi. You know what's Alawi? Yes. If you take him, if you take Bashar, then what happens to the Alawites? Yes? Is this democracy?"

I have to put my headphones in and when I unlock my phone it's still there: Doctor_02022012.mp4. I turn away from everything. I've turned away from you for so long. But if we have nothing left . . .

The beat of war submerges me, the clamorings of men, the hurling of rocks. Our war machine. It would stiffen my back once, propel me forward, but now I feel my spine curling into itself as I float through the crowd, the rock-strewn street, a ghost between the men and women racing forward and backward, the memory and the recording in sinister concert pulling me toward you. With each shotgun's report I'm listening for you, for your voice, a breath, a scream, a fall, something through the fog of gas and the fleeing bodies—anything. Could I have been there faster? A second earlier? Can I find you here, on the shores of this electric purgatory? Can I make you alive for just one second longer?

◆ ◆ ◆

"Do you want to leave?" Mariam says. "To America?"

"You always think I'm five minutes away from getting on a plane," I say.

"Sorry."

"But," I say, after a little while, "maybe I don't know anymore."

The familiar silence falls around us, wrapping itself around our shoulders, chilling the air between us.

"But this," I say. "Us . . ."

We both know it's coming. You've been waiting for it, thinking about it. We both have. And when it starts there's no stopping it. Who am I to you anymore? Just one word and the avalanche starts.

"I know," she says.

I can see it already. In a few minutes it will be over and I will never get her back. It's the only thing left in this world that we have any power over—so it must be destroyed. We are nothing now but the reminder of our loss. I will regret this moment forever but we both know the time for choices is over, both can see our futures empty of the other and once we start we won't stop. I'm going to be alone. I'm going to wake up every morning for the rest of my life and regret this moment. Take it back. Fight, fight for the revolution, fight for her, fight for all the things you said you believed in when belief came easily. Take it back. If you can't change the world at least change yourself. Take it back, it's not too late.

"Do you want me to move out?" she says.

"No."

I don't. Of course I don't. I love her and I need her and I want to run away with her to the past.

"I'll have to," she says.

You'll never wake up next to her again.

"It doesn't have to be now," I say.

"Of course it does."

◆ ◆ ◆

The taxi driver lights a cigarette. He looks out the window, quietly tuts to himself. "It's not right, these women. See how they're dressed. They come to Tahrir and what do they expect?"

I don't say anything.

The radio drones over hissing speakers:

> *We draw the martyrs of the revolution of January twenty-fifth and June thirtieth and the martyrs of the army. Graffiti doesn't have to be political.*

"Where in Downtown?" he asks.

I tell him Talaat Harb Square.

I don't want to see graffiti that I couldn't walk past with my mother or sister. The murals of Mohamed Mahmoud stand there for tourists to see the stories of January twenty-fifth. And, uh, of course, June thirtieth also.

I wish I could turn the radio off. I wish we had taken Maspero.

Suddenly, the buildings around us shut down, the block plunges into darkness. A power cut.

"A curse on the Palestinians," the driver mutters, as if in reflex.

"What?" I say.

The driver half gestures at the radio. "Our electricity. Morsi sold it all to Gaza."

I don't say anything.

"You look like you're not Egyptian," he says.

"I'm not."

"But you speak good Arabic," he says, suspicious.

"I'm from Greece."

◆ ◆ ◆

The heavy bound script sits on the table in front of me. Hafez's father called. There was only one thing I wanted from the apartment.

ALL WE GOT IS ROCKS
by Hafez Mansour
Draft 21.9.2013

He changed the title.

Each page is covered in heavy handwritten annotations.

Dozens of new pages are stuffed in between the old ones. Type-written, handwritten:

> SCENES STILL TO COME D2
> 5:00 Siege of Sayyeda Zeinab police station
> 5:27: State TV announces curfew
> 6:01 p.m.: NDP HQ in Cairo ablaze—man inside looking for papers
> 6–8 p.m.: Police retreat completely. Suez, Alex, & Cairo
> 10:12 p.m.: All flights suspended
> 10:57 p.m.: Army fully in position now
> Midnight: Mubarak useless speech

In hand, along the bottom, Hafez has written: *Just the beginning. Get out of Cairo.*

You're right, Hafez, it was a film, a cinematic dream of self-lessness where the good guys won; an explosion of light and sound and epic consequence with no room for ego or doubt; a narrative made by the bodies within it with no need for a narrator, as fragile and immortal as celluloid; a 75 mm memory to be relived together in our shared auditorium of triumph, our singular inheritance for the generations to come. If only you'd made it for us while it was still true. History changes as invisibly as the future, though more painfully in having tasted what is lost.

I flick toward the end.

INT. TELEVISION STUDIO - NIGHT

A CHAIR *crashes against a door, securing it shut.* KARIM *pushes at it again to double-check it. Satisfied, he picks up the heavy cane and turns to* MARWA, *sitting at a vast control panel.*

KARIM

Can you do it?

Above them the news feed plays on several televisions. The NEWS
ANCHOR *is reading the news as normal.*

MARWA

I need more time!

She scans the hundreds of buttons on offer before her.

There is a THUMPING *at the door.*

VOICE OUTSIDE

Open this door!
Open this door immediately!
You have five seconds to comply.

KARIM

We're running out of time.

MARWA

I've got it.

*She flicks a series of switches and the news feed on all the televisions
dies and is replaced by the* TV. COLOR/TONE CARD. *She presses
another button, takes a breath:*

MARWA

Do not switch off your television, this is not an error. The
Twenty-fifth of January Revolution is in control of the
country. The dictator has been toppled and the people's

demands of bread, freedom, and social justice will be met. Go out to the streets and join the revolution. Go out to the streets: our days of being ruled by tyranny have ended. Go out to the streets: reclaim what's yours, reclaim your country.

A thick red line crosses through the whole page. The words end.

◆ ◆ ◆

There is a cricket now, living outside my apartment. After midnight its call fills the night's soundscape, its tiny legs come together and in their music drown out the tens of millions of other lives and machines that make up the night. I come home ready for its conversation, its lament. I sit alone, with a glass of water and a cigarette, and just listen to it, to its unrequited call, its unanswered transmission into space. The cricket is patient. The cricket does not need validation from anyone or anything else. The cricket exists to act and so acts. The cricket makes its own meaning. And I keep thinking that one day soon it will be gone. Soon it will be gone and I'm not sure how I'll live without it.

◆ ◆ ◆

Dear Alaa,

I'm sorry I haven't written to you until now. I'm sorry this has happened to you. I'm sorry for Manal and for Khaled growing up without you. He will be fine, Manal will bring him up well. It will be hard for her, but she's so strong. I'm sorry we used to all be stood next to you and now we're cowering alone at home. I'm sorry they want you.

I can't tell you anything about the outside world, or the revolution or the future. I can't tell you anything that will give you comfort, can't tell you that five years will go by quickly, that there will be a better world out here for you to inherit, that we are all working with every breath we have for your release. I can't tell you that there is momentum building and an international outcry and diplomatic pressure mounting. I can't tell you that Sisi is weakening.

There is nothing. Just waiting. Broken by the obviousness of our defeat.

A word like solidarity doesn't mean anything anymore. So I can only say I am sending you love.

I don't know. I'm sorry for everything. I'm sorry I'm not in there with you. I'm sorry this is all I can do. I'm sorry I ran.

K

◆ ◆ ◆

I'm sitting in the long-abandoned roof bar of the Odeon Hotel. A single light flickers in time with the ancient radio playing the songs my father never taught me to love. The barman left long ago to catch his last bus home, leaving a boy inside in the dark corner, smoking cigarettes. Stella bottle caps arch over the ashtray in front of me. *To bloody battles and bruised arms.* The hot wind whispers over my back and shoulders, catching and trembling the small beads of sweat that have gathered, vibrating against my metal skeleton. When I scratch at my face I am surprised by how long my beard is. I haven't seen myself in a mirror for a very long time. I am losing my hair. It is long, messy, it is falling out and it is catching the heat and keeping it all around me, breathing on me, down my neck and through my body into my feet and suddenly I'm overwhelmed with heat, an urgent heat rising in my toes, around my ankles, the same heat that strikes now whenever I get home, an irresistible heat that has to be extinguished before it sears the soles of my feet, before it climbs up into the rest of me and I'm pulling my shoes off and my socks off and hoping no one comes in to see me sitting sockless and alone. I'm hoping my younger self can't see me.

Are you still a martyr if you don't die in the right place, at the right time? There are no flags with your face flying, Hafez, no graffiti of your words on walls but I see you everywhere, see you look up and ask: *Wouldn't you have been happy? To die in the 18 Days?*

Beginnings and endings. All we have left. All we will ever have. When did it really start? What a glorious start it was. When was it lost? What a terrible end it had. What could we have done? How could this happen to us? Again and again and again and again. Questions. Forever now. Questions. Beginnings and endings. You either win or you lose. Shell shock is a brain traumatized by sound, by violent vibrations detonating through the fabric of your mind, a sonic flood washing away your synapses and leaving nothing behind but an empty, dead plane with nowhere to hide from the police sirens and the flashing blue lights racing at you from the distance, nowhere to take cover from the threat sung through the teeth of watching neighbors, nowhere to run, only the flood, only the end. History has moved on, has left us alive with the cold weight of judgment pressing down on our chests like medieval torture: heavier, colder, more perfect with every inhalation and every *why?* Why me? Why not me? Why us and why now and what now? What, when you lose, is there left to do? We failed. All of us. And the whole world knows it and judges us for it and looks away as the undead past coils around our chests. No negotiation, no hope, only what will we fill our long and withering days with? What will we tell ourselves when we peer over the edge? What can we do to make it stop? What can we do to make it right? When will it be over? How do we carry on? How do we carry on? How do we carry on?

At least, they cheer, through the crackling TV, *we're not Syria!*

Beginnings and endings, beginnings and endings but at least

we know for sure that this is a fucking ending. You can say it just as much as you like, but you know it's over when everyone is either dead or in jail. And if you're neither of those things you were just never a player.

Even Talaat Harb Street, at this hour, is silent. The city is forever broken by those curfew nights. If I listen carefully I can hear an occasional car drive down it, I can hear the radio—

Bless these hands
Bless my country's army

In the eastern distance a loud, shaking noise bursts into the sky. A plume of smoke signals itself into the air. A bomb. I listen for the follow-up, the second blast that catches the first responders, the heroes; but it doesn't come. Hopefully it only killed police.

◆ ◆ ◆

I'm flying, flying away, running up into the air. You'll be back, I tell myself, it's not for long, you're weak, your body has given in, you're out, you've no place here, never, so you're free now, free to fuck off and I'm looking out the window at the perpetual yellow city and two green laser pointers flash up at me, searching through the darkness for the plane, searching in accusation. A happy family stare with shining malice at one another on the back of a magazine. I look away from the stewardess's pantomime with the life jackets. There is no surviving a crash landing on water. There will be no babies in little baby life vests floating to safety. Crashing on water is crashing and dying. This theater of possibility, what's it for? Why must people always think they're in with a chance? You are putting your trust in something higher than you, so why pretend we're still in the game until the very last miserable fucking breath slips into our dying lungs? You are not in control. You are not a player. You do not matter. You have come to the end of what you can do and here we are, in this dark whistling missile of goodbyes and broken promises stretching up into outer space, a band of strangers strapped in and breathing one another's air as the old men in the cockpit with broken dreams of martial glory lift us away from the city and the laser pointers and the memories and the police checkpoints. *Where you off to then, prince?* he said. The policeman at the last checkpoint before the airport held my passport in his hands and my blood grew hot but I kept calm and said I was just going to see my father and kept my face bland through my stomach's cramps. I've got an ulcer, I'm sure. I've had it for a while.

"And where's your father, then?" he said, and as I opened my mouth to answer I realized I'd been clenching my teeth down and a jolt of pain shot through my jaw.

"America," I said.

"Too good for Egypt, is he?"

I didn't reply. In my teeth I feel a future vision of bones worn to the raw exposure of an electric nerve, an invalid's future of slurped soup. He looked at my passport, then dropped it back in the car. "Go on then. Piss off to America."

I let go of the armrest for long enough to check in my bag for painkillers, but of course I have them. Aspirin, acetaminophen, ibuprofen, codeine, all the happy family, the gang giving me cancer, giving me stomach cramps, ripping at my bowels, festering a chemical rot in my gut. Is it better to have been abandoned, or to have always been alone and not known it? A ravine of sweat is running down my back and cooling my blistering skin and I see the video of Ramy Essam, how the camera lingers on the lashed map of needless suffering carved across his body, and I feel my skin reach for somewhere to hide as the long-healed scars pulse in familiar agitation.

There is a shared reservoir of pain that lies like an aquifer beneath us. When all else is lost, that will be all that binds us.

I turn the headphones up.

> *We hope,*
> *that you choke.*
> *We hope,*
> *that you choke.*

Roll credits. You're flying. You're leaving. You're running away. Maybe freedom . . . maybe freedom is nothing more than the taste of guilt.

◆ ◆ ◆

Abba Arsenius lived in the palace of Theodosius as a tutor to the two sons of the last emperor of a unified Rome. After eleven years of service Arsenius prayed to God and said, "O Lord, direct me how to live," and a voice came to him, saying, "Arsenius, flee from men and thou shalt live." And so he joined the men and women who found themselves called into the silent wilderness of the Egyptian desert to live the life of perfect self-denial.
—Saint Athanasius of Alexandria, c. AD 400

◆ ◆ ◆

A crane projects itself into the blue sky ahead. A mobile watchtower. Amsterdam and 125th. Harlem, Palestine. All around you it's the same, every step wading into the eternal swamp of conquest and cleansing and murder. They'll never stop chasing you, there's no way out of history's one long looping nightmare tripping through the dark bayou and it's the *things*, you're on the *things* and we want them: the army wants your land and the British want your oil and the Italians want your gas and the Americans want your airspace and your canal and your complicity and the Turks want your factories and the Australians want your gold and the Gulf wants your sweat and the Russians want your weather and the Israelis want your *name* so there's nothing left for you but to be gone. Gone, because we're coming and first we'll bring you war and you'll run and we'll seal iron chains around your neck and brand you with new names and drink your bodies in tea in your grandfathers' houses and when we're bored of war we will bring you peace and post-conflict resolution and interfaith dialogue and the United Nations and credit lines and television and when you choke we will grip your jaw firm in our hands and force open your mouth for structural adjustment and dialogue camps and off-Broadway plays and aid packages and first-party negotiations and mediated solutions and corporate social responsibility until your brain is reconfigured with our committee-designed computer-assisted algorithmically determined languages of unmeaning and you are finally and forever stripped of even the possibility of thought.

◆ ◆ ◆

The triumph of it all is the vanquishing of imagination.

There can be nothing new. No new music is imaginable, no new genre, no new memories to repackage and sell, no new stories or ideas or possibilities, no new happinesses. There is only nostalgia and kitsch and superheroes and heartbreak and a sealed fate and surrender. There is no reality other than this one and no past that wasn't marching toward it. They call it progress. It is undeniable, they tell us, it is all-conquering, it is this and it is now. The world is made. Countries are developed and others are not and so it shall be. A system is in place of such dominion there can be no imagining another. A system underpinned by a global network of trip wires, each tensed and primed to trigger self-destruction before evolution. Look around you. There is no other world. There can be no other way. Surrender. There is only the now. Whisper it to your children at night. It would be better for them to accept it.

◆ ◆ ◆

I sit invisible on the subway.

I can't stop myself from hearing the conversations around me.

"I'm pretty ambidextrous racially and can travel okay."

"I was just in India. It's disgusting, trash everywhere, but they were happy, you know?"

"Their religion probably allows them to be happy."

"We don't have that here."

"No."

"I was with my friend Sarah, though, and they're obsessed with blond hair and blue eyes."

"I know. I had a friend she wanted to go to the Middle East to get involved in politics and shit and I was like, yo, look: they will *never* respect you."

"No, never."

Sometimes I think I will throw up from all the words. Every idiot syllable spasms through my stomach and the only way to be clean of this language will be to vomit all over the ground between us.

◆ ◆ ◆

I keep thinking of the hospital waiting room. How many hours did we sit next to each other outside in that corridor of disease, so alone in each other's company? How many hours did I pass wanting to reach those few inches to my left and take your hand in mine? I kept my hand close to yours, close enough for you to feel it, I was sure, waiting for second after infinite second to see if you would lift your finger to make that first curl around mine. Could you feel the questions and doubts pulsing from my brain to my fingers and leaping and falling into the synaptic gulf between us? Would you have pushed me away if I'd reached out? Gently squeezed my hand and dropped it? Is that when we broke ourselves? It seems crazy, now, not to have reached over. It seems so crazy that now, in this instant, I would do anything to be back there and live it again and take the plunge and open that new road, begin that new universe that surely would have been born with the touch of those two fingers. It could have all been so different. We could have all been so much less lonely.

We could have, could have, could have.

◆ ◆ ◆

I'm standing on the boardwalk, waiting. Half waiting for someone to say something to me, or try to sell me something, or mutter something under their breath in a language they assume I don't understand. No one speaks to me. No one gives a shit about you here.

There's an outdoor bar. The barman opens a bottle and starts pouring it into a plastic cup and for a moment there's that reflex, that twinge, that plastic-cup twinge, that plastic cup that says to me drink whatever you like, drink yourself into the grave, please, but we don't trust you not to bottle someone after two beers or smash it and cut open a major pulsing vein of yours and lie there slowly bleeding out under the boards between the cigarette butts and the fallen toys of the children standing aghast in a semicircle around your convulsing body-offering to Murphy's Law, the twinge that reminds you you're strapped in with the nanny state and baby can't be trusted with the glass bottle, you're just supposed to drink the opiate inside, that twinge that tells you you're back home in the rat race and you've taken a wrong turn and you need to turn back and follow the sign that says fucking *Freedom* like the rest of the shirtless brotinis on the filthy beach whose only legacy is an ocean full of Solo cups, is the sea, now and forever, pushing their garbage up to the sand, begging for it to be taken away, begging with each wave for someone to, please, just take it away. How can we ever be any different? You have a peaceful revolution to topple a dictator but to have a peaceful transition you need elections and the only people with the resources and networks to win the elections are ex-dictators and dictators-in-waiting. We're trapped in an Escher painting. We had the fucking numbers. Seven million people voted for the revolution. If the vote hadn't been split between Aboul Fotouh and Hamdeen, if they'd put their pride aside for five fucking minutes, things would have been different. And now where do we go? Where are we supposed to go in this world where the only things that move freely are the floating refuse of fictional credit, where do we go when every inch of earth is already owned and valued and soon to be bought by Monsanto, when every cent spent holds another human in bondage before being smelted down to a bullet casing? What can we do with information or facts when the only currency that counts is guns and lies, when all anyone *wants* are guns and lies? Will we go on chattering forever in our digital echo chambers as Facebook throws up algorithmic borders around us uncrossable as the Berlin Wall, irresistibly invisible as gravity, corralling us into digital polities of irrelevant impotence that we occasionally emerge from, blinking, to discover the physical world of violence seething all around us? What use are our words when a republic of belief can be dissolved by a technician in California? Did we escape the mousetrap for those few months? Was there a moment when we were truly in charge of our own destinies or was it all a cinematic illusion? How do you win? How do you ever win? Without guns and Apaches and ranks of fighters and airwaves. How can any of us ever win? The world has taken centuries to build. You think an *idea* is enough on its own? No, you need a plan and you need patience and you need to meet their violence with your own. You can overwhelm them with numbers or you can kill them with precision. One unit, maybe that's all it would have taken. Get into Maspero, take it over and broadcast the new voice of the revolution. Two hours. In the end that's all you have. Two hours between the police retreating and the army taking up positions. Two hours and it was already lost. The right buildings have to burn. The right buildings have to be taken. Next time, you have to be ready to strike unhesitating. And will we be? Are we training, planning, preparing or will we go on forever only reacting? It was lost from the start, lost from the moment we didn't take Maspero, lost with the Molotov held back from the second army truck, lost when the square emptied after Mubarak fell. Next time you have to be ready. Next time? Next time we'll see the real revolution. Next time we'll see ISIS and we'll see organization and precision and the end of patience. The real flood is going to come. That real rain we're always being promised.

I put my headphones in to drown myself out:

> *People get ready*
> *There's a rain coming*
> *There'll be no saving*
> *So don't beg your Lord*

◆ ◆ ◆

It's better at night. The streets are quiet. I like to walk. It keeps the thoughts still. Walking is just about the next step. Flee from men and thou shalt live.

I walk for hours. I'll walk all the avenues. I'll walk all the avenues and something will change. Manhattan's great brick-work thicket crowds the sky. Jazz. The future. New York, New York. Isn't that right, Ned? Here we are. Maybe you were right. The heartache is a cliché.

Did we lose when we stopped selling ourselves? Was there a point in our tiredness and moral superiority and inexperience when we stopped trying? You can never stop. I remember a huge canvas in the Smithsonian: Bierstadt's *Among the Sierra Nevada*. The Edenic vista of the American frontier, an ice-blue lake, a noble stag, a mountaintop celestial in the distance. A great and wild and infinitely conquerable land. A fantasy for sale. A painting by a German of an imaginary lake crowned by an Alpine peak on sale in Rome along with everything the New World can offer to the battered longings of the Old. America never stopped selling itself, never stopped needing new bodies to crush into the dream's cement. And if America can't stop, then who are we to?

◆ ◆ ◆

A parked car's bass line vibrates through the cheap walls of this clapboard building, trucks' engines roar with a bellowing fury, early-morning arguments between drunks and the chemically confused loop louder and louder. Individual punctures of my anonymous solitude, alien and uninvited. I'm hungry and walk down to the slice shop too early to be respectable. I pay the dollar and sit down and above me is a poster, its colors faded, a smiling white nineties family grinning rigid. Behind them the great golden sunrise of the Dome of the Rock, before them the words *Visit Israel*. There's a whole collection of them. Future artifacts of an unsustainable paradox. Smiling family in the Dead Sea, smiling family in a Roman amphitheater, smiling family looking out at the Mediterranean. I walk out without eating.

A coil of razor wire twists over an overgrown lot. I hear the birds and I see the metal and I reach up to touch the edge and I am back outside Maspero, the army's steel sharp against me, and I pull my finger down and you feel it first, the warmth slipping down your hand, before you see the red darkness against your skin and I'm standing with Hafez, our hands gripping the razored coils, watching the soldiers, alert to their twitching fingers resting on their triggers. "What are you all doing?" a voice shouts. "Who are you defending? Mubarak? Are you with Mubarak!? You'll side with Mubarak against the Egyptian nation!?" Another voice shouts at the nervous soldiers. "Huh? Do you even know what you're doing here?" The soldiers aren't moving. The crowd isn't rushing them. Nothing is changing. We slipped into the crowd streaming into Tahrir. A group of girls' head scarves made an island of bright colors in front of us. Behind, boys pushed the crowd faster with their chants and drumbeats. All around were parents with their children, little children on their fathers' shoulders with the Egyptian tricolor painted on their foreheads or clutching on flags.

"You sleeping here or at home tonight?"

"I'll sleep in Tahrir tonight," Hafez said. "Two in, one out. You?"

"I need a night in my own bed."

"Good. No sense in burning out. This will go on for a long time."

"They say Mubarak flies to Germany once a year for a full blood transplant."

"So you're saying he's going to live forever?"

"I'm saying it's a possibility."

"God damn you, massive leaps in medical science." Hafez raised his fist to the skies. "Damn you all to hell."

He still makes me laugh.

"Sorry about this, brother," one of the security volunteers said as he patted me down.

"Not at all," I say. "Thank you for doing it."

And then we were in, and Tahrir opened up limitless before us, a sea of people and possibility and unknowable disappointments all brilliant in the late-afternoon sun.

Not at all, thank you for doing it.

I wipe the blood on my jeans. Pointless memories.

◆ ◆ ◆

The next war has begun.

> At least 121 Palestinians have been killed since Israel launched its Operation Protective Edge three days ago in what is shaping up to be a major offensive with 25 children among the dead already. Sherine Tadros reports for Sky News . . .

I sit alone through the night on the Greyhound.

I sit on the couch next to my father. We watch the killing together. We watch without words. There are only names now. In the night the same dream comes, the Ibrahimi Mosque, the death all around; the bullet holes are breathing, sighing, and I'm touching one, pressing my hand on it, and it is not cool to the touch but warm and I can't stop the bleeding. The doctor, as always, is next to me and everything is illuminated as a cloud of white fire spreads across the sky. There are more than can ever be named and you shall name them. All the names, from all the wars, all the names we carry with us, all the names on all the lists that keep on growing. Mohamed crouching, crying behind his helpless father. Aya breathing her last breaths alone with a sniper's bullet lodged in her neck. Munadel falling face-first into the asphalt of a settler road. Hamza playing football one moment and burning to death in sudden agony the next. Muhammed, gutshot, counting the minutes of his own slow death. Iman, whose heart slowly failed and died locked in Gaza. Haneen, Ali, Husam, Anwar, Mustafa and Islam and Khaled and Essam and Toussi more and more and more than can ever be named but you must hold them in your head and keep their faces next to you at night and hold and hold to give them some sliver, not of justice but at least of memorial. You'll join her soon. Will we be together next? Will I find a name for you? Will you take off the gas mask? Will I see your face? Will you hold my hand? Will your hand be cold? I am coming. It will happen. We will be together soon. There are more than can ever be named and you shall name them.

◆ ◆ ◆

I will go back to New York. I can't stay here.

"You need some new clothes," my father says.

I tell him I'm fine.

"Come on. Look at those shoes. Let's get you a pair of shoes."

We both stare for a moment at my battered Nikes.

"I don't need shoes."

"I know. But I'd like to get you some."

"Okay," I say. "Thanks."

◆ ◆ ◆

"Did you see the news?" The early dawning light is still blue. I close my eyes again. Diane is sitting up in bed, her phone in her hand. "They're going to release Mubarak."

I roll over, away from her. "Good."

◆ ◆ ◆

I am sitting in the Brooklyn Public Library. What little money I had is nearly finished. Prospect Park waits silent outside. The newspapers are full of a new name today: Michael Brown. They left your body out on the street, lying there on the hot summer asphalt for the world to see, for your family to see for four eternal hours. Another city burns tonight. Behind me, a man is whispering down into his chest, a running argument between the two halves of himself.

"Something's going on, yeah, I know, you don't have to tell me twice. Something's goin' on and Jones Jones is gonna find out what it is. Something goin' on in *my* house?! You need to— you need to—shut it up. You're in a library. Have some *respect*. I'm gonna find out. Obama? Obama? Obama's a fucking Muslim. We don't know shit, I know that much. I know you need something so you're weak. A man's gotta stand on his own two feet. I see the news. I see what's coming. This country's falling to pieces. Obama opening our borders. Syrians! Thousands! Did you get the milk? The milk? Shut up. Of course I got the milk. Jones was raised *right*. In the *European* mode."

I try to concentrate on the book open in front of me. A blue horse sits in front of me. If only this could be the end. Strong lines, bold colors combining in elegance and grace to give you a horse. A deer, cradled perfectly by unnaturally harmonious triangles of green. The monastery of the title, nowhere to be seen. Flee from men and thou shalt live. The man behind me keeps talking, there will be no resolution to his argument. Another man, his clothes dusty from his labors, is asleep, his bag serving as his pillow. They are together, the two deer, looking out for each other, in a world where the danger is still far away. A woman in a wheelchair is copying out the dictionary word by word. A deer looks over its shoulder, a mother nuzzles its fawn. No death. No hate. A blue horse rubs up gently against its companion. It is perfect, this world in this simple book. Is it strange to want to be a blue horse? To long to be a blue horse? To be loved with simplicity by other blue horses? To be frozen in your moment of definition, to never outgrow it, never fail it.

I cross the street to the park. I walk south. I cut off the main path and into the wilder, lonelier parts, find a bench to sit on in silence. Is it better to find meaning in endless struggle or struggle endlessly with meaning? It's quiet here. Down where the gathering dark is punctuated by the glow of the fireflies in silent conversation.

Was this, then, our full potential? What our new world of digital possibility amounted to? Nothing more than birds rising from the trees at dawn, a mass movement of synchronized unpredictability, a moment of stunning collective action followed by survival instinct. We were a flock of quelea birds, beautiful to behold from afar, impossible to organize from within, all moving forward in a pattern determined by a force we cannot comprehend, by principles forged over millennia of evolution and generations of psychology, each choice in concert with the tiny adjustments of thousands of other birds, each decision steered by the unsteerable flock, each pulling all others toward a fate unforged.

◆ ◆ ◆

My phone rings with an unknown number. My phone never rings. A dozen terrible scenarios play out in my mind.

"Khalil." It's Mariam. My heart freezes. "Listen, Khalil, I wanted to call you before you see it on the news . . . They arrested Rania and Rosa last night. Took them from their apartment. They're going to try them on spreading false information and, and, endangering national security and—what else—organizing a protest . . . They're okay. I think Rosa fought or struggled or something but the lawyers say she's okay."

"And you?" I say. "Are you okay? Are you charged?"

"We don't know. I don't think so."

"Is it about Chaos? But we haven't done anything for months."

"We don't know. It's probably more recent stuff. We're going to announce it all in a few hours with a release."

"Do you need my help? Shall I translate it?"

"No, it's okay. I just wanted to tell you."

And then she's gone.

◆ ◆ ◆

And so full of people running and of people searching did the harsh mountains of Egypt become that the desert became a city but not a city built to last but one looking for the city that is to come and it is there that the voice of the martyrs' blood can be heard and their burning spirit can be kept alive.

—Saint Athanasius of Alexandria, *The Paradise of the Holy Fathers*, c. AD 400

◆ ◆ ◆

I see her standing in the line, the lights of Omar Makram Mosque illuminating the faces in the crowd, the darkness of Tahrir behind us. She doesn't see me. There are so many people. Hundreds, here, waiting to pay their respects in forlorn silence. All these people we used to see all the time, together in grief again, waiting to enter the mosque, to give condolences to the family of another fallen friend. Ahmed Seif. Advocate of the poor and downtrodden. Ahmed Seif the tireless, the selfless, the godfather to every penniless human rights lawyer in the country. Ahmed Seif, who I never met but whose loss breaks my heart, whose loss we cannot afford.

His family receives the mourners. Alaa and Sanaa, his eldest and his youngest, are both in prison whites. Alaa's hair is short. He shaved his head on the first day of his hunger strike. How long before you can't stand up on your own? But he looks strong. He looks heartbroken. But strong. I watch as Mariam gets to the front and hugs him tightly and I can see her catch her breath and they hold each other. She squeezes his hand once more and moves down the line. The good keep dying and the evil live forever.

She's sitting toward the back of the mosque.

"You're here?" she says.

"Yes. There's nothing to do in America."

She laughs a little and squeezes my hand and I sit down next to her.

All these people. We used to see one another every day, at protests and meetings and press conferences and parties and the Greek Club. The whole revolution is in this hall. We cannot afford this loss.

I see Abu Bassem enter and I stand to shake his hand.

"How have you been?"

"Well, thank the Lord," he says. "And you, son? I haven't seen you for a while."

"I've been away."

"Good." He speaks slowly, carefully, as ever. "Good. It is good for you younger ones to get out if you can. Just for a little while. Let this time pass."

There's a noise and a rumbling and a gathering of people in the far corner. They are taking them away, taking Seif's children back to prison, taking Alaa and Sanaa back behind their walls and their guns. People start pushing to get closer, to shout goodbye and wave and reach out to touch them a final time. A dozen hulking men have closed ranks around Alaa and are bundling him forward into a waiting car and now they have Sanaa, two huge women officers gripping her by her thin shoulders and half marching her forward through the thickening crowd. Mariam climbs up on a chair to try to see but she's gone.

Then the air is punctured with the words:

Down, down with military rule!

The huge room electrifies in booming response:

DOWN, DOWN WITH MILITARY RULE!

Somewhere from within the crush comes Sanaa's voice again. *Down, down with military rule!* and again the crowd roars it back with everything they have: *Down, down with military rule!* and fists are thrust into the air and everyone's massed on the steps of the mosque as Sanaa's bundled into the waiting police car and the crowd is shouting at the ranks of police and their unmarked prison bus and foot soldiers and guns. *Down, down, with military rule!* and every face is streaming with tears, every fist is up, every mouth is bursting with these words that have never weighed so much, never mattered so much as they do tonight.

◆ ◆ ◆

ABU BASSEM

There are no new words for loss. They took everything from me. My boy, my brotherhood, my reasons for breath. He zips his coat up to the collar. He ties a scarf around his neck and quietly opens the front door, makes his way down the concrete steps, down the dark stairwell and past the faded graffiti. He slips into his seat in the corner of the cybercafe, places the headphones over his ears, and runs through the keyboard motions with muscle memory until the screen changes to the familiar YouTube logo and the waiting black video box and in these seconds a dread always takes hold of him. What if, today, it's gone? What if Bassem doesn't appear? What if it breaks or is lost or deleted and the last time was the last time I will ever see him and I didn't know it and I didn't watch it as carefully as I should have, didn't commit as much to memory as I will need to see me through the rest of these years of missing him? What if today is the day I find I have nothing left?

◆ ◆ ◆

Mariam sits across from me, her eyes down at her cup, her hand slowly moving the spoon in a spiral, the skin of her arm pale and tight up to her shoulder, her neck.

"The bastards put them in separate prisons," she says. "Just to fuck with them. Rania is in Qanater. Rosa's up in Damanhour. If they were together it would be a lot easier obviously."

"Is there a trial date?"

"No. Administrative detention."

"What can we do?"

"We're doing everything we know to do. But it's all the same problems. Media won't touch the story and protesting is impossible. And there are so many in jail now. How do you keep selling the same story?"

"Rania would have had a spin for it."

"That's probably why she's the one in prison."

"Do you think they'll come for you?" I ask.

"I don't care anymore."

She's stopped stirring the coffee but the spoon is still in her hand. How strange not to reach over the table and have her hand in mine. How unreal of us.

"You got a new job?" I ask.

"Yes. The Center for Economic and Social Rights."

"Workers' rights?"

"Farmers'. Land rights."

You can still undo everything. Throw the damned spoon down and declare yourself a revolutionist till you die. Stand up and take her by the hand and tell her you'll work alongside her, you'll work for the small battles and the great war, you'll work every day because that's all that's worth doing in this dying world. Commit. Commit to the revolution, to the struggle. Put your egoizing and your questions and your doubts aside and just commit. If you don't play, you can't win.

But, of course, I can't. It wouldn't be real.

"We need to be more organized," she says. "For next time."

The gaudy white sofa creaks and our silence is quickly filled with the shouted conversations of the triumphant fascists all around us.

Take her hand and commit to death on the barricades. Nothing else will do. I see Hafez sitting under the lamp in my apartment, Morricone playing in the background—*Wouldn't you have been happy to die in the 18 Days?* We could have all died heroes then. But not today. Death by whipping, death by electrocution, death by cigarette burns in the basement of a police station. She left you behind a long time ago.

"Are you happy?" I say.

"That's a stupid question."

"You know what I mean."

"It's enough, for now, to be doing something. Whatever it is."

"Enough for next time?"

"It's all we have."

◆◆◆

We're walking over the 6th October Bridge. A dust storm is blowing through the city. We haven't talked for a while, but it's okay, it's how it used to feel with Mariam, like you don't need to fill the silence with pointless noise. Her eyes are squinting against the sand. She says she has something to show me. We cross Tahrir. The square is empty. No signs, no celebration, no police, no nothing. Two kids with faces wrapped in scarves against the sandy wind sit on the defaced plinth in the middle of the square, the army's incomplete monument to the victims of their bullets. Look upon my works. To our left a terrain of air vents erupt out of the ground like termite hills on a Martian plain. The city's grand seven-year project to build an underground parking garage is finally nearing completion. The two boys watch us as we walk past in silence. Ahead, the downtown escarpment has been painted. All except one building. Our first home from which our words and demands poured proudly down from the top floor.

We turn left into the Estoril alleyway and I wonder what memory this street holds for you, do you remember when you buttoned my jacket against the cold and pulled me half an inch toward you or how we sat so close together at the bar that first night that our legs kept grazing each other's or the night before June 30 and our argument the next morning—then we stop. We're on Hafez's street. Mariam is looking at me, waiting for me to say something.

She glances up and I follow the look and it's the street's name: Hafez Mansour Street. I look back at her and it takes a moment before the words arrive and I understand I am reading Hafez's name in perfect white lettering on the royal-blue background of the street sign. Hafez Mansour Street. Hafez's street.

"Did you do this?" I ask.

"No," she says, and I see she's looking up at the sign in wonder, the same as me.

"Then who?"

"I don't know," she says.

◆ ◆ ◆

I'm driving us south through the city, each turn of the wheel taking us through time and the city's strata, older and older until the new towers of Maadi appear on our horizon.

We won't stay long. It's all prepared, all in the bag under Mariam's feet.

"You're sure it's working?" she says.

I am.

Ten minutes later we pull up outside the prison, and its high, dusty walls. The sun is low in the sky.

I reach down and take the camera bag, open it, and pull out a smaller cloth pouch. I check on the transmitter inside it and press play on the mp3 player. I put them in a plastic bag, get quickly out of the car, walk to a trash can, and carefully drop it in.

When I get back in the car Mariam has the radio on and is scanning through the FM frequencies.

> *The Egyptian Air Force has launched a series of clinical strikes against ISIS militias in Libya.*

She keeps scanning.

> *And tonight, darling, is the night of our lives*
> *Tonight's the most beautiful night of my life*

She keeps scanning.

> *. . . and that was just one of Sisi's recent mistakes. He has shown clearly that he lacks any new political or economic vision and that the country's problems will only worsen under him. Revolutionists of Tora, please do not think for a single minute that you are alone.*

"It's working."

> *This is a special broadcast for Tora Prison. We will not stop working until you have your freedom. We are sorry that we are not strong enough to get you out yet, but we will.*

*Coming up in this broadcast after the news of Sisi's
economic and political failures we have world news, new
music, and notes from the cinema. Stay tuned until they
work out how to shut this transmission down . . .*

"Let's go," I say, turning on the engine. The mp3 is three
hours long. It will loop until the army finds it or the player
dies. Ashraf and all the other revolutionists inside that he
could get word to will be scanning for it at sundown.

◆ ◆ ◆

A boat drifts slowly along the glinting darkness toward me,
floating in a halo of reflected pink tube lights, its arrival her-
alded by a low idea of music, a tango maybe, an accordion.
I watch it from the dark, sitting on top of Imbaba Bridge, alone.
The constant hum of the city flickers in the distance. The boat
comes closer. You are alone. They cannot touch you. I hold my
hand out into the night, strain to reach out as far into the nothing as I can. Bats click past in the darkness. The boat comes
closer, its music echoing off both banks, surrounding me and
reaching out with me into the breeze, the darkness. The bats
cut through the air around me like an innocent. I think, sometimes, that our martyrs live their second lives in them, the bats,
the true inheritors of the city. Khaled, Mina, Bassem, Toussi,
Ali, Nadine, Michael, Mohamed, Shaimaa, Gika, Ayman,
Hafez, Essam, Mahmoud, Karika, Mohab, Ramadan, and
you, Doctor, whose name I'll never know—sonic perfections
unseen around us through the night. I've built a bat box on the
roof of my building. They'll come when it's time. I put it up
yesterday and when I was coming downstairs I saw something
familiar. I couldn't believe it at first but it was really there: a

sticker on my neighbors' door. It says *Free Alaa*. The boat comes closer, the music rises, but I don't panic. I'm surprised by a sudden wash of calm. A true calm that can only come after brutality. The boat comes closer. It is, in fact, beautiful, this neon vision on the dark river. They cannot touch you.

◆ ◆ ◆

The courtroom cage yawns open and as the defendants are led in, the room explodes in greeting and waves and shouted messages. The ten women in prison whites file into the cage that runs against one wall of the crumbling, vaulted chamber. Rosa stands six inches taller than the other women. A plainclothes reaches over the judge's bench for the gavel and shouts for people to shut up and sit down. The judges enter and a line of policemen shuffle into position between them and the crowd. The head judge mutters inaudibly. I can't make out a word. Rosa stands tall in the cage, her face straining to hear, the whole audience leans forward, trying to catch their words.

"You!" the judge suddenly shouts. "Sit down!"

"There's no seats!" a young man with long hair shouts back.

"Then get out! Take him out! Out!"

Three policemen shamble over to the boy and grab at his shirt. "You have no right!" the boy shouts, but doesn't resist. "Close that door!" the judge yells, "with a key!" The policeman standing nearest to the door turns to look at it. He doesn't have a key, there has never been a key that he knows of, so he just holds the handle.

I can see Rosa scanning the crowd. I wave and she sees me and breaks into a smile. The judge mutters and a witness is called. A policeman. *Disrupting traffic.* Then another. *Disturbing the peace.* And another. I can hardly hear them. *Unauthorized protest.* And then everyone is on their feet and the judges quickly leave the room. The session is over. The crowd presses toward the cage, toward their friends inside and I slip past two people, grab on to the black wire mesh. "Rosa!" I shout.

"Khalil!" She steps toward me, puts her fingers through the mesh. "You're here?"

"Yes."

"Welcome back."

"Thanks."

"Okay, we don't have much time. Do you have a pen? This is what Mariam needs to know: There's a prisoner in here on death row who's never even had a lawyer, she's been here for three years, I haven't seen her but I talk to her through the wall and her name is Alia Magdy and she's from Port Said so someone has to get her a lawyer. They had an informal freeze on death row but that's over and they've started executing. Got it?"

"Yes."

Rosa is speaking fast and behind us the press of dozens of people shouting and joking with their friends in the cage, pushing at us to get closer to them, to reach the fingers stretching out of the metal wiring. "Now"—Rosa lowers her voice and leans in as close as she can to the metal—"this is the message for Rania. Word for word. Ready? I hope she's well. I have recovered and nearly everyone is better now. We are all eating watermelon, a little bit every day, until the end of the month. Her favorite TV actor is leaving us next month. Got it?"

"Yes." I nod, scribble, try not to look at the policeman watching me. My heart is pumping and there is an electricity in my body again as I race to keep up with her instructions.

"Now tell Mariam up front: We're all set for the strike to start on the first. Qanater prison is ready and we'll start on the first unless she gets me a message saying different. If the other prisons aren't ready, send me a message saying the mangoes aren't ripe yet. Got it?"

I'm writing as fast as I can, I feel the metal in my back alive again with excitement as my pen races to keep up with Rosa's instructions when a voice shouts, "ALL RIGHT, THAT'S IT!" Ten policemen start clambering over the benches to form a human chain between the crowd and the prisoners while another five gather by the cage door. Rosa is shouting on top of the noise: "Tell Mariam Samia's rashes are back and she needs to tell her family. And they've put Awatef back in solitary and they need to make some media noise so tell whatever press we still have on our side."

"COME ON NOW!" the front guard yells into the cage, and everyone freezes as Rosa turns to him, takes a deliberate step toward him and stops, looks him in the eye, and doesn't move. The guard is frozen for a moment, unsure what to do, Rosa's body pulsing confidence at him.

Then, on her own terms, Rosa steps forward, past the guard, and walks out of the cage and the nine other women follow behind her. She doesn't turn back. I feel it again, the current forcing my hands into a fist, but all I can do is watch as the women in prison whites follow her out of the cage and all questions and doubts and solipsisms fall away as I fold the paper with my notes into a tight square and slip it into my sock and run Rosa's words through my mind again in case someone finds it and the crowd all presses behind the women as they're led out of the courtroom and we follow for last moments of messages and instructions and jokes as the mass of people slowly spills out into the grand colonial atrium and through the doors down into the heat of the courtyard and a chant goes up against the military and the policemen twitch with tension and they're holding us on the stairs now as the women in white climb one by one into the waiting police truck, its engine already turning, and I watch the metal grille to try and catch another glimpse of her, primed for another signal, another job, another plan, another way of thinking but there is only darkness inside and the truck chokes out its thick gray exhaust as it turns to take her back to her prison far out beyond the city limits.

ACKNOWLEDGMENTS

I've relied on several sources to bolster both my memory and imagination: the Twitter timelines of Alaa Abd El-Fattah, Sarah Carr, Mostafa Hussein, Mona Seif, Salma Said, Sharif Abdel Kouddous, Bassem Sabry, Nazly Hussein, Hany Rasmy, Hossam Bahgat, Heba Morayef, Rasha Azb, Sultan Sooud al-Qassemi, Leil-Zahra Mortada, and Amro Ali are just some among many; the journalism of the old *Egypt Independent* and its reincarnation, *Mada Masr*, *Jadaliyya*, The Arabist, Jack Shenker, Khaled Fahmy, Ahmed Shokr, Mona El-Ghobashy, Evan Hill, David Kirkpatrick, Louisa Loveluck, and Robert Mackey; the photographs of Mosa'ab Elshamy; the archives of the newspapers *Al-Ahram* and *Al-Shorouk*. I referred to and quoted from the testimonies, evidence, and data collected by Wiki Thawra, Opantish, EIPR, Human Rights Watch, We Won't Forget Them, and Mosireen. Where I have used specific testimonies, I hope that the victims of the state's crimes will feel I have been respectful.

Finally, the writings of Alaa Abd El-Fattah, my cousin, to whom this book is dedicated, are a crutch on which I—and many others—regularly lean. Those writings have cost him his freedom.

THANKS

There is a large group of people without whom this book would not exist. My family, friends, and colleagues in Cairo and, in particular, those who came together to make the Mosireen Collective. Thank you to Lina Attalah for creating *Mada Masr* and the space for so many of us to start writing; to Mariam Said for that first essential breath of oxygen; and to Yassin Gaber for our Tuesday night salons in Stella. Thank you to friends who read the manuscript in its various overlong stages: Mai Saad, Sharif Abdel Kouddous, Susan Glynn, Khalid Abdalla, and Sherief Gaber. Thank you to Alexandra Pringle for her introductions; to Matthew Hamilton for always having the right advice; and to Ismail Richard Hamilton for helping me hold a chaotic life together.

Thank you to Lee Brackstone for his eye; to Sean McDonald for his confidence; and to David Godwin for his good taste in manuscripts. Thank you to Salma Shamel and Rodrigo Corral for their beautiful cover designs; to Ibrahim El Moallem of al-Shorouk, Marie-Pierre Gracedieu of Gallimard, Diana Gvozden of Hollands Diep, Luigi Brioschi of Guanda, and Eduardo Rabasa of Sexto Piso for their early enthusiasm; to my translators, Ehab Zelaky, Sarah Gurcel, Massimiliano Galli, Pon Ruiter, and Inga Pellisa; and to Marine Vauchere, Simona Lari, and Stella Nelissen. I have had the great honor of working with teams at the very best publishing houses, so thank you to Lizzie Bishop, Rachel Alexander, Hannah Marshall,

Maria Garbutt-Lucero, Eleanor Crow, and Emma Cheshire at Faber; and to Susan Goldfarb, Jane Elias, Sarah Scire, Nora Barlow, and Maya Binyam at FSG.

Finally, thank you to my wife, Yasmin El-Rifae, for the life that made writing possible, and to my mother, Ahdaf Soueif, for the life that made it necessary.

A Note About the Author

Omar Robert Hamilton is an award-winning filmmaker and writer. Based in Cairo and New York, he has written for *The Guardian*, the *London Review of Books*, and *Guernica*. He is a cofounder of Mosireen, a Cairo media collective formed in 2011, and of the Palestine Festival of Literature. *The City Always Wins* is his debut novel.